SEVEN DAYS
TO
GOODBYE

SHERI S. LEVY

BARKING RAIN PRESS

Seven Days to Goodbye

Edited by Cindy Koepp (www.ckoepp.com)
Proofread by Robin Layne Wilkinson (www.writingthatsings.com)

Cover artwork by Stephanie Flint (www.sbibbphoto.com)

Barking Rain Press
PO Box 822674
Vancouver, WA 98682 USA
www.barkingrainpress.org

ISBN Trade Paperback: 1-935460-74-9
ISBN eBook: 1-935460-75-7

Library of Congress Control Number: 2014914124

First Edition: August 2014

Printed in the United States of America

9 7 8 1 9 3 5 4 6 0 7 4 9

To Caroline,
    Enjoy a southern beach story and feel the warmth of summer!
        Sheri Shepherd Levy
            9-11-14

DEDICATION

In memory of Frank McGee and Neal Sopko.
And to my dad, Clayton Conner Shepherd.

CHAPTER 1

SUNDAY

Sydney and I wrestled in my bedroom until I giggled so hard my insides ached and his barking made me deaf. I crossed my arms on my chest and said, "Freeze!"

He stopped in motion, panting. His head tilted, eyes glued on mine, while he waited for the next command. I always made sure Sydney got to be a regular puppy. Even when he became someone's service dog, he'd still have playtime.

Momma's voice boomed through the door, "Trina, are you packed?"

"Sort of." I gave Sydney the release word, "Okay," and he pounced at me. I threw my arms around his neck, buried my face in his freshly shampooed red, brown, and white-freckled fur, and breathed in his clean vanilla scent. His trainer's words echoed in my mind, "Trina, you've done a terrific job with your first dog. He's ready to return to my kennel for his final months of training."

My stomach did cartwheels. I sucked in a breath and fought to hold down my breakfast. This week at the beach would be my last with Sydney.

Ever.

Using the bottom hem of my pajama top, I wiped the wetness from my eyes before I retrieved my duffel bag. While separating last year's summer clothes into two heaps, my dirty pile grew larger than the clean, minus one sock. "Syd, where's my sock?"

He darted back into the closet. Strutting out, he wiggled his little nub of a tail and dropped the sock on my lap.

"You're so smart, Mr. Sydney." Everything he did was a game.

Staring at my small stack of clean clothes, I shrugged, twisted a wild curl that didn't want to be included in my pony tail, and looked into his golden eyes. "You won't care if I wear some of these a few times, will you?" His tail jiggled.

I dressed in my regular jean shorts and concert tee shirt with the words *PINK & PURPLE* swirled across my chest. The front of my tee was purple and the back pink. My best friend Sarah's was just the opposite. We always wore these matching tops on special outings. Three years ago our parents had attended the band's concert and surprised us with the shirts as souvenirs. As ten-year-olds, we wore them as long tees with leggings. This year Sarah had grown so much, hers fit like a tee shirt should. Mine stayed a longer tee. But we still matched.

Minutes later, I rolled the bag into the garage.

Sydney's floppy ears drooped. During his year with me, he'd learned that the duffel bag meant a trip somewhere and he wasn't always invited. "Surprise, Sydney. You get to go!" His mouth stretched over his teeth like a grin as he spun in circles. Skidding into his learned Sit, he waited for the next command as I opened the car door.

His eyes locked with mine. Pointing at his face, I counted one thousand one, one thousand two, one thousand three in my head, and then said, "Okay!" He leaped onto the backseat. I climbed in and he nuzzled his forehead with mine. This summer we'd explore a dog-friendly beach, and I'd make Sydney an expert water dog.

Our parents spent every weekend together, but Sarah and I hadn't hung out since soccer season started months ago. Every time her team won, they moved on to the next level, eventually winning the championship. I had stayed busy training Sydney in public places, working at the barn, riding, and missing Sarah's company while feeding the horses apples at night.

Dad drove Momma and me down the street to Sarah's to caravan. As we went up her driveway, there she stood dribbling her soccer ball and wearing a baby-blue tank top layered over a green one with lace at the bottom. They matched the blue and green sea shells along the cuffs of her white shorts. I gasped, and my eyes widened.

She must have outgrown her PINK & PURPLE shirt entirely.

Sarah looked bizarre kicking a soccer ball in such a fancy outfit. Darby, her black and white Springer spaniel, chased the ball, barked, and wagged her stub of a tail. Sydney and I wedged our heads out the window. "Wow. You're all dressed up? Where are your soccer clothes?"

"Gone." She tittered, fluttered her eyelashes, and twirled, flinging her blond French-braid. "Mom took me shopping."

Her eyes matched her top, but I kept that to myself. No reason to add to her new coolness. Going to the beach had never required worrying about clothes or my red hair. But today, no way could I let on that my bathing suit was under my tee and shorts. Somehow, I just knew hers wasn't under those new fancy clothes like every other summer. I changed the subject. "So are you and Darby riding with us?"

"I will. Darby can go with my parents." She climbed in with her backpack. "Hi, Mr. and Mrs. Ryan."

"Hi, Sarah." Momma turned around. "You look very pretty."

I sighed.

Sydney wiggled onto Sarah's lap, but she gently pushed him off. Bending her head, she said, "Thanks, Mrs. R." and plucked dog hairs from her clothes.

With the air conditioner gusting and the radio blaring, Dad backed down the driveway. "Let's hit the road."

"Yay! We're off to the beach, Syd." Excitement spiked through my arms and legs like electric currents. His front legs stretched across my lap, putting weight on my thighs. I chuckled. "Look at you. Already sensing I need your calming techniques. That'a boy." I stroked his back and twisted toward Sarah. "Remember last year? How we buried each other in the sand. That was so much fun."

Sarah looked straight ahead. "Well, not this year. I just want to lie on the sand and work on my tan."

"Really? That'll get boring, quickly."

Sarah stared out her window. I used both hands and scratched behind Syd's ears, waiting for her response. Nothing. "Sarah, we need to learn to surf? Or boogie board? Even ride a wave runner?" My eyes pleaded with the back of her head.

Slowly she turned to me with a questioning scowl on her face. I swallowed. *Had she changed this much?*

Her head moved side to side. "Hmm... First, I'll have to see how cold the water is, or how many jellyfish I see on shore."

"But you know I can't go to the beach without swimming." When Sydney lifted his chin, I rubbed his neck. "The realtor said this house was kind of old, but right on the beach."

"Oooh! Being on the beach will make it easier to stroll up and down." Sarah's eyebrows rose and gave me a sideways smirk. "And meet guys."

I stared at her as if she spoke a foreign language. "Do WHAT?" Before blurting out something else crazy, I caught my breath and remembered back to the last day of school, only four days ago. Sarah and her class friend, Clayton, had huddled in a corner, talking, and passing pieces of paper. I guess I shouldn't have been so surprised. "But Sarah, this week is supposed to be about you and me and our dogs."

"Oh. Trina." She gave me a bright, cheery smile. "It'll be the perfect place to meet guys. No one will know us there. So it won't matter if we goof up and say the wrong things."

I scrunched my nose. *Yuck. What a waste of time.*

Sarah unzipped her pink backpack and pulled out a new pink cell phone. "Look. Here's my present for staying on the honor roll?"

"Wow. Let me see. I still have Mom's old phone. Why didn't you text me?"

"You're always busy with Sydney so I waited till today. Now you can see all my awesome apps."

It had never mattered that my phone was for emergencies while at the barn and an occasional text to Sarah. But I leaned closer and whispered, "It's almost my birthday. Maybe I'll get one that does all that fancy stuff."

I tapped Momma's shoulder. "Look what Sarah got."

Momma laid her book on the seat and turned around. "That's very nice, Sarah."

"Thanks Mrs. Ryan. It helps when I look stuff up for school and it has a GPS. Now Mom knows wherever I am." Then she snickered. "That part's a bummer!"

Momma eyed Sarah and gave me an apologetic smile. "One day, Trina," and returned to her book.

Sarah handed me her phone over Syd's head. It chimed, so she jerked it back. "Just a minute." She leaned over, started texting, and giggled.

Hmm. She can ignore me all she wants. I reached into my purple book bag, pulled out my book, *Socializing Your Australian Shepherd* and pretended to read. My eyes darted back and forth, hoping Sarah would talk with me.

Sydney moved between us and slept on the seat.

When Sarah set her phone on her lap, I asked, "Who was that?"

She exhaled and tilted her head on her left shoulder, then blinked her eyes and drew the word "C-L-A-Y-T-O-N" in the air with her finger. Then her phone chimed again.

This time I bit my lip and twisted the same straggly curl around and around.

The realization hit the pit of my stomach. Sarah was different.

CHAPTER 2

Sarah's phone beeped and chimed over and over, making me cringe. I pulled my game player from my backpack, turned up the volume, and clicked on *One Player.*

Minutes crept by. Sometime later, Momma glanced over her shoulder. "There's a rest stop ahead. We can stretch our legs and have lunch. How's that sound?"

"Hot." I closed my game player. "But good timing." I Velcroed Sydney's purple working-cape around his chest. Outside the car, he stood taller, head erect, ready to work.

Sarah bolted from the car, heading toward a clump of trees. I walked toward her with Sydney heeling, his eyes on me. Sarah stood with the phone attached to her ear like it was a new appendage to her body. I planted my hands on my hips and stood in front of her. Sydney sat.

Sarah shook her pointy finger at me, mouthing the words, "Just a minute," and turned sideways.

Sydney and I didn't wait but jogged toward tree-shaded areas. The hot, muggy air intensified the scent of freshly cut grass. Somewhere in the distance a lawn mower roared. As soon as Syd slowed to a walk, panting, I headed to the ladies restroom.

Sydney pushed the door to the handicap stall open, leaned his body against the door, and held it closed. He had learned to ignore the sounds of people, the noise from the hand dyer, and to watch me. I said, "Ready." He moved away from the door, letting it open. I washed my hands and held them under the blower. Sydney lifted his face with his mouth open and gulped the warm, rushing air.

We returned hot and thirsty to the cement table where our mothers had placed a small picnic of fruit, cheese, sandwiches, and chips. I grabbed an ice cold can of orange soda and a water bottle to fill Syd's bowl. Hoping Sarah would talk with me, I went to the opposite side of the table. Sydney crawled under by my feet, drank his cool water, and rested.

Our parents sat hunched together, deep in conversation.

While sitting in the shade and not moving, our damp clothes stuck to our bodies. No one complained. It was a normal summer in South Carolina.

But I was miserable.

During lunch, Sarah chattered on her phone to another girl from school, Lauren, about her plans to run for President of our eighth grade class. This was news to me. They talked about posters and campaign speeches, and Sarah acted as if she had no idea that she'd made me, supposedly her best friend, mad. I chose to ignore her, too. I alternated eating a red grape, and a piece of cheddar cheese on a pretzel, and stared off into space, dabbing at my face and neck with a paper napkin.

Our parents ate pimento cheese sandwiches. I had kindly said, "No thank-you," when offered, but what I really wanted to say was "YUCK" and giggle with Sarah, like we used to do. We'd make faces, falling into each other, pretending to gag, and saying, "How can they eat that stuff?" Obviously, Sarah wasn't thinking about those days. So I said nothing.

Finished with our so called picnic, we returned to the cars. I hustled ahead and tapped Sarah's shoulder, lifted my chin and said, "I'm going to take a nap. Why don't you ride with your parents?" She nodded and didn't miss a beat, talking on her phone. This time it seemed to be with Lillian.

I jogged to the car with Syd. "In," I said. He hopped up, circled the hot seat, lifting each paw quickly and holding it in the air for a second, panting. I slumped in the car, leaving the door open, and fanned the seat with my book. It must have been over a hundred degrees in there. I took off his cape and watched the words, *Please do not pet me. I'm working*, crumple into a pile on the floor, just like I wanted to do.

As soon as Dad turned on the ignition, I closed the door. "Come on, air conditioner." Sticky sweat trickled down my back and into the crotch of my bathing suit.

Momma asked, "What're you and Sarah arguing about?"

"Arguing? No way. I'm just tired of listening to her talking to everyone else."

"I'm sorry, honey. When we get there, perhaps you'll work it out."

Under my breath I said, "Maybe."

Sydney climbed on my lap and licked the corners of my eyes. I buried my face in his soft fur and scratched under his chin. He leaned into my hand as I whispered, "We'll have fun with or without Sarah. We just have to."

Staring through the side window, a deep blue summer sky flickered between pine trees covered in kudzu. Sarah's car passed on the right. I turned the other way.

Off the freeway, we headed east, and then south down a two lane road through sleepy little towns one after the other. Twenty minutes later, I leaned forward between the front seats, "Wow! Look."

Branches from gigantic live oak trees slanted toward the middle of the street. The trees looked as though they were trying to touch each other and some did. They reminded me of my cozy canopy bed where Sarah and I had spent many nights, giggling and whispering. But this canopy was made of tree limbs in different shades of green, dripping with grayish Spanish moss. The moss hung like long, ghostly arms swinging in the wind.

"This is kind of spooky beautiful. It's like being in a green tunnel." I cracked my window.

A whiff of salty ocean filled the car. Sydney lifted his head as the trees whizzed by. His nose twitched.

"We're getting close, Syd."

He squeezed into the same space with me and gazed out the front window.

Suddenly, the trees disappeared. The cloudless sky stretched with no end in sight. Pelicans flew in an upside down "V" formation. On both sides of the road, squiggly tidal creeks flowed through green marshlands. White birds with skinny legs stood statue-still in the shimmering water. This was a place I'd only seen in postcards.

"Okay." Dad straightened. "Look ahead. There's the bridge to Edisto Island." Dad drove higher and higher, like clicking up the steep incline on a roller coaster ride. We chugged up up, up, up to the top of the bridge. The deep ocean sparkled below. Small waves rippled, rocking the docks built along the intra-coastal waterway. Sailboats glided with the wind while motorboats buzzed under the bridge.

Dark blue water drew closer as we went down, down, down. Not fast like the roller coaster ride, but I pretended and closed my eyes. The impulse was too great; I had to giggle and let out a "Wheeee!" Then Dad started tapping his brakes. My eyes flew open and I moaned, "Ah. Come on Dad. Faster, faster." A sharp ring of my phone broke the spell. I pulled it out of my pocket, noticed the number and name. "It's Sarah." I sighed and answered. "Hey."

"This is way neater than any other beach we've been to." She rambled like there was no problem between us. "Do you see those people kayaking in the tidal creeks? Maybe we can do that."

"Yeah?" I whispered in the phone.

"I'm sorry I spent so much time on my phone. But I promise, we'll do all the beachie stuff together."

What came to mind was, "I won't hold my breath," but what flew out was, "Hope so. See you at the house." And I closed the phone.

Was that a glimmer of the old Sarah?

I stroked Sydney's back in the opposite direction, making his long fur stand up. As I removed my hand, the layers of different colors fell slowly into place. My heart was being squeezed like a stress ball and yet, I felt a tinge of excitement growing. "Sydney, here comes our first beach trip together."

And I swallowed the words, "and our last," promising myself to focus on each new and exciting day.

CHAPTER 3

D riving down Palmetto Boulevard, we passed a Piggly Wiggly grocery store, and The Pavilion, a restaurant and souvenir shop overlooking the ocean. Down one more block was the Edisto Sports Rental shop.

My heart beat so fast, I gasped. "Oooh. Bikes, kayaks, and surfboards. Won't that be fun?"

The quiet, main island road seemed to never end. Newer houses on the beach sat on tall cement pilings with carports underneath. They loomed majestically over the smaller and older houses. Those were built on shorter, wooden pilings and included a room on the ground floor and a small carport. They seemed out of place, more like houses seen inland. Name plates hung on most every house, old or new. For fun, we read them out loud.

Momma said, "Look. That one says, 'Sea Watch.' It's an older house on the beach, and seems okay." She grinned at Dad. "I bet ours will be just fine."

Pointing to the right, on the second row, I said, "There's a great name, 'Dad's Golden Nest.' Oh, Wow! It's really fancy, and so high off the ground. It looks like it's on stilts." I pointed toward the beach side. "I like that name, 'Sand Dreams.' Oooh, over there. That's my favorite, 'Pelicans' Perch.'"

We grew quiet, concentrating on the addresses. "Oh," I gasped. "There's ours, 'Edwards's Retreat.'" A rectangular name plate hung from the weathered front porch. My pulse quickened. "We're here. We're finally here."

Sydney barked. I touched my index finger on my lips. "Shh, Syd. Quiet." He pushed his nose and paws to the window.

We stared at the faded brown wooden house squished between two larger houses. A small area under the house was a carport, and the other side had an enclosed room. The front of the house had two small windows side by side, overlooking the yard. On the left side of the house, two windows had air conditioning units, sticking out and supported by wooden ledges.

"Hooray." I shoved my fist in the air. "It is on the ocean. I can see the sand dunes from under the house. And, who cares it's an older house? It's perfect."

Dad drove on a path of worn-down grass and parked in front of the carport. The Neals' car followed another path and parked beside ours. In seconds, car doors slammed and we stood, staring at the smallest house on the beach.

"Girls?" Dad glanced at each one of us. "Keep the dogs busy and out of trouble while we unload."

Sarah hopped to attention. "We'll do that, Mr. Ryan."

My head jerked toward her. *So we're going to be a team now?*

Noses in the air, Darby's and Sydney's bodies vibrated. I let Sarah go first with Darby pulling. Sydney followed with a tighter leash than usual.

I called, "Easy."

Out of the corner of his eye, he gave me a look and slowed through the grassy backyard.

Once again I called, "Easy," and got more slack in the leash, going single file, down the long, narrow wooden path.

At the top of the sand dune, we gazed at a wide open beach. We stopped at an abrupt, short drop where high tide had cut into the sandbank. The waves crashed, booming, one after the other. Sydney and Darby halted.

Sarah crinkled her nose and caught my eye. "There's lots of…" She looked to me to finish the sentence.

I hesitated, and then mumbled, "Beach." We had always finished each other's sentences. "We're still friends, huh?"

Laughing, she hooked her arm through mine. "Don't be silly, Trina. Of course."

Our weight collapsed the ridge, and the dogs rushed to a tidal pool. Darby walked around it, but Sydney jumped in and splashed his feet. "Sarah, I want to test the water before we head back."

Sarah stood back, but I kicked off my flip flops and stood ankle deep. "Oooh. It's perfect."

After Sydney pawed the foamy part of the wave, he licked his paw, leaned his head, and stared at the water as another wave broke.

Sarah chuckled. "How's that taste, Sydney?" His tongue swiped his lips.

The water rushed forward again and Darby backed up. Sydney leaped into the foamy surf. I shortened his leash. "Wow. Look at you. You may be easy to train as a water dog. But you'll have to wait. Come."

His ears sagged as we moved away.

Darby danced ahead on an extendable leash. Sydney stepped on one narrow plank at a time. I unleashed him, and he tried passing her. But Darby moved like a ballerina, flitting up the path, and never missing a step.

Eyeing the cars I said, "Sarah, let's get our bags. Then we can hurry back to the beach."

I rolled my duffel bag up the steps. Sydney sprinted to the top. A dull thump, thump, thump, came from behind. I turned around. Sarah heaved a huge, brown suitcase up each step with both hands. "Is that yours?"

"Yep." Her eyes focused on the suitcase as she huffed out one word after every step. "I... wanted... to... have... lots... of... choices."

"Sarah. We're at the beach. Where do you plan on wearing all that?"

"Let's just say, I'll be prepared for anything." Sarah blew out any breath she had left. "If you run out of clothes, I'll share. Darby, Come."

I shrugged and mumbled, "Nice."

The dogs rested on the edges of a round, braided rug in the middle of the small living room while Sarah and I searched for our bedroom. There were only five rooms in the entire house, which included two identical bedrooms, each with a queen bed and one twin against a back wall.

We stood speechless in the doorway of each bedroom. I dropped my bag, ran out to the front porch with Sarah following. I hollered, "Momma. Where are Sarah and I sleeping?"

She shouted back with her arms full of sheets and towels, "The real estate agent said there were only two bedrooms, so I guess you each get one of the twin beds. Just pick a room."

We froze and stared at each other. "Oh, no, Sarah. How're we going to talk at night?"

Sarah shook her head. "Have no idea. Maybe the couch makes into a bed."

We ran in, bounced onto an old couch at the same time, and fell into each other. Our outburst of laughter brought both dogs to our laps.

"Off, Syd." I stood and looked under the cushion.

"Yep! It does make into a bed, but I bet it's not very comfortable."

Sarah grumbled toward her suitcase. "I guess we'll be sleeping in separate rooms. I'll take the one to the left."

"I can't believe it." I dropped my duffel bag on the floor in the other bedroom.

While unpacking, I found Sydney's training aides that he used for pulling doors open, and placed them on a doorknob going out to the deck and on the refrigerator handle. I carried a box filled with scissors, glue, crayons, and brand new glitter magic markers to the picnic table on the screened-in back porch. "Sarah, look out here. This'll be a great place to scrapbook."

"Oh. My. Gawd!" Sarah hollered from the living room. "There's no TV. Anywhere. Not even one. And, there's no Wi-Fi. What're we going to do all week?"

"Sarah," said Momma, from the kitchen. "We're at the beach."

"That's right, Sarah." Mrs. Neal chuckled her high-pitched laugh and pushed her glasses further up her nose. "You may even want to read a book."

"This is too much." Sarah glared, crossed her arms and plunked them on her stomach. "What an old house." She puckered her lips and huffed. "At least, I have my phone, and we have our game players."

"Whatever." I rolled my eyes. "I just want to be on the beach and work with Sydney."

"Well, there's obviously nothing to do in here." She stormed to the bedroom. "I'm changing." And slammed the old door.

Five minutes later, Sarah moseyed out of her room. All the girls in my class wore bras whether they needed them or not. I was one of those nots. So when Sarah sashayed across the wooden floors in her hot-pink and white-striped bikini, my eyeballs rocketed forward like in a pinball game toward the target. Her suit revealed the real thing. Boobs.

I sat on the couch, gawking, and watched her plop into an old leather chair. As Sarah leaned backwards, she shrieked. The chair had collapsed into a flat chaise lounge, knocking her onto her back. Her pink foam flip-flops bounced onto the ottoman, making the plastic daisies jiggle between her toes.

I didn't dare laugh. I put both hands over my mouth, swallowing any sounds that wanted to sneak out.

Sarah's mom cackled like a hyena. Gasping for breath, she sputtered, "Thanks, Sarah, for being the first one in that chair."

Sarah didn't say a word. Then she let out a giant belly laugh. It was contagious, and the house shook with laughter. She snorted between words. "If I can get out of this chair, can we go to the beach? Like, today?"

Momma snickered once more and said, "That was too funny. Trina, go put on your bathing suit."

"Yay! I already have it on." I stood up, pulled off my tee shirt, slid down my shorts, swaying my skinny bottom, and threw my arms out to the side. "Ta-da!"

Sarah's eyes grew large. "Oh, Trina. Why are you wearing that one again?"

That blew the wind out of my ocean sails. I winced, sucked in more air as I twirled around. Fake-smiling, I walked like a model on the runway in last year's navy-blue, one-piece swim team bathing suit. "*I* like it."

"Oh my." Momma stepped back, scrunching her eyes, inspecting me. "I should've known. You and Sarah have always—" Momma stopped in mid-sentence and scanned both of us. "But I guess, not this time. Come over here and let me put sun lotion on you."

"Just my back. I can do the rest."

Mrs. Neal glanced at Sarah and then back to me. She cleared her throat. "You girls really need to watch how much sun you get, okay?"

Sarah moaned and walked away. "We know, Mom. Please."

"Don't fuss at me. I don't want a repeat of last year."

Momma shared a look with Mrs. Neal. "Amen to that."

Momma sprayed my blinding-white shoulders and back. "Honey," she whispered in my ear. "You could put on your new bikini."

Feeling a jolt in my stomach again, I lifted my shoulders to my ears. "Naw. I'm just going to get wet and messy. Can Sydney get sunburned?"

"Good question." Momma rubbed a blob of lotion into my neck. "There's a tube of doggy sun cream on the dresser. Dab it on Syd's pink nose before we head down. Be sure to do yours, also."

Smiling, I said, "With Syd's lotion?"

"Okay, smarty. You know what I mean."

I retrieved his lotion and painted Syd's nose. Mine, I covered with zinc oxide. He was busy licking off the lotion as we stood in front of Momma. "See. I'll be safe from more freckles. But I'm not so sure about Sydney."

With our arms loaded with supplies, we jabbered all the way down the stairs, sounding like a swarm of bees. Under the house, our dads grabbed beach chairs and an umbrella while Sarah rattled two mystery door knobs. "What's down here?"

Momma looked over. "The door to your left is a storage room with bikes and extra chairs. And the other is a small room with a bathroom and a bunk bed. The owner said we were welcome to use what ever we needed."

Sarah cupped her eyes and peeked in each window. "Wow, Trina. Check this out. We could stay down here."

"Yeah!" I stared straight ahead, already picturing the ocean. "But let's look later. The beach is calling."

At the top of the sand dunes, Momma stepped in front of me and made eye contact. "You're in charge of Syd. I plan to relax, read my book, and enjoy the sun."

"Got it." I scanned the coastline. "The beach is totally empty. I can't imagine Sydney getting into any mischief." He looked at me as I said his name, and I stroked his back. "Not my good boy."

CHAPTER 4

Sydney bit at the waves, which made him snort and cough, as Darby chased seagulls. Sarah found her sunbathing spot and flopped on her beach towel. I opened my towel, waved it in the air, and let it float to the sand next to Sarah.

Before I plunged into the sparkly ocean, I gave Sydney a hand signal, "Stay." The cold water took my breath away, but I had waited long enough. After a long, fast swim, I drifted up and over the waves, watching Sydney.

He slurped a couple of tonguefuls from the water bowl as something scurried across the sand. His eyes caught the motion, and in an instant, he was off. I treaded water, laughing at him. "What's he chasing, Momma?"

"A fiddler crab. It's burrowed in the sand close to my chair leg." Sydney's nose sniffed at the tiny opening. He turned one eye into the hole, looked up at Momma, and then placed his paws over the hole to keep it from fleeing.

One more time, he pressed his eye to the hole. Then his right front paw dug at the sand. He alternated left and then right. Momma's chair leg sunk into the hole, tipping over sideways. "Sydney. What in the world are you doing?"

She lifted her chair and moved it away. Sydney followed Momma's chair and started digging again. I sat in the foamy surf, tickled with his antics. Now he used both feet and the sand flew between his hind legs.

Momma moaned. "Sydney, stop."

He didn't.

She folded her chair, held it above the sand, and called. "Trina, please come in and get Sydney."

I stopped swimming and dashed to my towel. I draped Sydney's leash around my neck and grabbed his orange Frisbee. The minute he saw his favorite toy, he stopped digging, and darted toward me.

In both directions, maybe forty or fifty feet apart, rock jetties protected the beach from erosion. The wind blew in gusts, so I threw the Frisbee as hard as I could to the right. It took flight, but didn't stay in the air long. Sydney chased the disc as it rolled on its ridge, around and around, and fell to the sand. He pawed the edge, flipped it over, bit the lip of the Frisbee, and carried it back to me.

Darby watched, but with no interest in chasing the disc. She chased squawking birds.

This time I threw to the left. The wind lifted the Frisbee into the air. It looked as if the disc had sprouted wings and disappeared up and over the jetty.

Uh, oh.

Sydney halted, staring at me. He was used to chasing his toy, but his eyes asked for permission as his body quivered with pent-up energy. Letting him struggle for a minute, I giggled and said, "Okay, Syd. Find Frisbee."

I did a slow jog toward the rocks.

Seconds later, Sarah called, "Wait for me."

I turned around and stopped. "Wow, you're joining me! Good. I've got to find Syd's Frisbee. It's on the other side."

We climbed over the jetty. The dogs used their four-legged drive and moved much faster than Sarah or me. When we reached the top of the mound, Sydney stood a distance away with his Frisbee at his feet, leaning close to a small boy. The boy continued to pat the sand in his bucket and turn it upside down, making a row of mounds.

My heart did a triple beat in quarter time. I started running. Sydney's stub wiggled and jiggled as soon as the boy's sandy hands rubbed his back.

"I'm sorry," I said, running ahead. I bent, face to face with the boy. "I hope he didn't scare you."

The boy never looked at me, only at Sydney and back to the sand. He said in a monotone voice, "Doggy, doggy."

Sarah meandered up to us. I panted in fast spurts. Worried about the boy and Sydney, I never noticed the rest of the group. A little ways from the small boy, two guys around our age worked on a fort, or it could have been a sand castle. The one who seemed to be the oldest stood. He had long legs and was much taller than I expected. Using his hand, he shoved his longish brown bangs out of his eyes.

Oh, Sarah definitely noticed him. She smiled, pushed loose hair back into her braid, and pulled her bathing suit in place.

I rolled my eyes. *Okay. Here she goes.*

Sarah's flirty voice sang out the words, "That's going to be a great castle. How long have you been working on it?"

She did it!

The other guy with short black hair stayed seated and looked up. He stopped smoothing the sand around the sides and stood eye to eye with Sarah. "We just started this morning. Want to help?"

I hadn't noticed Darby lagging behind until she raced toward us. "Sarah, here comes your dog."

Sarah didn't move. I jumped in front of Darby, preventing her collision with their building. "Got you, Darby." I faced the group, but never made eye contact. My cheeks heated up, and I pictured my freckles multiplying. I froze. Not a single word entered my brain.

The easiest thing for me to do was to return to the small boy while holding Darby's collar. The boy's hands hung by his sides, and he held his head just high enough to see under his brown bangs and keep his hazel eyes on Sydney. I squatted to his eye level and said, "This is Sydney. Do you like dogs?"

He nodded.

Sarah's words floated in the breeze. "I love making castles. We make them every year. This is our first time at Edisto. It's really cool." There was a pause. And then she did what I hoped she wouldn't do. "Trina, come over here and meet these guys."

My heart stopped. What would I say? "In a minute. This boy's petting Sydney." I could only grouch for so long. Before I had figured out what to do, long, hairy legs were in front of my face.

The older guy stood over me. His deep voice changed octaves and crackled at the small boy. "Logan, what a nice dog." Then staring down at me he asked, "What kind of dog is he?" Again his voice squeaked, "I've never seen a dog like him."

I tried not to laugh and relaxed. Talking about my dog would be easy. I stood, and found myself having to lift my head and my eyes past his chest before answering. "He's a red-merle Australian Shepherd."

"He's cool. His colors are way different. Thanks for letting Logan pet him."

"I'm just glad he's not, or he wasn't, afraid of dogs. Some kids are. I gave Sydney, that's my dog, permission to find his Frisbee. It blew over the jetty. I had no idea he'd meet a boy. My dog, I mean. Although he likes children. So he's safe."

My stomach somersaulted. I had rambled and didn't know when to stop talking. I knew my red hair poked out like a porcupine after swimming and being in the gusty wind. I wanted to hide. Then I said something else stupid. "Sarah, we need to get back. Our parents'll worry where we are."

"You go on ahead. I'll be there in a minute."

I squatted to Logan's level, and caught a trace of freckles sprinkled across his pink cheeks. "Bye, Logan. I have to go." I stood and lifted my face upwards to the oldest guy. "I need to get back." Not waiting for him to reply, I called, "Sydney, Darby, time to go."

Sarah's giggly voice continued talking.

A few minutes later, Sarah called, "Trina, wait for me." I turned with my hands full, stuck my lower lip out, and blew the curls out of my eyes. Panting as she walked backwards, she kept her eyes on the guys. "Why didn't you stay? Did you see his green eyes?"

"You could have stayed. I've got the dogs, and I'm okay."

Sarah closed in on me. "I didn't want to be there by myself. It feels too weird."

There was only silence as we climbed over the jetty. Back on sand, I said, "Sarah, I'm not here to look for guys. I just want to be on the beach with you and Syd."

"It would be so much fun. We'll never see them after this week. And if we say the wrong things it won't be sooo embarrassing."

"I have enough to think about. Finishing Syd's training and with his leaving... and—" I took a breath. "Look at me. Do I look like a boy magnet?"

"Yes."

I dropped my chin and stared at her. "What are you talking about?"

"I've watched the guys at school look at you, but you're always in your own world. Never noticing them."

"You're just saying that to get me to do what you want me to do."

"Oh, Trina. You're hopeless."

"Well, I'm going swimming. That was so humiliating. I hope I never see them again."

Sarah opened her mouth, but I didn't wait to hear what she said. I ran to my towel, grabbed my orange raft, and waded out as far as I could before putting it under my stomach and paddling with my arms. I went farther and farther toward the rolling waves. Sydney and Darby played chase, barking. Then they grew quiet. I stroked the raft sideways with my right hand. Sydney, always alert to where I am, slammed on his brakes. My heart fluttered. Oh no. He's never been swimming. Or in the ocean.

I rushed to help him. He dog-paddled and stayed afloat. As soon as I felt rough sand under my feet, I stood, and put the rope attached to my float around my arm.

"Momma. Look!" I moved my eyes from Sydney and yelled. "Sydney's swimming." A sharp sting crossed my arm. "Ouch. Your nails scratched me." I moved out of the way.

He kicked faster, licked the water, and coughed.

Since the water was only up to my chest, I went behind him, put my hands under his stomach, and raised him away from me. "Sydney, no water. Momma said it'll make you sick."

Darby got wet half-way up her legs, pranced through the water, but never attempted to swim.

Sarah dipped her toes in the water and called out to me. "Miss Priss doesn't want to mess up her hairdo."

"You're hilarious, Sarah. You're one to talk." I had a quick laugh and let Sydney go. "Darby must take after you."

"Yes." She smiled, put her hands on her waist, and threw out her right hip. "We like to be neat and pretty."

Sydney coughed again, interrupting my next thought.

"Come on Syd. Let's go in before you drown."

He followed. Once his feet touched sand, he waddled onto shore. Sydney, with his long fur dripping and collecting sand, sprinted to the towels. Our mothers read magazines while lying on their stomachs, their backs to the water.

"Watch OUT!" I put my hands over my mouth. But it was too late.

He shook his entire body, flapping his ears. Sand and cold water hit their bare skin.

Mrs. Neal gasped. "Oh. Oh. Oh!"

Momma screamed, "Sydney, nooo!" Then Sydney shook again.

Sarah and I tried to stifle our laughter.

As Sydney headed to the pile of towels, Momma leaped to her feet and yanked open the towel on top. He lunged into the towel like a bull charging for the red sheet in a bull fight. He snorted in it as Momma dried his face, and then she handed it to me. "Here. You can finish."

"Sorry about that, Momma. Now we know he'll head for the towels before he shakes. I bet that salty water stung his eyes."

Momma took a deep breath and blew it out. Within a couple of seconds, she chuckled and said, "Whatever it was. We'll be ready, next time."

Bored with walking and getting her ankles wet, Sarah went to her towel. She lathered her bare skin with more sun lotion and laid down, glancing at *Teen Life* magazines. Darby joined her and rested.

I sat on my mat, crossed-legged, munching on cheese crackers, and staring across the sea. Sydney lay at my knees, scanning the area.

Several seagulls nestled into the sand to rest, and others flew over the water looking for food. Darby watched, trying to figure out their routine. In a surprise attack, she rushed toward the sleeping flock.

They screeched and fluttered off as Darby chased and barked. Sydney hurried after her. Once the gulls disappeared, the dogs chased each other, making figure-eights up and down the beach.

I walked close to the water's edge. Every time they got close to the jetty, I called, "Come here. No rocks!"

They'd turn around and race back for a peanut butter treat.

Our dads competed to see who could body surf the longest, and our moms borrowed our rafts to float up and over the waves. Once in a while Sarah lifted her head to see what was going on, or pressed on her pale skin to see if she was sunburned.

After Momma and Mrs. Neal had dried off and rested in their chairs, I heaved a sigh. "Momma, I'm ready to take Sydney up to the house. I'm worn out watching him."

"Honey, you've done a wonderful job. Syd can stay right here with me. You and Sarah go swim or walk."

Sydney lay on his stomach with his front paws crossed, acting like he was still on duty. One eye was always open. He watched me float out into the ocean but followed my command, "Stay."

With the game of chase over, Darby stood in the foamy waves. Sarah sat on her raft, squishing it into the sand, and looking toward the left jetty. Small waves guided my raft into her legs. She flinched.

Darby gazed at me and back to Sarah.

I stared at Sarah's braid. "I know what you're thinking, Sarah. And I don't plan on changing my mind."

CHAPTER 5

The sun crept west, bringing larger waves and moving the tide closer to our belongings. The umbrella leaned sideways with all the grown-ups clustered under the shade and discussing going out to dinner. Sarah and I lay on our towels, soaking up the last rays of sun as the late afternoon wind peppered us with sand.

Sarah sat up and touched her hair. "Yuck. I must look terrible. Does my hair look as bad as it feels?"

Lying on my stomach with my arms glued to my side, and my face squished on the towel, I purposely had looked away from Sarah, and mumbled, "I don't know. How does it feel?"

She giggled, "The loose pieces of my hair feel like straw. And you?"

I poked my matted hair. "Mine feels stiff." I knew what was coming next. When I was younger it didn't bother me to be teased about my curly red hair. But now it made me feel different in a weird sort of way.

"You look like a fuzzy, red-headed poodle."

I didn't move. "Thanks for the info. That always makes me feel better."

Once again Sarah was oblivious to my reaction. "Gosh, listening to our parents talk about going out to dinner is making me even hungrier. I'm starving."

Fighting with my feelings, I let her comments roll away. "Me, too."

"Won't a shower feel wonderful? And tonight I'll wear one of my brand new outfits."

I thought back to the contents of my duffel and sighed.

Under the house, a sign hung:

The House Rules

PLEASE! No Beach in the House

That meant every time we went from the beach to the house, we had to rinse our feet and the dogs' feet.

I moaned and studied our dogs. "That'll be a lot of feet."

The dark, wet carport contained a shower with hot and cold water faucets and a hose. I rubbed Sydney's chest, loosening the sand hiding in his thick fur and watching it sprinkle to the ground. "Oooh! Sydney. You have half the beach in your coat. You're going to need more than your feet cleaned. Ouch." I slapped my leg and looked around. "Something bit me."

Momma clapped her hands at the air. "There are mosquitoes down here. Let's hurry it up."

Sarah ran into the sunshine. Before Darby got away, Mrs. Neal grabbed her collar. "Oh, no, little girl. You'll get bathed just like Sydney."

Sydney mouthed the squirting water. At home he'd ruined many hoses this way.

"No bite, Sydney." I pulled on his collar. Again he snapped at the hose. I pulled his body away. His eyes squinted, full of glee. "I'm glad you're having so much fun, but you'll ruin the hose. No bite. Stand."

He spread his legs in a stand position. His long hair soaked up the warm water and vanilla-scented shampoo. Once it foamed, only his pink nose poked through the white bubbles.

I slapped at my arm while rinsing. Mosquitoes swarmed. "Hurry Sydney, Shake." Water flew everywhere.

"Okay, Darby. It's your turn," said Mrs. Neal. "She'll be quick. And then we can get out of here. Sarah, come help."

But Sarah wandered to the bunk bed room, and peered in the small window. "We really need to check out this room, Trina."

I waved my arms in the air. "Later. Let's get out of here. I don't want any more bites."

Darby led the way up the stairs. Sydney pushed by her at the screen door, wanting to use his skills. Darby growled, but backed up. Sydney pulled the grip, opening the door and letting Darby and then everyone else enter. Inside, both dogs circled the wooden deck, found their spot to rest in separate corners, and waited for their dinner.

I wished I could find my own space.

Syd lay on his stomach with his hind legs stretched behind and his front paws around his bowl. He filled his mouth with kibbles, and then spat them on the floor. Some rolled. Without moving from his position, his tongue reached each piece, one at a time.

Darby inhaled her dinner and paid close attention to Sydney's game. She hoped to snatch a stray piece of kibble, but once his bowl emptied, she disappeared to her napping zone.

Not Sydney. He grew excited, listening to our conversation, knowing the words, "going out to dinner." He had a job to do. First I blow-dried his damp fur and brushed it smooth. Then I wrapped his cape around his chest. "Now you look very professional."

Everyone squeezed into our van. Sarah and I went to the third row with Sydney sitting at my feet. Every time I read the writing on his cape, I sat a little straighter and held my chin a little higher. Showing off his skills to people who had no idea about service dogs gave me a warm, fuzzy feeling.

All the windows went up. The air conditioner blasted hot air.

"Ouch! Dad, everything's burning hot. And I can't put on my seatbelt."

Momma checked the vents on the right. "Carol, see if they're open behind you. Give it a minute, girls. It'll cool down."

I put my hands under my bottom. "The seat's melting my legs inside my pants."

Since Sarah had modeled her baby blue Capri outfit, the least I could do was wear my one pair of khaki Capris and my lilac flowered, Hawaiian-looking blouse. I had even taken extra time to blow-dry my hair and straighten it with a flat iron.

Sarah tipped forward, keeping her back from touching the seat. "Come on, cool air."

It didn't take long before the same buzzing sound I'd heard in the carport caught my attention. "The car's full of mosquitoes."

Dad slapped his cheek. "Hang on, everyone. I'm opening the windows. I'll blow them out."

A burst of wind gusted into the car, blowing my straightened hair into my mouth. Instantly, I grabbed all of my hair, bunched it behind my head, and hoped to prevent it from recurling.

After a few minutes of fresh air Sarah yelled, "The wind's messing up my hair, Mr. Ryan. I think they're all gone."

Dad closed the windows.

"Wrong. Wrong. Wrong." Sarah looked at a spot in the air and clapped her hands. "Let's see how many we can catch."

We sat like statues until the buzzing noise got close. We clapped at the air and laughed together. Sarah caught one, and I caught none. I smelled strawberry hair shampoo and soap. Being squeaky clean felt good. And my friend, Sarah, seemed to be back.

I put both hands on my stomach to silence its growling. "I can't wait to eat fried shrimp and hush puppies and coleslaw." I caught myself really smiling at Sarah. "And I bet they have sweet tea."

Sarah chimed in with a huge grin, "Then we'll have ice cream."

At the restaurant door, the hostess walked outside and closed the door. "It's against the law to have animals in the restaurant."

I removed the legal document carried in the side pocket of Sydney's cape, handed it to the lady and said, "He's a service dog in training and cannot legally be turned away."

She read the document, looked at Momma, and said, "Please wait a minute." She sprinted inside, disappearing behind swinging doors.

Everyone paced outside, famished. Sarah window-shopped at the souvenir store.

I turned to Momma. "I hope we don't have another argument like last month. I've got the phone number if we need help."

A few minutes later, the manager popped out of the swinging doors and met us outside. He rubbed his hands up and down on his pants, apologizing. "I'm so sorry to make you wait. Please come in. We've never had the opportunity to have a service dog in our restaurant. How about a seat by the window?"

Dad looked to me for my approval. I smiled. And then he nodded to the manager. "Thank you. That's very nice." He waved his arm, motioning for everyone to go ahead.

Sarah and I slid into opposite sides of our own booth. Sydney lay under my legs, peering out. Our parents took the booth behind Sarah.

The waitress brought menus and handed them to Sarah. When she returned, she asked Sarah what we wanted. I ordered for myself, but the waitress never made eye contact with me, just jotted notes on her pad.

I remembered other times when people assumed I was blind because I had a service dog. Their eyes showed pity, not knowing I could see them. One time the waitress even began reading what was on the menu. I smiled and said, "Thank you. I can read the menu." Then I explained I wasn't blind, only training a service dog for someone else.

This time, I tapped Sarah's hand on the table. When she looked at me, I grinned. "Sarah, the waitress thinks I'm blind. I'm going to play along."

Sarah's eyes gleamed, and a silly grin crossed her face. "Okay. I'll help."

I fumbled for my fork. Sarah reached over and unwrapped my silverware and handed me my napkin. I set it on my lap. My parents faced me from their booth. They knew what I was doing.

I read Dad's lips, "Stop being so dramatic." He shook his head from side to side and mouthed the words, "Not nice to tease the waitress."

Sarah and I ate our entire dinner, pretending. Through the window, I enjoyed the waves crashing through the pilings under the pier. And when we chatted, I looked to the side of Sarah's happy face, or I'd start laughing.

The waitress brought us chocolate ice cream and said to me. "Your dog's very well-behaved. Can I bring him a treat?"

"Oh, no thank you," I looked straight into her eyes, smiling. "He never eats people food. That's why he can sit without begging."

The waitress took a step backwards, stared at me for a moment, caught on, and then approached the table with a smirk. "What kind of dog is he?"

"He's an Australian Shepherd. He's training to be someone's service dog. In six months, he'll be matched with his special companion. It could be helping someone in a wheelchair, or who needs an alert dog, or who has other special needs. There are many kinds of service dogs nowadays."

Wow." She bent over, looked at Sydney under the table, and then stood up. "I had no idea dogs could be used for so many jobs. He's really nice."

Sarah laughed as the lady walked away. "I thought you'd play blind all night. You gave it away."

"Yeah. I changed my mind. I thought she should know the truth."

Sarah and I pulled chairs from an unused table over to the end of our parent's table. They spoke about looking for Loggerhead turtles as we scooped spoonfuls of ice cream.

I bumped shoulders with Sarah. "Oooh. That'll be fun."

Sarah shrugged. "I guess. There's nothing else to do."

"Well, I can't promise we'll find any, but it'll be an adventure," said Dad. "Something we couldn't do at the other beaches with their hotels and tourist attractions. The hard part is that you'll have to stay awake. Turtles won't come ashore until it's really dark."

"We love staying up late. Right, Trina?" Sarah poked me in my ribs.

"Yeah!" I sat up taller, put a smile on my face, and willed myself to have more energy. "I can do it."

CHAPTER 6

Before going turtle hunting, Mrs. Neal pulled out a large book from the house bookshelf called *Loggerhead Sea Turtles on Edisto*. "Have a look at these pictures, girls."

I sunk into the squishy couch and read. "Oh, I had no idea this kind of turtle was so big. Sarah, listen to this." I read out loud. "Adults can weigh two hundred to three hundred fifty pounds."

Sarah leaned over the book. "Look at the size of its head."

"Here." I scooted over. "Want to read with me?"

"That's okay. You read it out loud. I'm going to paint my toenails." Sarah bustled around getting her supplies.

I wanted her to hear, so I raised my voice. "Lights from the beach homes actually scare the turtles away from coming ashore. If the mama turtle gets frightened by noise or lights before she lays her eggs, she'll swim back to the ocean and must start all over again."

Mr. Neal bent over, looked at the picture, and added. "Because it takes a lot of effort for the turtle to drag her body out of the water, that's one of the reasons the beaches aren't having as many turtles laying eggs. People aren't being careful enough."

"Wow. Wouldn't it be cool to see one?" I wiggled to get more comfortable on the lumpy couch. "Let's stay busy, Sarah. You know I'm not very good at waiting."

I moved to the picnic table in the screened porch. "Bring your stuff out here. The smell won't be so bad, and we'll work on the jigsaw puzzle."

This time she rolled her eyes, sat on the other side of the table, and opened the polish bottles. "I'll just watch."

Our heads bopped back and forth to the beat of music coming from the iPod Station. I would say out loud, "I need a puzzle piece with a head and two arms. Look, this place needs a heart shape on the right foot."

Sarah would glance at me, and then the puzzle. Did she remember doing this together?

After painting one toe hot pink, and the next purple, she slid next to me. "All right. You've worn me down. I'll do it for a little while."

An hour and a half later, Dad announced, "Okay, everyone. We've waited long enough. We have a full moon, and the tide's coming up. That'll bring the turtles closer to shore, and we won't have to cross the jetties. Go put on long pants, and spray mosquito repellent over any skin showing."

I squirted my arms, neck, and face. The repellent was sticky, and smelled like rotten oranges. So much for being squeaky clean.

"Sydney, you'll need to *Stay*." He sniffed me, snorted at the new smell, and marched straight to my bed. Darby had already disappeared to Sarah's.

On the beach, the moon lit our way like a giant flashlight. The tide was coming in, causing waves to ripple one after another. Sarah whispered to me, "Crabs are running every which way. I'm afraid I'll step on one. What if one climbs on my foot?"

"Oh, don't be such a wimp. They're afraid of us, too. See, they're running the other direction."

Sarah moaned, and moved away on tip-toes, looking only at the sand.

Mrs. Neal's and Dad's flashlights scanned for a trail coming from the ocean and heading into the dunes. We continued walking, listening to Sarah complain. "I'm ready to go back. This is getting boring."

Ten minutes later, Mrs. Neal pointed and whispered, "Check this out. The shoreline looks as if someone's dragged a chair or something heavy out of the water. But there's no trail going back in the water."

Mr. Neal inspected the wet sand. "That might mean the turtle's still there, laying her eggs." Flashlights clicked off.

Momma put her fingers to her lips. No one spoke. Our eyes opened wider. My heart thumped faster.

Momma got there first, and waved for us to come. Once again she shook her finger, and then covered her mouth.

One at a time, we snuck into the dunes, and stood motionless, hardly breathing. The enormous turtle had begun digging her hole.

The turtle's flippers scraped the sand, flinging sand out of the way. The hole deepened. She glanced sideways, making sure it was safe. No one moved. With the quiet all around us, I couldn't help staring up into the starry sky. It was like watching a 4D movie with every sensation magnified. The waves exploded onshore, leaving florescent white foam and sending a salty, fishy odor into the misty air, onto our skin and lips.

Sometime later, the turtle backed up to the hole, and an egg popped out. Within seconds, another and then another fell into the nest. We stood, watching for over an hour. Once the eggs were falling, we had read, she couldn't stop until she was empty. Sarah pointed her phone camera at the turtle's face and clicked, bent down, and clicked the egg emerging.

After the last egg dropped, the turtle used her flippers to pull sand over them. Then she patted it down. Once the eggs were snuggled in, she pulled branches and leaves over the nest to camouflage the newness.

Sarah and I stepped closer. "Trina, lean down next to her. Let me get you and the turtle. She has a crusty line coming from her eyes and down her cheeks. Okay. Perfect. Look."

"Oooh. Great picture," I whispered. "Here let me get you." As Sarah kneeled, I aimed the camera. "Okay, got it. I wonder if those tears are because it hurts or she's just exhausted. There must be over a hundred eggs."

Dad spoke, knowing the turtle had completed her mission. "That's how she keeps her eyes moist while being out of the water for so long. Now, she'll go back and swim until her next hatching season."

I ran over and put my arm through his. "What happens to the babies when they hatch?"

"In sixty days or so, the ones that aren't eaten by other animals and make it to the ocean will live on their own. If the females live to adulthood, they'll find their way back to this exact location, and lay their eggs. Then the cycle begins again."

With the eggs safely hidden, the momma turtle turned her huge body around, and started her slow trek back to the ocean. "Hurry, Sarah. Take some more pictures as she heads to the water."

We scooted along with the turtle in slow motion. Now the sand had two trails, going up and coming down. But all evidence of her march on shore would disappear as soon as the tide washed up to the dunes.

Momma looked at her best friend, Carol. "Wasn't that was incredible?"

"Absolutely "Mrs. Neal's face sparkled in the moonlight. "Wouldn't it be fun to come back in two months, and watch the hatchlings come from their nest?"

I bounced in front of Momma. "Can we? Can we?"

"I doubt we'll be able to come back," Momma said while hugging me. "But it would be exciting."

Mrs. Neal handed her flashlight to Sarah. "Here, you girls go on ahead, but not too far. We'll meet you at the house."

Sarah chattered and skipped all the way back. "I'm sure glad I didn't turn around. What if I'd gone home? I would have missed all that. Did you ever see so many eggs? And her face. Wasn't she amazing?"

I grinned. She babbled so fast I didn't have a second to comment.

Sarah started again. "Wow. I can't wait to text all my friends, and forward the pictures. We've got to check the nest every day. Just think! After all that work she'll never see any of her babies."

Never once did Sarah mention looking for guys. I skipped ahead, saying, "Yes, yes, yes, to all that you said. We'll start tomorrow."

CHAPTER 7

MONDAY

S un leaked through the cracks of the window blinds. The minute I rolled over, Sydney leaped on the bed and snuggled up to my neck. Whew. He smelled like the ocean, fishy. I hugged him anyway and then said, "Off, Syd."

His nails clicked on the hardwood floors as he walked in circles, panting. No way was I going back to sleep. "Okay. Okay."

My bathing suit hung from the rounded chair spindle. Squeezing the bottom of the suit, I whispered, "Yuck. I'm not putting you on." I picked up my shorts and tee shirt lying on the floor and snuck out.

In the living room, I told Sydney, "Wait." I poked my head into Sarah's room and softly called, "Darby." She lifted her head from the end of the queen size bed, but didn't move.

Sarah needed a jolt, a shove, or an explosion before she'd ever wake up early in the morning. I closed the door and dressed. Scratching and whining at Sarah's door let me know Darby had changed her mind.

I reopened it. "Good girl. Come on."

On an empty beach, the dogs could run unleashed, but by nine o'clock, Edisto had leash rules. I hoped to find the turtle's nest, safe before that time. Then we'd practice some training skills. I put my phone in my pocket and stepped softly out the screen door. It squeaked, and then slammed. So much for being quiet!

At the top of the dunes, the dogs stood at attention, their ears perked at the whistling wind and the crashing waves. Then a flock of squawking sea gulls soared across the sky. The dog's eyes never wavered from the birds, until they coasted out of sight.

Wishing I had my camera, I tried to store the images of the sun reflecting on the water like a large mirror and how the sparkling light rolled with the waves. I'd sketch this when I returned.

Sydney had watched long enough and ran, barking at the waves. On the exact moment he put his nose level with the water, a wave broke. With a face full of sea water, he turned away, snorting and coughing. Then he dashed back to the water's edge to do it again.

Darby ignored Syd and dug into the wet sand.

I started in the direction of the turtle's nest, splashing through the shallow water. Sydney chased me, and Darby trailed after Sydney, but higher on shore. All of a sudden they disappeared into the dunes.

Keeping an eye on what they were doing, I followed. Sydney squatted, and then he looked to his rear end, twisting around and around.

I bent, close to his face, "What's wrong, Syd?"

He stared at me as a steady brown stream squirted from his bottom.

"Oooh. Nasty!" I waved my hand in front of my nose. "Momma said you'd get diarrhea if you drank that salty water."

Darby sprinted from bush to bush sniffing new smells, and then did her morning business. I pulled out a baggie and scooped it up.

After rinsing my hands in the ocean, I turned to check on the dogs. Sydney sat in the sand with a droopy face. I hurried to him and bent, eye to eye. "You'll be okay. We'll go home and Momma'll give you some medicine." He licked my face.

A trash can with a painted yellow smiley face stood next to the pier. I made my hand signal and called, "Come." Both dogs followed as I threw away my nasty morning souvenirs.

Spotting a large bird on the sand, Darby ran ahead. I didn't think twice about her chasing a bird. They always took off to the sky. But this bird didn't move. Sydney, distracted by a crab, didn't notice.

The bird's black and white speckled wings opened and caught the wind. Two black, skinny legs with webbed feet stuck out sideways, as it tried to lift its body. Flopping up and down, it showed its white belly, shook its grey head, and poked a duck-like beak in the sand. Dark eyes stared back at Darby. "Darby, come here. You're scaring the bird." Darby's nose continued working overtime.

Sydney stopped digging, raised his head, sniffed the scent in the air, and looked to me. "Good boy. Stay."

The bird flapped harder as Darby prodded it with her nose. She was lucky she didn't get nipped. And suddenly, the bird's head drooped, and lay perfectly still.

I ran to leash Darby. A small crowd formed around the bird, gawking and whispering to each other. I pulled Darby next to Sydney. His nose twitched, trying to get a whiff. Darby squirmed and whimpered.

I gave her The Look. "Darby, Sit."

She glanced up, and knew I meant business.

"Oh, no," I mumbled under my breath.

The two sand castle guys ambled over, talking quietly about the bird. My heart hammered, and I wanted to disappear. Out of the corner of my eye, I saw the dark-haired guy move closer to me. He poked the older boy with his elbow and nodded in my direction. I held my breath.

He turned to me and said, "Hi. What're you doing out so early?"

For a split second, I peeked up. His green eyes meet mine. I inhaled and spoke to the sand. "I wanted the dogs to run free." Trying one more time to look him in the face without blushing, I added, "There aren't many people on the beach this early."

Then the taller guy moved closer. "Where's your friend?"

"Oh, she's still in bed. Early morning isn't her thing." I had barely finished my sentence when the bird screeched. My head spun to the bird, and I blurted louder than I ever intended. "Someone needs to do something. That bird's going to die."

The crowd, hovering over the bird, lifted their heads and stared at me. My cheeks heated up, and I'm sure my freckles stood center stage and took a bow. Great. I dropped my head, hoping my embarrassment would dissolve.

The older boy pulled out his cell phone. "I'll call the beach ranger. He'll know what to do." His voice didn't croak this time.

The smaller guy said, "My name is Chase. That's my brother, Peyton. Your friend called you Trina. Is that right?"

I lifted my face for a moment. "Yes." Sydney looked at me when my name was said. Darby had given up moving and lay on the sand. "How'd he know to call the ranger?"

Chase smiled. "We used to live here."

I actually spoke to him. "Really?"

"Yeah! For four years. It was great."

"Wow! That's lucky." I let a smile grow. "Where's the little boy?"

"Logan? He's at home with Mom." He paused, looked around, and then lowered his head. "He has a hard time with changing places and new people. Even though we come often, it takes him a few days to get settled."

I had wondered about Logan's behavior yesterday and started to ask, "Does he—" But the noise from the ranger's jeep alerted the dogs. "Quiet, Syd. Down." Darby crawled between my legs. In seconds, the jeep had rolled across the sand, leaving deep tire marks. With no doors on the jeep, the ranger jumped out, sideways.

I didn't take my eyes from the ranger. He walked directly to the bird. It flapped its wings, but never budged.

"Oh, I hope she's okay." Once again, the words flew out of my mouth.

Standing by the bird, he said to the crowd, "It looks as though the loon was pulled in with the high tide and stayed too long. Since her legs can't support her body on the sand, and she needs a running start to fly, she got trapped. She'll be okay. She's just exhausted from trying to free herself."

The ranger picked her up with both hands and carried her into the water. Once in the waves, the loon swam away.

Not prepared for any more conversation, I let a heavy sigh escape, and I turned to the guys. "Well, it was nice meeting you." I twisted a loose strand of hair, looked at Chase, and tried to find the right words. "I need to get back. See you on the beach." I took a step and released Sydney from his down. "Come, Syd."

"W-w-wait." Chase stammered and then continued, "Can I ask you a favor?"

I stopped, gripped my hands together with the leash in the middle. "I guess so."

"Yesterday, Logan petted Sydney. You'll never know how happy that made him. He has trouble talking, and yet, all day he said, 'Dog' and smiled. Is there any chance that you'd bring him down again for another visit?"

"So Logan likes dogs?"

"He's never been around dogs before, but he certainly enjoyed yours. He has, um—" He looked down at his feet, groping for the words and then said, "He has autism."

My heart skipped a beat. Sydney's special skill. I nodded my head. "I know all about that."

Chase's eyes flickered. He moved in closer. "You do?"

"Sydney's training to be a service dog, maybe for a child with autism. We had two classes with special needs and autism in our school. Sydney and I helped in those classrooms once a week."

"Really." His smile widened. "So, maybe, you wouldn't mind?"

"No. Not at all. Sarah always wants to go for walks on the beach. This is her dog, Darby."

He looked down at Darby and patted her head.

My front teeth grazed over my bottom lip. I swallowed my concerns about talking, and lifted my chin. "I'll tell Sarah. And we'll definitely come down later."

"Great. See you then."

While walking home, I replayed the conversation. No reason to tell Sarah about our meeting. Not yet. The idea of meeting those guys would totally distract her from all we had planned for the morning. And I did say, "Later."

CHAPTER 8

Closer to our house, I unhooked Darby. "Who's ready for breakfast?" Darby and Sydney's ears raised to attention at the word "breakfast." They looked at me with sloppy grins, raced up the path, and waited for me on the deck.

Towels hung over the side of the porch, drying. As I pulled the orange and purple striped one down, they shoved their faces into it at the same time. Darby growled. Syd backed up and waited his turn like a gentleman. Once the dogs were dried, Syd pulled the door open and backed up. Darby and I walked into the screened porch.

I held the door for him. "Thanks, Syd. Stay here and I'll get your food." I cracked the inside door just enough to let me move in the house and keep the dogs out. The smell of coffee and sausage drifted out, telling me everyone was up.

Detoured by food, I first snagged a sausage biscuit, and then whispered to Momma, "Sydney has diarrhea. He might need some medicine."

Sarah gave me a puzzled look. "What have you been doing?"

My eyes darted around the room. I wasn't good at lying. I didn't dare look Sarah in the eyes, or the truth might spill out. My heart beat like a snare drum and I worried my face would give me away.

Casually, I said, "Walking the dogs on the beach and watching a Ranger save a loon stuck on the sand." Then I answered her questions about the loon. *Whew. I did it. No guys mentioned.* I turned a happy face to Sarah. "Want to see if the Turtle Patrol found the nest?"

Sarah's hair was in a ponytail and she wore a red tie-dyed tee with splatters of white and pink with white shorts. "Yes. I'm ready. And thanks for taking Darby. You must've gotten up really early."

"Yep. You know it's my favorite time to be out there."

Momma hustled around the kitchen. "Sydney needs to stay here. Did you already feed them?"

"No. Just took them out for a quick run."

"Well, that's actually good. I'll boil rice and spoon in some pumpkin. If that doesn't help we'll try some medicine. It's going to be difficult, but you must teach him not to drink the salt water."

In between sips of coffee, Sarah's mom said, "I'll feed Darby, Sarah. Take your phone and go have some fun."

My stomach growled, reminding me I was still hungry. I wrapped one more biscuit in a paper towel, stuffed a boxed orange juice in my shorts' pocket, and we flew out the door.

It creaked, and Momma called, "Don't slam the door."

I flinched as it banged. "Oops!"

While running down the beach, Sarah showed me a half-empty bag of potato chips, and a baggie full of crackers. "I want to feed the seagulls before we look for the nest."

I halted, and glanced toward our intended destination. "Aren't you anxious to see if the turtle's nest is safe?"

"Yeah, but it can wait a little longer."

If I have to wait to see the nest, she can wait to hear about the guys. "All right." We stood on the beach gazing into the sapphire sky. Not a bird flew over us. "I wonder where they are."

Sarah threw chips into the air, and the wind blew them into my face. We giggled. "Try again, Sarah. Let's see if I can catch them."

As I opened my mouth to catch a crumb, a large seagull flew toward us. Sarah threw more crumbs into the air, and it swooped down with its beak wide open. I fell to my knees, clamped my mouth tight, and let the gull eat them.

Then another seagull zoomed close. Holding a cracker in the air, I let the gull pluck it from my fingers. Before long, the birds sat in a circle around our legs, eating what had fallen. One bird took flight, pecking those lingering in the air.

When a fat gull waddled closer to Sarah, she complained. "I'm not letting that bird have any more. He's a hogger."

Another large gull flew overhead, waiting for the next toss. I dropped the last of the crumbs over by the smallest birds and pushed the bully away with my foot. "Did you see that? It actually tried to peck my toe."

Sarah shook her head. "You better be careful. It may decide to attack."

Suddenly, a familiar barking sent the seagulls soaring into the clear, blue sky. Our parents carried large mugs of coffee for their morning walk.

Sarah's dad called ahead. "Sorry about the dogs. We thought you'd be finished with the gulls and over at the nest."

"It's all right, Dad. We just ran out of food."

I ran up to Sydney and gave him a hand signal, Sit. "And it was definitely something we couldn't do with the dogs around."

Dad unleashed Syd. "That's very true. I brought a tennis ball to keep him busy for a while."

"Perfect, Dad." I grabbed Sarah's arm. "Come on. We've waited long enough. Let's check the nest."

Momma stepped over to join us. "I'm glad you didn't go without us. It's a ways up the beach. I'm dying to see it, too."

Sarah's shoulders slumped. She stared at the sand, making deep, straight lines with the heel of her foot.

Mrs. Neal patted Sarah's shoulder and looked at Momma. "I think the girls want to explore by themselves. Sarah's got her phone, and this is such a family beach."

"Yeah." Sarah's head popped up. "That'd be good. We'll be fine."

Momma shrugged. "I don't know." She nodded sideways, scrunched her eyes, and pressed her lips together. I knew she was trying to find the right words to say. "I'm not used to you taking off by yourself." She paused, and I could see her brain spinning with all the terrible things that could happen. Then her eyes locked with mine. "I'll let you go. But only if you'll call in a few minutes. I'll want to know where you are and that you're safe."

Sarah rolled her eyes and puffed out her breath. "Mrs. Ryan. I promise we'll text you. I'll even send you a picture of us."

Mrs. Neal put her arm around Momma's shoulder. "They'll be fine." Her eyes zeroed into Sarah's. "You better pay attention." I just stood there watching their interaction. It was obvious this had been discussed before.

Once more Momma spoke. "Trina, do you have your phone?"

"Yes. And I charged it last night. I'll call when we get to the turtle's nest."

The moment we moved away, Sarah groaned. "Whew. I didn't think your mom was going to let you go."

We started jogging and chatting about my mom being overprotective. I was used to it and had never really questioned her. I even defended her. Sarah rolled her eyes once more.

It was kind of a thrill to have some Sarah time, alone. Having the dogs at the beach was more work than I'd ever anticipated, and I wanted Sydney to have the time of his life. But right now, I was free.

Free to inhale sea air. Free to run in the sand, and free to collect sea shells.

"Sarah, look at the scallop shell I found." I parted its two sides. "Aw. It's empty."

Sarah had moved to a new spot, and yelled, "Look at this one. It's huge."

I ran over. It had a swirly cone shape with spikes on one side and a skinny end. "Oooh. I saw that kind in the shell book. It's called a whelk shell. The book said a sea snail wore this and crawled around on one foot."

I scanned the shore in each direction and laughed. "At this speed we'll never get to the turtle's nest. But I don't care. Sydney's having fun with Dad, and I'm having fun." I whispered to myself, "With you." I took a deep, deep breath, calming myself. I knew I needed to say something about the guys, but just couldn't bring myself to do it. Not yet.

Sarah bent close to the sand. "Look. Do you think it's a shark's tooth? It's tiny, tiny, black and sharp."

"Yep. I bet it is." I stopped moving. When Sarah gave me her full attention, I held her glance. "Why didn't you want our moms to come?"

"It's more fun on our own."

"Oh." Another little pang of guilt pricked at my conscience. But once I confessed, our fun would stop. And I reminded myself I had said "later."

Sarah pointed toward the dunes. "There's a nest. I see the orange ribbon." She sprinted to the stakes that barricaded the nest. "Wrong date. Can't be ours. Let's keep going."

As we rushed back, the dune caved in, dropping Sarah onto her bottom. While cracking up with laughter, she stared out to the calm sea. Then she shrieked, "Dolphins. Look. Trina, look!"

My eyes searched the ocean. Nothing. Just waves.

Then she screamed again, "Keep watching. They're under the water."

Smack in front of us, a pointed fin peeked out of the water. And then a head. A body. And then a two-sided tail. It jumped in a curved position and splashed back in the water. Sarah and I bounced up and down. I squealed, "I see it. And there's more."

Sarah clapped. "I see one—two big ones."

"Look. One—two babies. Hurry, Sarah. Take a picture."

Swishing our bare feet back and forth, we buried them in the scratchy sand, not wanting to move. The dolphins put on a show. Their tails patted the sea, sending a shower of shimmering water into the air. The time between their jumps became longer and longer. Sarah and I waited for them to leap above the water. "There." Sarah pointed farther to the right.

"Yep. They're following the shrimp boat." We watched until the boat was a speck in the water. I turned from the ocean to the direction of the turtles. "All right. It's time to find our turtle's nest."

Again my stomach jolted at what I hadn't told Sarah. I'd have to do it soon.

CHAPTER 10

I glanced at every path and up every deck looking for something familiar. "It was so dark last night. I'm not sure I'll recognize the spot."

Sarah folded her arms and concentrated. "I kind of remember a long walkway that came out close to the dunes. Mom spotted the trail soon after that. Let's keep looking."

We walked and walked.

"I sure wish I'd worn my bathing suit." Sweat streamed down my back. "Sarah, I can't wait any longer." I dashed into the shallow water, getting my legs wet to my knees. The water cooled me a bit, and I tried to look innocent.

As Sarah dunked her toes, I impulsively kicked at the rolling wave. I really aimed to miss. The salty water only sprinkled one of her legs, but she gave me The Look and moved toward the dunes.

While up there, Sarah checked out the mound of sand surrounded by orange ribbons and hollered, "It's here. I found our nest! It has last night's date. The Turtle Patrol is protecting our nest."

I ran up. "Good eyes, Sarah. Remember the book said, 'Approximately sixty days from now, little hatchlings will emerge.'" I squatted and patted the sand. "I sure wish we didn't live so far away. I'd love to see the babies swim into the ocean."

"Me too. I feel like they're our turtles, and we'll never know how many make it."

"It's great the Turtle Patrol keeps an eye on all these nests. We can relax and know they're safe."

"But," Sarah interrupted, and put her hands on her hips. "Maybe, we should still check it." She gazed up the empty coastline and then chuckled.

"This'll give us a reason to jog on the beach and maybe meet others." She gave me sideways smirk.

I gulped. "That's true. Which reminds me, I need—" I had planned to tell her about the guys, but instead I remembered Momma worrying. "Sarah, send a picture of me with the turtle nest and text Momma. I'll sit right here."

As soon she clicked the picture, Sarah's head bent over the phone texting, and I waited until I had her attention.

Two loud barks made me lose my train of thought, again. I spotted a couple with a golden Lab, his tail waving back and forth and his tongue lolling. I jolted toward the dog and, not wanting to alarm him, I slowed down and found out it was a her.

"Dis is Golee," said the tall man with a throaty voice and dropped consonants, similar to the deaf students at school. "She lobs to pay."

I turned directly to him so he could see my lips while I spoke slowly. "We have two dogs back at our beach house. May I pet her?"

He nodded.

I stroked Goldie's back and smiled at the lady walking with him. "Mine's an Aussie. My friend," I turned to Sarah who was bent over the sand, looking at sea shells, "has a Springer spaniel. Dogs sure have fun on the beach. Don't they?"

The lady used sign language. Then she answered. "Yes. We can't keep Goldie away from the water."

"Sarah!" I called loud enough to get her attention. "You need to meet this dog." I turned back to the couple. "Ours are puppies and never run out of energy. Is Goldie a lot of trouble?"

"No, she's an older hearing dog. She stays very close to my husband and clues him into sounds. Just this morning, a beach ranger raced his Jeep along the sand. Goldie stopped my husband. She wouldn't let him move until the Jeep had passed. But she doesn't have as much energy as she used to."

Sarah must have overheard the conversation about Goldie being a hearing dog. She bounced over, threw her arm around mine, and proudly announced, "Her Australian Shepherd's going to be a service dog, too. She's a puppy raiser."

I tingled inside. *So she does know what I'm doing.* I turned to look at her face. *And she's proud of me. Who would have ever known?*

The lady smiled a big, toothy smile, making her happy eyes squint into slits above her puffy cheeks. "It is so nice to hear that you're a trainer. I'm Mrs. Walker and this is my husband." She looked at him and signed.

Mr. Walker nodded his head and said with slurred speech, "You're a very special person to do what you're doing." I understood him completely.

Mrs. Walker spoke to Sarah. "You have a very courageous friend." And then to me. "I know it's got to be hard to give up your puppy, but you're doing a wonderful thing for others. I'm impressed."

"Thanks. It's been fun raising a puppy, but a lot of work, too. This week, Sydney's on his first beach trip." I smiled, but it slowly faded. "On our way home this Sunday, I have to return him to his kennel." I dug my feet back and forth in the sand. My heart ached as I thought about the day coming. The rest of my thoughts just spilled out. "Depending on his personality, his trainer will decide what kind of service he'll do." I paused and glanced out to the shiny waves, blinking to clear my eyes, and tried to think about something else. I looked at Mr. Walker and back to Mrs. Walker. All that came out was, "It's going to be really hard."

Mrs. Walker signed again to her husband. He peered at me and signed back. His wife said, "This is what he wants you to know. Goldie has been my ears. I know someone did what you're doing for me, and I want you to know, my life changed completely. I've never been able to thank them. Those two words will never be enough. Please take my thanks and remember on Sunday what I've said."

We stood face to face. I wanted him to read my lips as I used a couple of hand signals. "Okay." I sucked up my sadness, and wiped my wet cheeks with the backs of my hands. I needed to move. "It was nice meeting you. I'll try to remember. Come on, Sarah, let's go rescue our dogs. Bye, Goldie." I patted her head.

I stuffed my sad thoughts away, heading home. I knew I couldn't wait any longer on telling Sarah about the guys. "Oh, by the way, I kept trying to tell you the sandcastle boys want us to come down."

"What?" Sarah interrupted, folding her arms and halting. "The ones we met yesterday?" She glared at me.

"Yes." I nodded, but kept my eyes on the scraps of shells in the sand. "Every time I started to tell you, we got busy, and then we met Goldie."

She took two steps ahead, turned around, and pointed at me. "All morning you never shared this piece of information. What'd they say?"

I swallowed. "They want us to bring our dogs down to play with their little brother this afternoon."

"When I asked you what you'd been doing this morning," Sarah's voice grew louder and louder, "you never mentioned guys." Her chest and shoulders lifted as she gulped air. Her eyes glared as she mocked my voice. "How convenient to mention—" Her head flopped side to side with each word, "'—walking the dogs on the beach, and watching a ranger save a bird.' But nothing about." She made air quotations. "'The Guys.'"

Sarah chugged ahead. I stopped walking and watched her go. I had really blown it this time. She had every reason to be angry with me. After a few minutes, Sarah did an about turn and stomped her way back. She stood face to face with me. My cheeks warmed.

"How could you not tell me? You knew I wanted to see them."

"I'm sorry, Sarah." I swirled my big toe in the sand, shamed. "I should have told you earlier, but I knew you'd be more interested in them than me."

"Well." Sarah's eyes gazed off. There was a giant pause. Neither one of us said anything. Then she grumbled, "I'm still mad that you didn't tell me."

"I know I should have—"

Sarah interrupted. "I guess I have been a little obsessed with meeting guys." She had held up her finger and thumb as if measuring two inches as she spoke. "But I told you I could have fun with you, and meet boys at the same time."

"I really didn't believe you."

Sarah's eyes met mine. "Okay. Okay. I don't like it, but you're probably right."

"So, you're not mad at me anymore?"

She glanced out to the water and then to the sand. "Hmm." She lifted her head to me, "I guess not." She scowled for a moment. "Now, tell me again what they said. I don't think it sunk in the first time."

Relief swelled through my body. I wanted to laugh, but just smiled. "The guy you liked is named Chase. His tall brother is Peyton. The interesting part is that Logan, their little brother, has autism."

"You sure learned a lot about them." Her eyes narrowed. "Never mind, never mind. Go on."

"The little boy, Logan, has been asking to see Sydney. Chase pleaded with me to bring him back down the beach." I paused. "So, do you want to walk down?"

"I've got to go home first. I can't go this way." She looked down at herself. "I'm a mess. Of course, I want to do it! Let's get cleaned up and then walk down." She inhaled. Smiled, then her eyebrows crinkled. "I have to take Darby?"

I nodded. "Sarah, the whole reason they talked to me was about bringing Sydney to see Logan. And Darby should come, too. It gives us something to talk about."

"But I won't be able to visit with the guys and supervise Darby." Sarah stomped her foot. "I still can't believe you didn't tell me. If I had known sooner, we'd already be there."

"I know. And we would have missed all the fun we had. See. I was right not to tell you earlier."

Sarah's eyes told me she got it.

CHAPTER 10

I retrieved my bathing suit from the deck and sprayed sun lotion on myself.
Our moms flew up the stairs, laughing, and our dads and dogs were close
behind.

Momma asked, "Anyone ready for lunch, and then a swim?"

"I'm ready, but Sarah is still fixing up in the bathroom. The guys we met
on the beach yesterday asked us to come down with our dogs."

"That's nice." Sarah's mother knocked on the bathroom door. "Hurry up,
Sarah. We're all waiting."

Five minutes later, Sarah opened the door and moseyed out in a sky-blue
bikini with a white net cover-up. Her long hair hung loose in the back, and
the sides had been pulled into a small pony tail on top of her head, and tied
with a blue ribbon.

"Hey, supermodel." I shrugged. "I'm wearing my same bathing suit. I'm
going to get wet and play in the sand."

Momma gawked at Sarah and glanced back at me. I knew her thoughts, I
should have put on my new suit, but I planned to visit with Logan—and he
didn't care what I wore.

Mrs. Neal shrugged her shoulders. "Your new clothes were meant to be
worn."

Momma smiled and moved to the kitchen. "Absolutely. You do look pretty,
Sarah. Let's have lunch."

I could have been a ghost, listening to their conversation. *Was I invisible?*
Tomorrow, maybe I'd wear my new suit.

Single file, everyone hauled beach supplies down the wooden path. "I bet
today will be easier, Momma. The afternoon's half over, and now we know
what the dogs will do."

One by one, we halted at the top of our sand dune. The tide had started back down, and we had a wider beach. Patches of people covered the beige sand, some under umbrellas, and others sunning themselves on colorful towels. Several families swam, a few children threw skim boards and balanced on the surf, and Frisbees flew in the wind on their own courses.

Sarah and I leashed our dogs. Sydney barked, pulling me toward the water. I looked down at him and said, "Quiet. Have you forgotten your manners? Sit." Sydney's ears flattened out and he sat. After making him wait, I said, "Okay." He stood. "Forward." And he heeled down the beach.

Darby moved closer to Sarah's legs as she yelled back to our parents. "We're going farther down." I glanced at Sarah.

We wore our towels around our necks. I juggled Sydney's leash, shoved a chair under my left arm, placed a heavy denim bag over my shoulder, and carried a plastic jug of water in the other hand. Sarah slid Darby's leash around her wrist, and had a free arm for her chair, and a small beach bag.

Sarah's parents waved, but Momma shouted, "Don't go too far. I want to be able to see you. And don't forget sun lotion."

"Okay," Sarah answered for me. Turning back to me, she said, "This worked out great. Yesterday, I tried to think of a plan to get you to walk down and see the guys. I still can't believe you didn't tell me. I'll get up early tomorrow. Maybe they'll be running again."

"I have to see that to believe it. I'm only interested in letting Sydney get to know Logan. You can have either boy you want." I moved my eyes from the sand to the boys' direction. "Sarah, I see them. They're on this side of the jetty making another sand castle. Let's not get too close."

Sarah wiggled her shoulders and ducked her chin. "OO! I see them, too. We *are* going to visit with them. Aren't we?"

"Of course. But let's put our stuff down. Let them come over and talk. Anyway, there's way too much going on to let the dogs go free."

"How about, we put our chairs right here?" Sarah stopped and nodded toward the birds nearby. "Darby will sit next to me and watch the birds."

"That's a good spot." I dropped all my stuff and looked around the beach. "Wow. More people today. I guess they all just got here like us."

"Let's make a sand castle." Sarah smiled as she leaned closer. "They'll notice and come help."

I frowned. "Really, Sarah. For a little while, can't we just enjoy the beach?"

"No. You already talked to them this morning. And I've waited all day."

I held up both hands palm out. "All right, all right. But first, let's get settled."

Sarah opened her chair and hung her beach bag on the back. Darby sat, watching the birds. "So far, so good."

"Syd. I'll unhook you. Stay. This will be a great lesson for you." Sydney scooped sand, leaving a bowl-shaped hole, and laid in his nest. "Good boy." I patted him, gave him a treat, and opened my chair. "Okay, Sarah. I'm ready."

Sarah walked backwards toward the water. "We'll need water to mix with the sand. Then we can dribble it the on the sides of the castle, and make fancy spires. Ask Sydney to dig a hole. He likes to dig." Sarah peeked sideways toward the guys, trying not to be obvious, and ran to fill her bucket with ocean water. Darby trotted back and forth.

I didn't look but also wondered.

"Sydney." His gold eyes peered directly into mine. "Dig. Right here. Dig." I used my hands and showed Sydney what I wanted him to do.

His ears went up and he barked once, telling me, "Okay." He put his bottom in the air and his front feet started digging. Sand flew.

"Good boy," I said, proud of his intelligence. "Okay, all done." Sydney continued tunneling to China. "STOP, Sydney, STOP!" He dug once more, looked at me, crept to his nest, and rested his head on the sandy edge. "Now we're not going to have a castle, but a manhole."

"I've got it," said Sarah. "We'll call it a lake."

"Sydney, Stay." He watched us fill our buckets. Every time I got close to the water, I'd go for a quick swim. I held my bucket in one hand and swam with the other. A wave splashed over me, burning my eyes, but I brought more water to the lake and went out again.

Only going knee deep, Sarah caught water in her pail. Darby followed her back and forth. On each trip to the water, Sarah glanced toward the guys. She'd whisper to me on her way back, "I wonder how long it's going to take until they come over."

The dogs panted with their tongues hanging. "I think we better get them wet, Sarah. They're getting too hot. I'm taking Sydney swimming."

Sarah filled her bucket and poured ocean water on Darby. Darby flinched and wrinkled her nose at Sarah. "Don't give me that look. This is better than making you swim. And I'm not ready to get wet, either."

Sydney dog-paddled beside me with his head and chin jutting out of the water. His little legs kicked. We went just far enough, where the waves only rolled and didn't break. As the water leveled, I touched the sandy floor. Syd's mouth went under the water and he slurped.

"Oh, no. Sydney, no water." I lifted him higher. He snorted and coughed. I moved to shallower water, holding him around his stomach until we reached sand. "Go back, Syd. Go see Sarah and rest."

He walked to shore and followed Sarah. Darby paced, avoiding the foamy waves, watching Sydney. Then Syd noticed I wasn't following. He halted, did an about turn, waded into the water and dog paddled out to me. Knowing he was tired, I swam toward him. One wave rolled, lifting him up and over. He kept coming further out. Another swell of ocean grew. I believed it would move under us. Instead, the wave broke, crashing on top of Sydney.

I scanned the water inch by inch, screaming, "Oh no! Oh no!" My head jerked every direction. *Where is he? I don't see him.* I kicked as hard as my legs would move. *Hurry. Faster.* I swam to where he had been. Once my feet touched the sand, I caught my breath. Everything looked dark. I shrieked out to the ocean. "Sydney, where are you?" I turned toward the shore. "Sarah!" I shouted, fear filling my entire body. "Do you see Sydney? He went under."

CHAPTER 11

Treading and keeping my head above the deep, dark water, I gasped for breath and still had no clue on Sydney's location. Chase and his brother must have heard my plea for help. Peyton hurled one long leg after the other, crashed into the water, and dove in. Darby howled. Chase held Logan's hand and pulled him toward the water's edge. Dad and Mr. Neal swam out. Momma and Mrs. Neal paced on shore. I took another deep breath, clamped my mouth shut, and got ready for another wave.

Dad plunged through the wave. With long strokes, he quickly made it to me. Nothing. Still no sign of Sydney. The suspense made me want to cry, but I needed my breath. Mr. Neal swam against the current.

I floated up and over a wave, calling, "Sydney! Sydney!"

"There he is! To your right!" Chase screamed out to us.

Off in the distance, Syd's head bobbed with his nose in the air, and then he disappeared.

Dad swam straight over and lifted Sydney enough to keep his head above the water. Once Dad touched the ocean floor, he clutched Syd's body to his chest. Sydney looked like a small porpoise, spurting water from of his nose and mouth. He sneezed twice, each time splashing his nose into the water, and then coughing.

"Hey, fella." Dad's words rebounded in between waves. "Let's get you in. You've had enough water."

Mr. Neal swam with me to shore. Sarah clapped, jumping up and down, and everyone cheered. I hugged Dad around his waist. "You saved Sydney. You're a hero."

"Well, I don't know about that. Those boys helped, too."

Peyton bent his head between his knees, and flung water from his long brown bangs. After catching his breath, he stood and used his fingers to comb the hair out of his eyes.

"Way to go, Pey," called Chase, walking over with Logan. "You were fast on your feet."

With Darby at her heels, Sarah stepped in front of the guys and swished her skinny pony tail side to side. She put her hand on her heart and said, "That was sooo scary. Thanks for helping."

Once Dad had rubbed Sydney all over and seemed satisfied Sydney had no injuries, he turned to the guys. "Thanks a lot. He kinda blended into the water." And to me, with his face still frowning. "T, we better keep an eye on him when he goes swimming. I don't want to have to do that again."

Sydney licked his arm.

"He's saying thank you, Dad." I grinned at *my* Sydney.

I faced Chase and Peyton and looked them straight in their eyes, one at a time. "And, thank you for noticing what was happening. I think Sydney's going to need some more practice on being a water dog."

Chase asked with a nervous laugh, "Can I help you get Sydney settled?" His green eyes connected to mine.

"Okay." I knew my face glowed, but I hoped he'd think it was from the sun. "Come on, Syd. You need to rest." I walked Sydney to our place on the sand, opened another towel, and told Syd, "Down." He circled until he had the right spot, and then lay on his sandy paw prints.

In and out, Darby weaved through Sarah's legs while Peyton visited with her. I sat next to Sydney and stole tiny peeks. I didn't want her to think I was flirting with Chase. And then Chase sat next to me. I gasped a short, guilty breath as her jaw dropped.

Logan plunked down next to Sydney and stroked his wet fur. Sydney sighed and moved his head onto the boy's lap. I never saw Logan's eyes, but his grin wallpapered my memory bank.

With my little bit of knowledge about flirting, I'd say Peyton spoke to Sarah with a lot of interest. Sarah had jerked her attention back to Peyton, balanced on one leg, drew circles in the sand with her other foot, and seemed to be sliding toward us. Peyton and Darby inched along. As they got closer, I heard her say, "Let's check on Sydney."

Usually Syd kept one eye open as if on duty, but this time he slept. Darby lay next to him on his towel with her face on her paws, staring at Logan.

Chase and I had begun filling the manhole with ocean water. Sarah snickered as they closed in. "We've come to see the champion swimmer. How's he doing?"

I don't think Chase heard Sarah. I sort of ignored her. I'm not sure why, but I didn't want to stop collecting water, laughing, and encouraging Logan to help.

When Logan abruptly decided to join us, Sydney's head fell onto the towel. He woke, shook his head, glimpsed at his surroundings, stood, and then waggled his entire body.

Logan grabbed his bucket, saying, "Wah-der."

Trailing behind, Sydney scuttled close to Logan's legs.

"It's awesome to see Logan joining us." Chase beamed at me.

Out of the corner of my eye, Sarah approached. "Hey, you guys," She swung her hip to the right and placed her hands on each side of her waist, waiting for us to notice her presence. Then she put her pointy finger in her cheek, and cleared her throat, "Am I interrupting?"

Peyton teased Chase about something at the same time and caught his attention. Peyton roared at Chase's response and said, "Looks like you've got it under control, dude."

"Don't just stand there," Chase sassed back. "Get a bucket and help us fill this lake. Logan's having so much fun. Come on, Sarah. You can help, too."

Laughter emerged, water splashed, and somehow the hole was filled without Sarah ever getting wet or sandy. Sydney jumped in and Logan followed.

Momma walked over with her arms full of beach supplies, visited with the guys, and then told us to come in soon. The crowds thinned. When we were the only group left on the beach, Peyton put his hand on Logan's shoulder and said, "Five minutes. Then it's time to go."

"NO!" Logan shook his head. "NO! NOO!"

I remembered a technique the teachers used in class. "Logan, Sydney's hungry."

He patted Syd's head.

I continued. "Ask Sydney if he wants dinner."

After standing motionless for a few seconds, he leaned over Sydney and asked, "Dih-er?"

Sydney barked and spun in circles. "See, he's hungry." Every word I said came out slowly and precisely. "Tomorrow, we'll come back. Say goodbye to Sydney."

Logan started to wave, dropped his hand and then shook his head left and right. "Doggie, go?"

"Yep!" Chase gently took hold of Logan's hand. Logan twisted his head again, his calm, quiet manner vanishing.

I quickly knelt to talk to him. "It's been a fun day, Logan. Sydney's tired. Can Sydney see you tomorrow?"

Staring at the sand, Logan lifted his eyes for one second, made eye contact, and added a quick nod. Two seconds later, his face turned violet as he held his breath. From my time in class, I could tell he was holding back an ear-splitting scream.

Chase held one hand and Peyton the other. As they headed back to their house, I watched them go, and listened to Chase saying, "Good job being quiet, Buddy. Take a breath. That's it. Sydney and Darby are nice doggies, aren't they?" A few moments later, Chase turned and called to us. "We'll meet you here tomorrow. Okay?"

I stood, rubbed the sand from my knees, and waved. "Yes. See you tomorrow." I turned to Sarah.

She was leaning against the edge of her folded chair, her bag hanging from her shoulder, her eyes glaring. If looks could kill, I'd have been a goner.

CHAPTER 12

Once the boys passed over the jetty, Sarah shoved her folded chair under her arm and chugged past me. "How dare you flirt with Chase! I told you yesterday. I liked HIM. Now you've screwed it all up."

Ten steps behind, I called, "Sarah, I can't believe what you're saying. He's just being friendly because of his brother."

Sarah stormed toward the house. One arm swung at such a fast pace, she looked like a soldier, marching.

"You're being ridiculous," I said as Sarah moved so fast the space between us grew. I yelled the next time. "Was I supposed to get your permission to talk to him?"

She didn't answer.

I jogged ahead of her and walked backwards. "I didn't do anything. Chase offered to help me. That's it. I'm only grabbing this chance to train Sydney with Logan. It'll give him more practice around kids with autism."

"Right." Sarah finally spoke. "No wonder you never told me about the guys this morning. See, you really DIDN'T want me to be with Chase." She plodded further toward the house.

I let silence fill the air. After a few steps, Sarah turned and pointed her finger at me. "I saw the way you looked at him. Don't act so innocent."

"What?" I stared at her like she had lost her mind. "Sarah, I don't want a boyfriend. You can have him. I promise you. He's yours. Come on. We have a few more days to have fun. Don't let a guy ruin our trip. I'll try harder not to talk to Chase anymore."

Sarah slowed her steps.

I walked in a daze. *Did I really look at him in a different way?*

Eventually, I caught up to her, but stared straight ahead. Sarah started to laugh. I couldn't believe my ears. Her head turned toward me, I frowned at her and moved forward, never saying a word.

Sarah dropped her chin, and gave me her actress grin and persuasive voice. "Okay. Okay. You're right. I'm making a fool out of myself. They're just some guys we'll probably never see again. I don't know what's gotten into me."

"I don't know, either."

"Tomorrow I'll get up early with you, and we'll jog on the beach. We'll feed the seagulls and check on the turtle's nest. If we see them, great. If not, you and I will have fun. I'm sorry I got so upset. Don't say anything when we go in, okay?"

I nodded, but with no eye contact. *Can I really trust her?*

The dogs darted up the steps, making so much noise Mr. Neal opened the door. The grown-ups had already showered, and the iPod played Oldies music.

Momma's head popped up with a grin. "We'll feed the dogs. Go clean up and meet us on the porch. Dad's barbequing tonight."

Sarah and I traveled to our rooms like strangers passing. I heard Sarah open her door and go into the only bathroom. I plopped on the bed and buried my face in my pillow. *Why haven't I ever thought about guys? Chase was nice. Could it really be that he liked me? It doesn't matter. I just want Sydney to learn his special skills and Sarah to be my friend and be happy.*

The gush of water stopped and the door banged open. I grabbed my clothes and waited to hear Sarah's door click.

After a warm shower, I felt better and dressed in my uniform for the beach, my jean shorts and a tee. Tonight it was a gray tee with two black Lab faces on the front. My hair would air dry and my curls could do as they wanted. Our parents laughed on the porch, never tiring of each other.

Dad cooked hamburgers outside, and the aroma seeped in through the screen, making me lick my lips. I eyed the pretzels, potato chips, and onion dip.

"Hi, honey." Momma rocked in the chair. "Did you have a good time today?"

"Yep. It was fun." I slid onto the picnic bench and dug into the snacks. "After Sydney almost drowned, he made friends with the guys and their younger brother, Logan. He has autism, and I'm supposed to see him on the beach tomorrow. I can't wait to tell Ms. Jennifer what Sydney's doing."

Momma's chair squeaked every time it rocked backwards. "Yes. She'll be proud of what you're teaching him. But, if you're planning to go visiting tomorrow, you'll have to do it before lunch. We've rented a boat to go out to Pelican Island."

"Are we taking the dogs?"

"Absolutely! Ms. Jennifer wants Syd to know about boats and swimming. We'll do a better job of keeping him safe. And he and Darby can run free."

"Sounds like fun. After dinner, I think I'll go to bed early. I'm tired."

Sarah stepped out to the porch wearing her *PINK & PURPLE* shirt and jean shorts. I hid my surprise. *Was she wearing it to tell me she hadn't forgotten being best friends? Maybe, the old Sarah is still in there.*

Neither of us said a word.

She sat on the other side of the picnic table, dipping potato chips into the dip. Mrs. Neal handed us each an ice-cold Coke.

I glanced up. "Thanks. This tastes great."

Sarah took the drink and mumbled, "Thanks."

Momma said, "You girls are sure quiet."

"I did a lot of swimming." I dipped my potato chip in the onion dip. "And the dogs kept me busy."

Sarah didn't say anything and gazed out the screened porch. I should have said something else but didn't.

As soon as dinner was cleared from the table, Sarah went in to help. Each family had a night for preparing and the other for cleaning. Tomorrow would be my turn to do the dishes. I moved to an empty rocker and swayed back and forth, careful not to crunch Sydney's paw that stretched close to the rocker's feet.

After a few minutes I faced Dad. "I'm going to potty Sydney and then say good-night. I'll read for a while and then go to sleep. I want to be up early for a run on the beach."

"Okay, honey. If that's what you feel like doing." He watched me walk away.

Lying on my bed with Syd curled next to me, I listened to laughter and music and replayed the day. *Will we argue for the rest of our trip? We're supposed to be having fun. Not fighting about guys.*

I fell asleep and dreamed about the ocean pulling me further and further out. The waves wouldn't let me get back to shore. As I tossed, kicked, and flung my sheet, Sydney jumped up on the bed and pawed my arms, waking me. "Uh... I'm okay, Syd," I whispered. I swung my legs over the bed and sat for a minute. "Come on, Syd. I need a drink." And I tip-toed out of the room.

There sat Sarah on the couch reading a magazine. She looked up. "What're you doing up?"

"I just had a terrible dream. I need some water. What are you doing up?"

"Couldn't sleep."

As I walked toward the couch, Sydney lunged forward with his front paws. He'd trapped a bug. He put his nose carefully under one paw, not letting it get away. His curiosity took over his judgment and he lifted his paw. A giant, rusty-red insect with two long antennas dashed across the floor. Before he could swat at it, it disappeared under the couch. "Oh no! That's a Palmetto bug."

I leaped onto the couch. Sarah stood holding a small square pillow to her chest. She gasped in small spurts.

"Where's Darby?"

"In bed with Mom and Dad." Sarah's ragged breathing sounded like an engine trying to start. "There's probably more under us." She latched on to me, hugging me tight, muttering in my ear. "Oh, this is so gross. What're we going to do?"

I started laughing. Then she joined in. We looked like we were crying, and that made us laugh even harder.

Sarah stammered, "This really isn't very funny. And I'm sure glad you're out here with me. I'm sorry about what I said today. Really, I am."

We marched up and down on the old, squishy cushions and our feet slid under the seats. I wiped a tear away and said, "Well, I think those bugs will stay under the couch. I wonder how many there are?"

"Oh that's even grosser. It gives me the heebie jeebies."

In between giggles, we tried to figure out what to do next. Neither one of us wanted to step down. Then Momma opened the bedroom door.

"What in the world are you two doing?"

Sarah tightened her grip on the small pillow squished to her chest, and my eyes went to the door. "We couldn't sleep. When I walked out, Sydney caught a roach."

Momma froze at the door. "Oh no! Where there's one, there's more."

Sydney skidded across the hardwood floor, and put his nose under the front of the couch. Sniff, sniff. Then he put one paw under the couch and slid a small, black, plastic round container out into the open.

"What do you have?" I leaped down and grabbed it before he put it in his mouth. "Momma, what's this?"

"That looks like a roach trap. There must be roaches everywhere. Honey, don't let him eat any of those. They could be poisonous. I'll check under our beds and then I'm going back to sleep."

Sarah put one foot on the floor and looked around. "Oooh! Chills just went up my back. I'm going to bed, too. I'll feel safer. Trina, please wake me when you get up. I really want to run on the beach, too."

I raced to my door. "Okay."

Sarah did the same and put her hand on the door knob. "You promise?"

"Yeah. I'll wake you. You know it'll be early."

"I know. But it'll feel good. Once I wake up. Have you forgiven me?"

I had cracked the door open and spoke in a whisper. "I'm trying, Sarah. It's just I don't know how long your nice mood's going to last."

Sarah hushed her voice. "I don't know, either. One minute I feel silly, and the next I'm mad. Mom said I was starting to 'mature.'" Sarah took her hand off the knob and used her fingers as quotation marks around the word mature. She took my hands and made me look directly in her eyes. "You may not believe me. I really do want to have fun with you. But, I have to say, I really do want to meet those guys, too."

I nodded, but thought "maturing" really meant moody.

CHAPTER 13

TUESDAY

Darkness encased the window when I tossed and turned under the covers. The clock glowed. 5:52. *No. No. No. I can't start this early.*

Sydney, always aware of my movements, thought it was time to start the day. He sat on top of me and licked my face.

"Lie down, Syd. I'm going back to sleep."

He crawled to the end of my twin bed. I moved my legs to the side and let him curl into a ball. As I forced my eyes closed, the image of the ocean shimmering under the pink sunrise wouldn't go away. I squeezed my eyes tighter, telling myself, *Go back to sleep. Don't open your eyes. Think of something else.*

It didn't work.

Now the clock said 6:16.

Sarah's not going to like getting up this early. I'll wake her later. The minute my legs hung over the edge of the bed, Sydney jumped down and danced in circles.

Dad whispered, "T, please take Sydney out and let us sleep."

After sliding on my flip-flops, I found my gray tee and shorts at the end of the bed. They were warm from Sydney's body heat and something else crunchy.

"Oh, yuck." I wadded the clothes into a heap, keeping the sand tucked inside. On the deck, I shook the sand over the railing. Sydney stood on the porch, expecting me to open the gate. "You'll have to wait. I need your leash."

Sydney knew the word "leash" and retrieved it from the porch floor. "Thanks, Syd. Good boy."

The sun had crept over the horizon. A fiery orange-red light spread across a line where water met the sky. "Go potty, Sydney. Stay on the grass. No beach."

Once he finished his business, I said, "Good boy. Breakfast." Hearing his favorite word, he flew up the stairs.

He gobbled like a hungry cub. For the first time, he stood eating, not spitting kibbles on the wooden floor. His dish slid to the other end of the deck under the picnic table. He licked and licked. Finally, convinced there was no more food, he backed out.

I dressed in my now sandless clothes and scooted over to Sarah's door. When I opened her door a couple of inches, my breath drifted in like fog. Their window air-conditioner blew icy-cold air. Mr. Neal snored lightly and Sarah lay totally still as if she was frozen under her covers. I lifted the blanket and patted Sarah's arm. Sarah rolled onto her side, facing away from me. I tried again. This time Sarah rolled toward me.

"Time to get up," I whispered in her ear.

Sarah rubbed her ear as if a mosquito buzzed.

I tried again. "Let's go. The sun's up." No response, so I muttered, "Do you want to see Chase?"

Sarah rubbed her eyes and stared blindly at me. "It's so early. What'd you say?"

"Do you want to see if the guys are on the beach?"

"What time is it?"

"6:40. I've already fed Sydney, and we've been outside. Come on. Wake up, or I'm going without you."

She didn't move. I waited one more second, maybe two, and then it sunk in.

She whined, "Oh, don't go without me. Give me a minute to wake up." She sat, leaned her head against the headboard, and rubbed her eyes. "You've got to be crazy to be awake at this hour," she moaned as I headed for the door. "Okay, I'm moving. I'll get dressed. Meet you in the living room."

Darby lifted her head from Mr. and Mrs. Neal's feet, and then burrowed back down.

Scrounging around in the kitchen for seagull food, I found the baggie of leftover potato chips and pretzels. "Perfect! Now we need people food." As I spoke to myself, I stuffed one package of pop tarts into my sweatshirt front pocket, and opened every cupboard and then the refrigerator. "Bummer! No more cartons of juice. This will have to do."

Sarah stepped out of her room wearing another new outfit, white shorts and a garnet tee with a black and white soccer ball painted on the front and the initials of USC. Almost like one of her old shirts, but newer. In the bathroom she brushed her long hair. Her tan made her blue eyes stand out.

I inhaled, and pressed my lips together. *She always looks beautiful.* "Sarah, are you planning on running?"

"Of course. I'm going to wear my cap. It'll keep my hair out of my face."

"Okay. Me too. My curls are totally wild this morning." I grabbed my purple Clemson cap and pulled my hair through the hole to make a pony tail. I spotted my phone on the kitchen counter and plugged it in.

"Sarah, grab your phone in case we want to take pictures." She did and grabbed her USC cap and did the same with her hair. After picking up her soccer ball and moving toward the door, she explained, "After we feed the seagulls, I want to practice dribbling."

Racing ahead, Sydney stopped at the top of the dunes. "Good boy. Wow. There's no one out here. Let's walk on the wet sand. It's low tide." I looked back and forth. "I don't see any seagulls."

"Maybe they're not awake yet," Sarah said, poking me in the arm and smiling. "I want to go find the turtle's nest. The guys live that direction, too."

"All right. Maybe they'll be coming our way."

Sarah looked serious. "I promise I won't let them wreck our day."

"This way, Syd." I ignored her comment. Sydney splashed in a foamy wave as it rolled on the sand. It was deep enough to wet the long, feathery strands of hair on the back of his legs and under his stomach.

Sarah ran ahead, "Hey, seagulls, where are you?"

Looking up into the sky, I called. "Here, seagulls, we have potato chips. Come and get it."

Concentrating on looking for the seagulls, I didn't pay attention to what was happening around me. When Sydney barked his happy bark, I looked ahead, just before bumping into Peyton. He dribbled a soccer ball and had it aimed at Sarah. Sarah beamed and had her foot ready to kick the ball to him.

Sydney chased after the ball, but it was too big to fit in his mouth. I jumped to the side and watched without being noticed. "Sydney, here. No ball." He stayed. While close enough to hear, I hoped I might learn from watching and listening.

In between laughs, Sarah and Peyton passed the soccer ball with their feet. Sarah spoke so easily. "I didn't know you're a soccer player."

"I was on a travel team, but now I'll play on our high school team. What about you?" Peyton continued to dribble the ball.

"I'm on the rec team." Sarah caught her breath. "We won divisionals, and I'm going to soccer camp in two weeks."

Peyton stopped in front of Sarah, her head at his neck level. "Which camp are you going to?"

"Furman." Sarah lifted her chin to talk with him. "We'll practice all day, every day, for five days." Sydney woofed, telling them to continue playing. Sarah smiled at Sydney and then to me and turned to Peyton. "Where's Chase?"

"He's on his way. Logan woke early, and Chase is helping him get ready. Guess what?" His long eyelashes blinked over warm brown eyes. "That's my camp. I've been going since I was eleven. Is this your first time?"

"No, this'll be my second, but it's the first time my parents are letting me stay in the dorms. What grade are you in?"

I was impressed at how relaxed Sarah seemed.

"I'll be a freshman. We'll both be at the same camp, but on different teams. That's cool. It'll be a lot of work. Kind of tiring, but it's fun. How old are you?"

Sarah stood taller and held the ball between her feet. "I'll be fourteen in November. Starting eighth grade."

"How about Trina?"

"Trina and I are in the same grade. She doesn't play soccer. She's into training dogs and riding horses." She didn't mention *my* birthday was in September.

"That's cool." They both glanced at me. I pretended to see something in the water.

"Yeah." Sarah lowered her voice, but I still heard. "But it takes a lot of her time. She's always busy. Logan's been good practice for her service dog. How old's Chase?"

Peyton rolled the ball from Sarah's feet and dribbled it away. "He turned thirteen in January. He's not much into sports."

Sarah followed, but didn't run. "Do you live close to Furman?"

"No. We're in Columbia. About an hour and a half away. How about you?"

Sarah stopped in her tracks. "I can't believe it. I live below Furman. In a little town called Simpsonville."

Peyton picked up the ball and walked closer. "I know exactly where that is. We drive through it every time we go to Furman."

Their conversation grew silent, and they looked up the shoreline. Sydney's ears lifted to attention. And so did mine.

CHAPTER 14

Logan screamed in a high-pitched voice, flinging his hands in the air. "Syd-ney, Syd-ney!"

Syd looked to me for permission; I, of course, said, "Okay!" And he darted to Logan.

Not wanting to interrupt their greeting, I walked slowly toward them. "Hi, Logan. You're awake early."

He jumped up and down, repeating, "Syd-ney, Syd-ney, Syd-ney!"

Laughing at his excitement, my eyes accidentally met Chase's startling, lime-green eyes and held his steady gaze.

Sarah rushed over. "Guess what! Guess what! These guys live in Columbia. I was just getting ready to tell Peyton about you training Sydney in Columbia."

"That's great!" I returned my attention to Chase. "It's something for your parents to check into."

"You definitely need to come to our house and tell them about it." Chase's eyes stared into mine.

Sarah's voice broke our spell. "Let's take them to the turtle's nest. Peyton and I are going to practice soccer on the way."

I hesitated for a moment. "Sarah, first you should call. Mine is at the house being charged. Our parents will want to know what we're doing."

"Naw. It'll be okay. They're probably not even awake, or they're just getting up. Mom will call if she has any questions. And she can check my GPS."

I smiled at Chase. "Do you want to see the turtle's nest?" He nodded with a grin. My pulse zoomed. Giddy and afraid that my face had colored another shade of pink, I spun around, acting as if I spied something out at sea. I gave myself a couple of seconds and returned to his gaze. "On the way, I'll show Logan how to call Sydney."

"Sounds like a plan." Chase's eyes twinkled with mischief. "And you can tell me more about where Sydney trains."

Sydney entertained himself, splashing the foam with his front paws. "First, let me show Logan one thing." I squatted to his face level. "Logan, do you want to call Sydney?" He nodded without looking at me. "Okay. Say it loud, 'SYDNEY, COME.'"

Logan lifted his face, glanced at Chase, and then at me for a split second before his head went back to his original position. Only his eyes lifted to watch Sydney play in the waves.

"Try again. Say, 'Sydney.'"

This time the words came out a little louder than a whisper, "Syd-ney."

"That's great. Now say his name again. And then say, 'Come.'"

Sydney peeked at Logan and waited for his command. Logan repeated, "Syd-ney, come." Syd raced straight to Logan, sat, and stared at him. And Logan's whole face smiled.

"Good job, Logan. Here. Give him a treat."

Logan stretched his arm to touch Sydney's head, scooting one small foot at time. Sydney didn't move, lifted his nose close to Logan's, and looked straight into his eyes. Logan gurgled and rubbed Syd's back.

"Good boy, Sydney." I handed small treats to Logan. "Give one treat. And say, 'Good boy.'"

Logan opened his hand, and Sydney nibbled every treat. Logan giggled. "Like cookie."

"Yes, he does. You're wonderful with Sydney. He really likes you."

"Like Syd-ney. Friend."

Chase stood taller and his shoulders straightened. "That's the most words he's ever spoken. Sydney's working his magic already. You've got to tell me more about this kennel. My parents have to meet him."

I sucked in a long breath, stretched up on my toes, clamped my hands together, and felt my heart stutter. Adrenalin rushed through my body. "I'd be happy to, but today we're renting a boat to go out to Pelican Island. Our parents plan to spend the whole afternoon on the island. How about tomorrow?"

"That'll work. Let's walk to our house, and you can see where we stay."

"All right." I glanced back toward our house. Momma's words about taking chances kicked around in my head. I imagined those thoughts galloping over fences and out to pasture. I smiled, held my head up, and continued walking. "It's so cool that you used to live here. How old were you?"

"I was six and Peyton, seven. We went to school here and had really small classes. It was hard going back to the city. I love this quiet place. Every summer Mom brings us for a month and Dad comes down on weekends or cuts his work week short. He'll come on a Thursday or he'll stay until Monday or Tuesday. We spend holidays and long weekends here."

"Ball incoming!" Peyton's baritone voice yelled.

But it was too late. The stinging blow hit me in the back of my right knee, buckled my leg, and I fell to the sand. "OW!" My head snapped around to see what had happened.

Sarah and Peyton raced over. Peyton squatted, squinted, and puckered his mouth. "Are you okay?"

"I guess so." I glanced behind my knee, touched the spot and kind-of-winced, more for their concern. "I have a red welt, but I'll survive. So, which one of you kicked that ball?"

Peyton hung his head. "It was me. I was trying to make Sarah run faster and get in front of it. I guess that maneuver didn't work."

Sarah chuckled. "Trina, maybe while we practice, you guys should be on higher ground."

I rubbed the back of my leg. "Sarah, maybe you should hold your soccer ball and walk with us. Chase wants his parents to meet Sydney, so he needs to show us where they're staying. Tomorrow, we'll visit."

Peyton picked up his ball and grabbed Sarah's. "I'll hold them so I know they won't get away."

Her sparkly, blue eyes narrowed and shot heated rays at him. "Well, that's either thoughtful or an insult. Do you think I can't carry my own ball?"

"Nah." Peyton stared Sarah down. "But it's a sure way to keep you following me."

"OH!" Sarah's face suddenly streaked with pink. "Okay."

Logan ran with Sydney at his side. If Sydney stepped in the water, Logan put his feet in the water. "Oooh, cold."

Chase stamped the water. Logan laughed and stomped his feet. Sydney bit at the splashing water. "Syd-ney funny. Like much," and he held his arms wide apart.

"I know. I like him, too. Sydney's going to walk to our house." Chase tried to hold Logan's hand, but Logan flung his hand loose and chased Sydney.

"That's our house. The yellow one with a green roof." Chase pointed ahead. "Tomorrow just walk up the deck and we'll be watching for you. What time do you want to come?"

Before I had a chance to say anything, Sarah answered. "How about later than today? We got up early this morning, and I don't want to do that two mornings in a row."

Peyton hopped in front of Sarah. "That'll work for me. I like sleeping in, too."

I called to Logan.

He did a one-sided skip toward me.

"Do you want to practice calling Sydney?"

He nodded and his eyes rose for a moment.

"Say, 'Sydney... Come.'"

Logan clapped and bounced.

I patted his shoulder and said, "Stand. Don't move. Then Sydney can listen."

After a couple more hops, his hands grabbed his shorts and squeezed. He gulped short breaths of air and then shouted, "Syd-ney." He started to clap and then put his hands back on his shorts and said, "Come."

Sydney raced to Logan.

I said, "Good boy, Sydney."

Logan's eyes caught mine before he bowed his head.

I finished saying, "Logan, you did great."

Logan held a treat in front of his Syd's face. "Good doggie. Good Syd-ney."

I tingled inside. This was a perfect example of Sydney's talent. I stretched taller, seeing the happiness in Logan's face. "Can I hug you, Logan?"

He nodded without looking up.

I got on my knees so we were almost eye to eye. "Logan, look at my eyes."

He glanced up.

"I'm so proud of you." I wrapped my arms around his thin body. "You said it perfect. Logan, look at me."

His eyes stayed on mine for an extra second.

As his eyes drifted, I continued, "Tomorrow, we'll learn one more word." I stood and turned to Chase. "I have to get permission to go to your house. My parents will ask me a thousand questions."

He took out his phone and added my number to his contacts. "I'll tell my parents to call."

"Great! Bye, Logan. Have fun on the beach."

He lifted his head, almost made eye contact, and then dropped his head with a muffled, "Bye."

Sarah and I scooted down the beach after promising to return around ten. Sarah jigged. I started to ask, but swallowed the words. She never spoke, just grinned from ear to ear.

My curiosity got the better of me and I blurted, "So, are you happy being with Peyton? Or are you angry with me because I spent so much time with Logan and Chase?"

"You know—" Sarah spun in the sand with her arms out. "I think you're right. Logan needs Sydney. If Chase chooses to be with you while you help train Sydney, it's okay." She swayed side to side. "Peyton's really cute. And he likes to play soccer. And, he's older. Did you notice his brown eyes?"

"Uh-huh." I nodded and squinted my eyes, while my stomach tied in knots.

Sarah's mind was off in dreamland.

"Hello in there!" I clicked my fingers in front of her face. "Are you ready to go on a boat ride for the day with just me?"

She snapped her head up and acted if she was waking from a dream. She grabbed my hand and pulled me toward the house, beaming. "It's going to be great. Just us and the dogs."

CHAPTER 15

Sydney's head tilted, listening to my words. "Today we're going for a boat ride. We'll be on an island. You can run and run. Won't that be fun?"

He knew the word "beach," and today he'd learn the word "boat." Sydney's vocabulary was like that of a two-year-old child's. He listened to everyone's conversations and acted as if he understood.

I dashed into the house, and the door slammed. The dogs scampered across the wooden floor, and we stood breathless.

Momma lifted her head from packing. "Good timing, girls. I assume you've been walking on the beach?"

"Yeah. I'm sorry we didn't call, Momma. We literally bumped into the guys from yesterday. I asked Sarah to call. But she figured you knew where we were. So—"

"It's fine, honey. You weren't gone too long."

My chin dipped, but my eyes focused straight ahead. *My over-protective mom wasn't worried? The beach is doing her good!* Then I realized she was still talking and I hadn't been listening.

"—one cooler full of food. Go put on your suits. Then, see if your fathers need anything."

I got the gist of what she had said and headed to my room.

Our dads had packed another cooler with drinks and water.

Mr. Neal said, "You girls grab the straw mats and towels and put them with the shade tent under the house."

We didn't have far to drive, but needed two cars. Darby and Syd sat in the rear of our van. Sarah and I rode in the backseat. Darby pressed her nose to the side window. Sydney's front legs, chest, and head hung over our seat. He dripped saliva down my neck, panted, and looked out the front window.

"Ewww," I wiped my neck with the edge of a towel and said, "Sydney, Sit."

At the marina, small ripples swayed a small boat side to side.

"Is that what we're riding in?" Momma asked with wide eyes.

Dad grinned. "It's perfect for the short distance we're going. Perfect."

While I held the dogs, Sarah helped unload supplies. Dad and Mr. Neal climbed into the boat, and our mothers handed things to them.

The dock rolled back and forth. Darby stopped walking, but Sydney pulled toward the boat.

"Sydney, wait. Darby, Come. Come on. Walk." Laughing out loud, I said, "Sarah, look. I'm being split in two. Darby won't move, and Sydney can't wait to get on the boat."

"Poor thing." Sarah hurried over. "She's afraid."

Sydney trotted to the boat and jumped in. Sarah pulled Darby, inch by inch, down the ramp. Finally, they stood overlooking the boat.

Darby gazed up at her as if saying, "How do I get in?"

"Dad, I need help."

Mr. Neal climbed onto the dock. With his arms under Darby's chest and stomach, he lifted her and teased, "Hey, little girl. You've had too many treats." He stepped over the railing and Darby grunted.

Across the channel, the island poked its sandy head in the middle of the ocean.

Momma gazed out. "Thank goodness. We don't have far to go. This boat is more like a fishing boat than a snazzy, cruising boat."

With only four seats, Sarah and I sat on the coolers, wearing goofy orange life jackets, and holding tight to the dogs' leashes.

Captain Neal floored the engine, sending us soaring ahead. Darby stared straight. Sydney's yellow eyes gleamed; he gulped at the air and grinned.

Sarah caught Darby's unhappy look and held the poor dog's flapping ears down. In baby talk, she said, "Darby, honey, we're almost there. You'll be okay."

I screamed, "This is so much fun!" The clear blue sky shined on the water. "Since we're going to Pelican Island, that's what the local people call it, we should at least see some pelicans and hopefully more dolphins."

The waves rolled, making bumps for the boat. Dad took a turn at driving. The faster we went, the smoother we flew over the waves, but our moms kept saying, "Slow down. Slow down."

I squealed. "No faster, faster." Sarah managed a teeny smile. The salty water splashed our faces, and Sydney snorted as it splashed his. Darby gazed at the floor of the boat and her ears hid her face.

The ride didn't seem long enough. We drove straight onto the sand of the island, jarring the boat to a sudden stop. Mr. Neal jumped off, grabbed the line, and held the boat in place.

Darby was first off the boat and Sydney followed, ready to explore. Dad handed the sun tent to Mr. Neal and climbed off. They hammered the stakes into the sand while Sarah and I tossed the moldy life jackets into the boat and then lifted one side of each cooler together.

Our mothers camped under the tent, organizing all the supplies. Darby chased the birds. Sydney chased her, making figure eights up and down the beach. I giggled, pulled off my green cover-up and shouted, "Yes. Have fun! Run to your hearts' content."

No one commented on my new green and purple bikini. I stood, waiting for someone to notice, and then ran into the water for a swimming workout. Sydney did a U-turn and swam out to protect me. When he came close, I lifted him, keeping his legs away. He kicked, but couldn't swim. He squirmed and whined.

"I got the message, Syd." I put him back into the water.

Dad came out with a boogie board and slipped it under Sydney's body. He growled, jumped off, and went under the water. "Uh-oh. Don't think he liked the boogie board."

I caught him and waited for him to stop panting. He was too tired to be angry. "Okay, Syd. Go back." I laid across the board and rode a wave into shore.

Dad bugged Mr. Neal until they had another body surfing contest.

While Sarah sunbathed, I walked up to her, leaned over, and shook my wet hair. She shot up. "Why are you always dripping salt water on me?"

"Oh, come on. Get wet and have some fun."

"I don't want to get wet and sticky."

"I thought we were going to have some fun together."

Sarah laid back down, shading her eyes with her hand. "Does that mean it has to be swimming?"

"You used to swim. What's happened?"

"I look a little stupid wearing a plastic ring around my waist."

"What are you talking about?"

"Think back, Trina. Have you ever seen me actually swim? I've always had something keeping me afloat."

"Wow!" I screwed up my face. "You don't know how to swim?"

"Nope." Sarah sat up, crossed her arms, and huffed.

"Why didn't you ever tell me?"

"You're such a good swimmer. You ride horses and train dogs. I always thought you'd think I wasn't good at anything."

"No way! Really? You play soccer, look like a model, and are popular with a capital P. All right. Forget about swimming. What would YOU like to do?"

Sarah glanced right and left and then grinned. "Let's explore the island."

I moved my head, mimicked Sarah's inspection, and put on a cheesy grin. "That sounds like fun. But I don't think there are any guys."

"Okay, smarty. I told you I wanted to hang out with you. Let's see what's on the other side. And by the way, your new suit looks great."

CHAPTER 16

Sarah and I climbed over sand dune after sand dune. The dogs roamed. Once in a while, I'd splash into waist-deep water or take a quick swim. And then we'd continue discussing our separate lives. We discovered our favorite bands were now totally different. We shared about next year's classes.

I moaned, "So you're not taking computer? What about Spanish?"

"No, to both. I'm taking tennis and algebra. I have enough trouble with English. I can't imagine learning another language, and I know how to use the computer. The math will help me with programming. What about you?"

"I'm taking art again. And Spanish. Wonder if we'll have any classes together? Or, the same lunch schedule?"

Sarah stopped a few feet in front of me, and turned around with a horrified look. "Gosh, I hope so. Then you can meet some of my new friends. Last week at our soccer party, they ganged up on me and convinced me to run for class president."

"Uh-huh. Heard that while you were talking on the phone." I caught up to Sarah and linked my arm through hers. "Thanks for finally telling me."

At a good distance from our parents, Sarah stopped and spread her towel. I did the same. We laid on our stomachs, facing the water, elbows bent, with our hands propping our heads under our chins. Sydney explored the water, and Darby watched.

I looked down at the towel and quietly said, "So you think we'll still be friends next year?"

"What did you just say?"

Afraid of her answer, I said it only a little louder. "Do you think we'll be friends next year?"

"How can you ask that?" Sarah rolled over sideways, leaning on her elbow, her eyes piercing through me. "We've done everything together for, let's see—" She counted on her fingers. "—seven years. I can't imagine you not being my friend. I'm sorry. I know I've been acting different and we're not spending as much time together. From now on, I'll try harder not to be so, as you say, moody."

"Well, maybe it's time for me to change, too."

"Oh. No! You can't be moody, too."

We both laughed.

"Tell me about your campaign. Can I help? I'm good at writing speeches."

"Would you really help me with my speech?"

"Absolutely. And you know I love to draw. I'll design your posters."

"Lillian and April are going to have a poster party before school starts."

"Oh. Okay." I looked out to the ocean and twisted a curl behind my ear.

"No, Trina. That came out wrong. We need your ideas, too."

I stood and waded into the water.

Sarah trailed along the wet sand. "It's okay, Trina, if we have different friends. We'll still do things together. Our parents will make sure of that!"

"That's for sure. They're so funny. On Friday nights, Momma waits for your mom to call. Her face lights up, and she says, 'Let the fun begin.'"

"It's great they're such good friends even without us." Sarah smiled and walked back to her towel.

Once we settled on our towels, I braved the guy subject and asked, "So Sarah, what about Peyton? Do you like him?"

"He seems nice. Seeing him makes my stomach kind of sparkle. That's it! When I'm with him my stomach fizzes like a Fourth of July sparkler. It's a weird, new feeling."

"I never thought about talking to guys. They always seemed like jerks. And I have to say it's been really scary." Then my words got so jumbled in my head, I didn't know how to say what I wanted to tell her.

Sarah leaned forward, smiling with her eyes, waiting for me to continue talking. She picked up on my frustration, and pulled her knees up to her chest. "Do you like Chase?"

I hesitated, then tried again. But the words didn't want to come out.

"Come on, Trina. It's *me*. Your best friend. We share all our secrets."

I sat up, bending my legs to the right. "Do we?"

"Trina, you know things are different now because you're always training and off to places with Sydney. He's taken my place. But you're still my oldest friend. We can't let that get away from us."

I stared at her. "You're right." My stomach sank, and I swallowed. "I guess that'll change next week. I'll have more time to do things with you." I heaved a sigh and lowered my head.

Sarah picked up on my mood. "Not if you get another dog."

My head shot up. I looked into Sarah's eyes. "Well, I haven't totally decided."

"Really?" Sarah put her face close to mine. "I thought you wanted to be 'the best dog trainer, ever.' What about all your plans?"

"I don't know anymore. I hate that we're not doing stuff together. You're busy with your activities, and I know what I'm doing is really important. But my heart aches like when I lost Gretchel. I didn't ever want to hurt that way again, and here I am feeling the same."

"You knew you'd be sad, but you thought it would be temporary, until you got another puppy."

"Yeah. But now, I know how it feels."

"Okay. Let's change the subject. Let's talk about this kind of stuff later. Today is supposed to be fun. Back to my question. Do you like Chase?"

I drew in another deep breath. "All right, Sarah. Yes. Let's talk about the important stuff."

Sarah frowned.

I straightened my legs, pointing my toes up and down, and waited a minute, telling myself Sarah had only one thought right now: Guys! And I needed to go along with it. "Well." I paused again, but made myself spit it out. "I thought it was because training Sydney made me excited, but now I realize I get the same feeling in my stomach that you talked about when Chase looks at me."

Sarah's eyes twinkled. She pulled her knees to her chest, and rubbed her hands up and down her legs, staring out to sea. "I thought so." And then her eyes got fixed on my reddish-haired legs. "Trina, don't you shave your legs?"

"No. Do you?"

"Yeah. Momma let me before spring break. They made my legs look prettier during soccer season. Do you want to try it?"

"I don't know. I guess." And rubbed the hair on my legs. "Let me feel yours."

Sarah laid her hairless leg over mine. I ran my hand up and down. "Wow! They're so smooth. Does it hurt?"

"Naw. Only when I cut myself, but I learned fast."

"Will you show me how?"

Sarah smirked "We'll do it tonight. When our parents are on the porch. We'll go into the bathroom and you can use my razor. Don't tell your mom. See if she notices."

"Okay. Back to having secrets."

Sydney raced across the sand, breaking our train of thought. He had spotted something lying on the beach. His nostrils opened and closed. In seconds, he was rolling on it.

I rushed over to his discovery. "No. Nasty! You're going to smell like rotten fish."

Darby, of course, chose not to stink. She only sniffed and watched.

Then a humming noise filled our ears. Syd stopped rubbing his neck on the fish carcass and stared with us as brown pelicans packed the sky. Some glided close to the water with no wing movement and others flew high in an upside-down V formation. One bird led with two behind, spread farther apart. The rest followed, two by two, widening the shape of the letter V.

If a pelican spotted a fish, it did a beak dive, splashing into the water. When its head came up, if it was a lucky bird, it floated with a fish hanging from its pouch. A second later, it would stretch its wings across the sky, swallowing the fish whole. But the birds that didn't catch anything flew around and dived again.

Both dogs plopped on their bottoms and watched. Sarah and I wrapped our towels around our necks and sat, not moving, afraid we might startle the birds.

"I've never seen so many pelicans," Sarah murmured.

I leaned into Sarah and whispered, "Yes. Stay still. It's amazing."

In a couple of minutes, the flock of pelicans flew to the end of a pointy piece of land. Their brown bodies covered the white beach, turning it bronze. Most pelicans wiggled their feathered bottoms into the sand to rest. Some stood. Those pelicans must have sensed the dogs.

In the same amount of time it took for the birds to settle, Sydney and Darby made the stillness disappear. They cantered to the point, doing a barking duet. With plenty of noise, the pelicans rose to the sky.

"Wasn't that incredible?" I breathed a happy sigh. "Uh-oh, Sarah. Momma's calling. She sounds kind of frantic. Must be time to go."

We stood, and Sarah linked her arm through mine. "Don't you worry about us not being friends, Trina. Just let me know how I'm acting."

"I'll try. And thanks for finally sharing about not swimming and your political plans."

I called our dogs, and we ran, giddy with laughter.

"Momma, we need to come to this island every day," I panted, trying to catch my breath. "The dogs can't get into trouble here, and it's a lot more fun."

"I agree. It's been nice, but speaking of next time—" Momma turned to Dad, with her eyes looking sideways. "—the ocean looks like it's getting pretty choppy."

He looked out to the waves breaking and the foam rebuilding into new waves. "It's a short trip. It shouldn't be a problem."

Our moms eyed the sky, nodded at each other, and rushed to start packing.

CHAPTER 17

Winds gusted, and the clouds clumped together, turning the skies gray and eerie. The dogs paced, peering every direction. I played in the crashing waves until the current towed me out without my consent. After a hard swim to shallow water, I touched the bottom, and hurried onto shore. Sarah's lips curled in a scowl as the conditions worsened.

Finally, Momma had everything packed. "Girls, call the dogs. It's time to go."

Dad continued to sit. "Ah. It's just a little wind. Relax. It'll blow itself out."

Mr. Neal surveyed the skies. "Are you comfortable boating in a storm?"

"This storm may never even get to us," Dad said.

Then the wind made its own noisy announcement, swirling the sand like little tornadoes. Our dads hopped to their feet and caught the tent poles just before they became airborne.

"All right, Neal. Let's get this down before it blows away."

The dogs' instincts kicked in. Darby jumped into the boat by herself and Sydney followed. They hunched down on the floor, away from all the commotion.

Momma grabbed the life jackets. "Put these back on. Hook the dogs to their leashes and keep them close."

The wind howled and whirled. Tired of spitting hair out of my mouth, I reached into my shorts pocket for two cloth-covered rubber bands and handed one to Sarah. We held the leashes between our knees and, in a rush, pulled our hair into pony tails.

Mr. Neal shoved the boat off of the sand, and with such a sudden lurch, we jolted backwards. The sky had patches of black. Sarah held her breath as Dad started the engine. This time it didn't seem as loud with all the noise from the ocean.

The dogs sat, staring at the water. I shivered. "Where'd the sun go?"

Dad patted my shoulder. "We're going to be fine. Look ahead. I see clear skies on the other side of the channel. This is just a quick thunderstorm."

"Really?" Momma glanced right and left. "Just have to get to the channel, huh?"

Mr. Neal took the steering wheel and stared forward.

Dad stood next to Mr. Neal. "Point the boat straight into the waves. That way they can't tip us over."

With no sides on the boat, just a metal railing, cold water splashed over the edges. The coolers Sarah and I used as seats slid back and forth.

I screamed to be heard, "Well, this is better than any ride I've ever been on!"

Sarah's face puckered. "I don't like this. I want to be on land, not in this deep, deep water."

The boat drove through some waves, and rolled up and over others. I patted Sarah's hand and tried to cheer her. "It's just a little bouncy. I'm glad no one's getting seasick, though. That would not be good."

Sarah eyes widened and never veered from looking straight ahead. Then the rain started. Mr. Neal pushed the throttle forward. We zoomed across the water. "OW!" Sarah almost started crying. "The raindrops feel like needles."

Mrs. Neal reached for towels under the dashboard and handed them out. We wrapped our legs in one towel and tucked it under our bottoms. Using another towel, we covered our heads, shoulders and arms.

I yelled to be heard over the boat motor. "If I cover my face, then I won't be able to see!" When I couldn't stand the stabbing on my face any longer, I completely covered up. The dogs had crawled under our legs and stayed close to the floor. The clouds dropped on the water. I lifted my towel for a quick look. "Now it's so dark, I can't see anything."

Sarah stayed under cover. "Our beautiful, sunny day has blown away."

Off to our right, white flashes zigzagged across the sky. I began counting to one thousand five when the thunder boomed. "Thank goodness. The lightning's a long way away."

Sarah's muffled voice came through the towel. "How do you know that?"

"When you see the flash, you start counting by a thousand one until the thunder rumbles. Each number tells us how many miles away the storm is."

Sarah lifted her towel to peek with one eye, and we both saw a brilliant flash. I counted out loud to one thousand four. "Uh-oh." I turned to Mr. Neal. "The storm's getting closer."

Sydney crawled onto my lap. Every couple of seconds, his body shook. After the second boom, he shoved his face under my towel.

Sarah stifled a scream. "Are we almost there?"

"Hang on, honey." Her mom screamed over the noise. "We're almost there. I see the sand bar that juts out in front of the channel."

Dad put his hand on Mr. Neal's shoulder. "Good job, Captain."

I laughed. They stood together grinning like little boys on a wild adventure.

As we rounded the point, a short distance in front, the skies shined blue and as we boated closer, the wind died.

"I'm glad that's over." Momma's shoulders relaxed and her breathing slowed.

Dad took over driving in the narrow channel. "Let's get some gas. We still have some time left on this boat. We could drive through the tidal creeks and look at the scenery."

Since we were safe and needed warming up, our moms agreed.

A boat wasn't supposed to make a wake, a wave that followed a boat, while coming in to the gas dock. Wave runners buzzed up and down the waterway making only tiny wakes, but their noise caused Darby to bark. Sydney's nose was too busy inhaling new scents.

We all oohed and awed at houses in the inlet. Going slow brought no breeze. Sarah started to complain about getting hot and sunburned.

"All right, girls. Cover up." Dad turned the boat around. "We'll call it a day."

I teased Sarah. "We could jump in and get wet. That would cool us off."

"Yeah! That's just what I want to do."

I grinned at her. We were friends, and we had a secret.

CHAPTER 18

At the back door, Sydney waited for his command. I turned the knob, cracked it open, and made him wait. As soon as I said, "Open," he pushed the door with his paw and moved to the side. He let everyone enter, then he walked in and stood. I paused and then said, "Close." He repeated the same motion. "Good job, Syd."

Momma stroked Sydney's head. "We thought we'd go for pizza tonight. There aren't too many choices on the island. What do you girls think?"

"That's the best." Sarah winked at me. "Then we can come back and hang out."

"Yeah! And listen to music." I giggled inside, nodding, and exaggerating a silly grin. "I'll get ready. What're you wearing, Sarah? Another new outfit?"

"Come into my room. I'll show you what I have. Maybe you'd like to choose something fun to wear."

Sarah opened her suitcase and my mouth fell open. "Oh, my! You did bring a lot." I rummaged through layers of clothes. "How about this cute tie-dyed tee shirt? I'll wear it with my jeans. No shorts tonight. I already have enough mosquito bites."

"Me too. I'll wear jeans, like you." As an afterthought, Sarah beamed, "Maybe we'll see Peyton and Chase there."

I shrugged but smiled. "Maybe. You know I'm bringing Sydney."

"That's fine. It actually gives us something to talk about."

Dad lifted his chin and jangled his keys, smiling. "Tonight there shouldn't be any mosquitoes in the car. I've kept the windows closed, and I'm on my way to cool it before you pretty girls crawl into the back seats."

"Thanks, Dad. That's nice." I patted his arm, and started into the room to dress. "We'll meet you down there.

A few minutes down the road, Dad turned his head sideways, "So how is it back there? Did I do better this time?"

"The air feels great, Mr. Ryan." Sarah chuckled and pretended to examine every nook inside the car. "I haven't seen one mosquito. It's almost a boring ride."

Dad winked at me through his rearview mirror. He drove a couple more blocks, turned into the small parking lot, and hunted for a parking space.

"Wow. Trina. There's a quite a crowd here." Sarah scanned the people as we looked for a place to sit. She spotted an opening on a bench, sprinted ahead, and waved me over. Our parents stood by the side of the building.

Sydney's eyes followed the younger children chasing each other. His body language said he wanted to play, but he sat and only moved his head. "Good boy, Syd." Two heads in the window of the restaurant seemed familiar and I jabbed Sarah. "Look. Look. Isn't that Chase and Peyton?"

Sarah's eyes followed to where I was pointing and grabbed my hand. "Don't point." Her eyes glanced up one more time. "Yeah. That does look like them. What if they saw you pointing? That'd be embarrassing."

"Darn it! Everything I do is wrong."

Sarah leaned into me, covered her mouth, and whispered. "I'm sorry. We just don't want them to know we're talking about them."

I spoke in a hushed voice. "I don't think they saw. But when they come out, they'll recognize Sydney. So, do you want to say hello?"

"Of course. We'll act surprised. Oh! Oh! Here they come. Talk to me, Trina. Act like we're busy, discussing something really important."

I rattled on about Sydney, and all the new words he knew. When Chase tapped my shoulder, I jerked an inch off my seat.

Sarah turned and faked being startled to see Peyton. "Well, hey, you guys. Did you just get here?"

"No, we've already eaten." Peyton flashed a handsome smile. "Their pizza's really good."

Chase added, "We were starving, and Logan loses it if he gets too hungry. He's with our parents. If he sees you, he'll want to come and see Sydney."

I stroked Sydney's head. "That's okay. He'd actually enjoy the attention. Maybe your parents should come over and meet mine. That would make it easier for my parents to let us visit tomorrow."

"Well, we're in a hurry to get back." Peyton squirmed and looked at his watch. "We're connecting with some friends on the Internet at 8:00."

Sarah moaned. "It must be nice to have Internet. We don't even have a TV."

"Whoa!" Peyton shook his head. "That would be tough. When you come over tomorrow we'll let you get on our computer."

Sarah's face lit up. "That'll be something to look forward to. See you around 10:00."

The boys raced to the parking lot, waving.

I looked at Sarah. "Do you think you just said the computer was more important than seeing him?"

"Oh no." Sarah's sunburned face grew even pinker. "I told you I needed practice talking. I hope he didn't think that. Oh, I should've said something else."

"Don't sweat it. I don't think he took it in a bad way. What's done is done."

After dinner, Sarah was still obsessing over what she'd said.

In the car, Dad glanced back at us before leaving the parking lot. "Is there anything else you girls would like to do? There's an arcade at the end of this block."

We looked at each other, shook our heads, and said, "Naw," together, and giggled.

"Dad, we just want to get back."

Sarah added, "We have some things to do."

Momma smiled at Mrs. Neal. "I guess we'll have to go back, put on some music, and sit on the deck."

"Sounds like a plan to me."

Then Momma turned around. "Trina, are you planning on taking Sydney to the boy's house tomorrow?"

"Yep. Chase said he'd have his parents call."

"That's good. I want to make sure they're expecting you."

"Momma, when we get back, would you mind taking the dogs for a walk? I want to go through Sarah's stash of clothes and see what I might want to wear tomorrow."

"We can do that. Then we'll sit on the deck."

Back at the house, I followed Sarah into her room and closed the door. Once the screen door slammed, Sarah said, "Okay. Quick, into the bathroom."

Sarah pulled out her bathroom bag from under the sink, and slid her hand around inside. Then she peeked down inside the bag. "I have a brand new package of pink razors. They're here somewhere. Oh, I've got them."

I slid my jeans off and onto the floor, shoved the shower curtain away, and sat on the edge of the tub. "Now, what do I do?"

"Wet your leg under the faucet. Then squirt some shaving cream on your hand and rub it all over one leg."

I did as I was told. "This smells good. It feels good, too." I rubbed my left leg up and down. "Okay. My leg has disappeared under the foam. Is that enough cream?"

"I think so. Now here's the razor. The trick is to move the razor on a slant and slowly bring it up. Lift the razor before you move it another direction. Did you get that?"

"I'll find out in a minute. I lift it before I change direction. Okay. Here I go." I placed the razor above my ankle and started pulling the razor upward. In seconds, I cringed. "Ouch. I've already nicked myself." Blood seeped through the white cream. "I must not have the right angle."

Sarah grabbed the razor. "Let me show you. She put the razor on my leg and said, "Watch." She pulled it up, making a path through the white lather. Skin peeked out. "Now feel how I have the razor. Got it?"

"I think so. Let me try again." I started at my ankle again and made a new path. I got to my knee before I cut myself one more time. "I may bleed to death before I finish." I giggled and looked to Sarah for encouragement. "I hope this is worth it."

"The knee area's kind of tricky. You'll get the hang of it. Then you'll like how it feels."

When the screen door thumped, the dogs barked, and I jerked the razor, making a new slit. "Uh-oh. What do we say?"

Sarah hollered, "We're in here. I'm doing something with Trina's hair." She grinned at me and whispered, "That is the truth."

We covered our mouths and snickered.

CHAPTER 19

After we rinsed off the shaving cream, small spots of blood oozed every few inches on both of my legs. Sarah squinted, and her mouth puckered. "Oh, dear. We're going to have to stop the bleeding or your jeans will be messed up. Let's see if there are any Band-Aids in this medicine cabinet." Sarah pulled on the side of the mirror and the cabinet opened. She pulled out two boxes of Band-Aids. "Hmm. You're not going to like any of these."

I stared at her hands. "What'd you find?"

"Sponge Bob. Or Dora!" She showed me the boxes. "I guess the last people here had little kids."

"Well, I'll have to use them. My jeans will cover them up, and no one will know."

"You won't feel the cuts in a few minutes. Just wash your legs with soap and water, one more time. Make sure all the shaving cream is gone. Then I actually need to do something to your hair so your mom won't wonder what we've really been doing."

Minutes later, our laughter roared from the bathroom. My legs were covered in Dora's orange and yellow butterflies and blue and yellow Sponge Bobs. Momma came to the door. "Are you girls okay? What's going on?"

"We'll be out in a minute." I giggled in between words. "Sarah's having fun making me pretty."

Ten minutes later, I tugged on my pants and walked through the living room. I covered my mouth, giggling sideways to Sarah. "Sponge Bob and Dora-Dora are stuck to my skin and the insides of my jeans. They're pinching me."

At the door, Sarah whispered, "Hurry, get behind me. I don't want anyone to see you moving funny."

Stiff legged and trying to contain my laughter, I stepped onto the porch.

Momma stood up. "Let me see you." I stood still for inspection. "Why, don't you look gorgeous! I love your hair French-braided. What's the occasion?"

"No occasion. I just like it when Sarah wears hers this way. She tried to show me how to do it. I'll never get the hang of it. I have way too much curly hair."

"Well, maybe I can help when you decide to try."

"Yes. I'll definitely need an extra hand." I turned to Sarah. "Okay, what do you want to do now? The wind is really blowing and our dogs seem restless."

"Let's go downstairs and look at the extra room. It might be fun to stay down there."

"Oh yes." I bounced on my tip-toes. "That'd be fun. Momma, where's the key to the bunk bed room?"

"Look in the kitchen, in the Charleston basket. The one made out of the different colored sea grass on the counter."

Sarah rushed in. "Got it."

"Be back in a few minutes, Momma. I'm taking the flashlight since we don't have any outside lights. We're going for a walk, too."

"Honey." We halted and Sarah grimaced. "I really don't want you going too far. I hate thinking about you girls out there by yourself in the dark."

"Oh. They'll be okay." Dad winked at me and added for Momma's sake, "No one will want to get tangled up with two dogs. But stay close."

I wanted to tell Momma, "I thought you'd relaxed," but I sighed and said, "Momma, you worry too much. You know Sydney'll bark if someone gets near us. We'll be fine. I'll let you know when we're leaving, and I have my phone."

Sarah added. "I have my mine, too. You'll be able to track us if we're kidnapped." Then she pushed me ahead, worrying someone might notice the way I was walking.

Going down the steps, I giggled. "Sarah! That wasn't nice. Why'd you tease about being kidnapped? Now Momma will worry until we're back." The music blared from above as we turned the key in the downstairs door.

Sarah flicked on the light. The room was a skinny rectangle. There was hardly room for the two of us, let alone our dogs. Sydney leaped onto the bottom bed. Darby wandered into the bathroom. The bunk bed was pushed next to the wall leaving a narrow passageway to the bathroom. It had a shower, a toilet, and a sink.

"This is perfect," squealed Sarah. "What do you think?"

I looked at the bunk beds and the floor space, and said with a straight face, "I'm not sure there's room for all your clothes."

Sarah punched my arm. "That's probably true. I'll bring just what I need for the night, and leave the rest in the house."

I stuck my head under the top bunk bed. "I'd want to sleep on top. I'd feel suffocated under here."

"Good. I'd rather be on the bottom. You know I don't like heights. So, do you want to do it tonight?"

"Yeah. Why not? But, where will the dogs sleep?" I surveyed the room.

"I'll leave Darby upstairs." Sarah bounced on the mattress. "Will Sydney sleep without you?"

"He might, but I'm not sure I can sleep without him close by. I'd feel safer, anyway, if he's in here. Let's take them for a walk and then we can get our stuff."

Dark clouds covered half of the full moon. Giant waves crashed and broke in the leftover moonlight making glow-in-the-dark foam.

"Uh-oh." Sarah spotted flashes off in the distance. "I'd say the storm is coming this way."

"It'll be okay. We'll walk to the jetty and turn around. The storm can't get here that fast."

"How do your legs feel?"

"If I had on shorts they'd feel a lot better, but then I'd be getting more mosquitoes bites. When we get back, I'm peeling off the Band-Aids."

Strolling across the sand in the moonlight, Sarah glanced up and walked in a circle. "Look. There are so many stars. I wish I knew more about the constellations."

"I've read about Sirius, the Dog Star. It's supposed to be the brightest star, but only shows itself before dawn. We'll never see it that early."

"You might." We both laughed.

Sydney charged toward the water. I called him, "No water, Syd. I'm not bathing you again. Come here." He came and walked next to me. "Good boy."

Darby never showed any interest in getting messy.

"Trina, let's sit and listen to the waves. It's really pretty at night."

I found dry sand and sat. "I've been leaving my window cracked and falling asleep to this sound."

Darby sat next to Sarah, and then Sydney stretched his back legs straight behind, lying on his stomach beside me. Sarah and I leaned into each other, gabbing about the beach, and talking about our dogs, and all the things we'd already done. We didn't talk about the next week. I didn't bring up the subject of Sydney leaving. It stayed on my mind every minute of every day. And the day was coming soon enough. I'd have to make a decision about training another. But not tonight.

After a few quiet moments, I asked, "So are you excited about tomorrow? Wonder what we'll do?"

"I like that we're getting up later and not wearing bathing suits. I'll pick out something casual for a visit. Did you see something else you'd like to wear?"

"I've decided I need to be me. I'll wear shorts and a tee shirt. I can't pretend to be something I'm not. It makes me too uncomfortable. You'll get on the computer with Peyton, and I'll work with Logan and talk with his parents. Then we'll figure out what to do with the rest of the day."

Out of nowhere, a huge clap of thunder shook our peace and quiet. Sarah and I watched as the fireworks zipped across the sky.

Sarah took a deep breath. "I'd say that storm is finding us again." She counted out loud. "One thousand one, one thousand two."

BOOM.

Sarah popped up. "Oh, boy. It's really close. Let's go."

We dashed up the stairs and into the house, ready to pack our belongings for the night. This time, lightning hit and all the lights in the house blinked. Sarah gasped. "Hmm. I'm not sure this is a good night to move downstairs." Then the flash flared through the windows again. Sarah closed her eyes. "I'm not counting."

"You know, tomorrow night might be better." I counted to myself. "Let's make a cup of hot chocolate."

During the night, the rain splashed against the house. With my window closed, the sound of thunder and the flashes of lightning lulled me to sleep. When I woke, Sydney lay on his back with his furry tummy showing, his legs wide apart, and his head on my pillow.

The clock glowed 7:00. Shocked that I had slept in, I lifted the blinds. *Uh-oh. Our first dark, cloudy day.*

CHAPTER 20

WEDNESDAY

Before my parents and Sarah woke, Sydney and I snuck out to walk on the empty beach. We ran in and out of the water with not a soul around to distract us. Clouds swirled in the sky, and the wind blew. "Isn't this a fun way to start the day, Sydney?"

He woofed and ran in circles. "Let's do some nose practice." I first turned him toward me with the ocean to his left, saying, "Heel" and then called, "Front" which brought him in front of me and sitting on the wet sand with an eager expression. I put the palm of my hand to his face, his signal to Stay. With his back to me, I ran the opposite direction, and he waited for his next command. Once I was hidden behind a dune, I called. "Okay."

He raced right and left, weaving closer to the dunes. As he approached, I took shallow short breaths, not wanting him to hear me, only smell me. His nose sniffed every inch of the sand, and then he snuck around the sea grass and woofed.

I giggled. "Yes! You found me!"

He gobbled a few treats, ready to do it again.

After a couple more practices, I headed toward a small pier and found some unusual hiding places. When his tongue drooped, I said, "Time for breakfast."

We jogged home with Sydney in the lead, but from time to time he'd turn around, check his distance, and stay only a couple of feet ahead. Panting, we rushed into the living room, hungry.

Sarah sat on the edge of the broken lounge chair, reading a book.

"Wow, Sarah. This is a surprise. What's gotten into you? What are you reading?"

She showed me the book cover, *Nightfall*.

"I'm reading the same one. Do you like it?"

"Yep. It's a little scary when the vampires and werewolves fight. We'll have to read together tonight. It'll be more fun. Has Sydney eaten?"

"No. But he's hungry as usual." Sydney guarded his food bowl, waiting for me to fill it. I shook my head, giggling and heading into the kitchen. "Every night he recharges his batteries while he sleeps. And then the minute his eyes open, he's ready for a new day."

"Sounds like you."

I chuckled "Yeah. I guess that's true, but today I'm kind of tired."

Syd's nose disappeared in his bowl. There were three pieces of food stuck in his dish. It clattered across the floor until it hit the wall. His tongue licked sideways and around inside the dish until all pieces had been captured. He looked up at me as if saying, "I need more."

"You probably are extra hungry after all that running and swimming. I'll give you just a little more."

He followed me inside the kitchen, his stub wiggling, and his rhythm growing faster and faster. He watched the food pour into his bowl, waited for me to set it down, and inhaled the extra food like a vacuum.

Sarah had called Darby over to her and held her head. "I can't let Darby see Sydney getting any extra. She'll beg for more, and I'm supposed to be keeping her lean and trim."

Standing at the counter, I ate two bowls of cereal and a banana. "Wow! I feel better now. Are you excited about going to Peyton's house?"

"Duh. Do you ever see me up this early? Just think! They get to stay, and we only have three more days. Tonight we'll sleep downstairs. Okay?"

"Yep!" I knelt in the overstuffed armchair, and hung over the back, looking out the porch window.

Sarah joined me in the same chair.

"Today looks rainy, Sarah. Maybe it won't mess up our day too much. We'll be inside, visiting. But I sure hope it's our only rainy day."

Sarah looked over her shoulder and down at my legs. "Are your legs better?"

"Yeah. I took the band aids off before I went to bed. They felt funny last night, like they were naked under the blanket, but I'm getting used to the feeling. Wading this morning, the salt water stung and I cried 'Ouch' a few times.

Sydney watched me taking baby steps, tilted his head, and worried something was wrong."

"What time do you want to walk down?" Sarah looked at her wrist watch.

"Maybe just a few minutes before ten. We don't want to be there too early."

"Yeah. You're right. Don't want to seem too eager. If it's raining, we may not be able to get there. We never got the address." Sarah moved to the squishy couch.

"We'll find a way." I sat next to Sarah. "Do you realize we haven't fought for a whole day?"

Her eyes widened. "You're right. Maybe I should change that. I'll have to think of something to fight about."

"That's okay. I'm kind of getting used to the way you are." We both chuckled, and all my tension hiding inside vanished. "So, have you heard from any of your other friends?"

"Only a couple. Clayton and April are on vacation. Clayton has texted a couple times with pictures. Lillian texts me at night when she can."

"I think I'll call Mrs. Brown and see how the horses are." I dialed the number twice and nothing happened. "My phone's not working. It's totally silent. This is the first time I've used it besides in the car on the way down."

"I bet you have no reception here. What plan do you have?"

"I think it's from a discount store. Dad has a company phone, and his is working. I've seen him making calls. I'll have to tell Momma. Can I use your phone?"

"Sure. You can text her, if you want."

"I'll just call. Mrs. Brown probably doesn't text."

We spent the next half-hour phoning. Mrs. Brown said she was fine and had Heather helping with my barn chores and riding my schooling horse, Chancy. After that phone call, my stomach had a new ache. *What if Heather buys Chancy?*

Sarah told me more about her school friend, Clayton, shared his pictures from The Grand Canyon and April's from Williamsburg. And then she texted Clayton. He responded immediately. Sarah let me read his messages, and even let me add silly comments.

Then I had an idea. "Can I call Ms. Jennifer? I could tell her about Logan and Sydney swimming."

"Sure."

Ms. Jennifer answered on the second ring. In my excitement, I stumbled over all the words I wanted to say about Sydney working with Logan. When I hung up I told Sarah. "She liked that I had found a child to work with, and she's really happy we took Sydney on the boat. Some people have actually requested dogs that like the water."

One by one, our parents strolled out of bed and sat around the kitchen table, drinking coffee. I had retrieved my backpack from a corner in the living room and began rounding up Sydney's supplies. As I replayed Ms. Jennifer's conversation to Momma, I grabbed treats, undid the rubber strap on the deck door, and found a carton of juice in the kitchen cabinet.

"That's wonderful news, honey." She stood at the deck window and said, "It sure looks like this will be an inside day. I guess we'll go to the store and redo supplies. There's a museum here. Do you girls want to go?"

Sarah and I looked at each other, shook our heads, and in unison said, "We've got plans."

Momma returned to the kitchen and poured another cup of coffee. "Hmm. We've never gotten a call from the boys' parents. I'm not comfortable with you two showing up with Sydney and Darby. What if their parents don't know you're coming?"

"My phone's not working here. Is yours, Momma?"

"I don't know. I haven't used it. Let me try calling your phone." We waited to hear a ring; but nothing happened. "Well, that's not good. All this time I've thought you were safe. It's got to be our phone plan. We'll fix that next week. Dad's service must be better. He'll let you use his."

"I gave Chase my phone number, Momma. That's probably why we haven't heard from them. You've met them twice now. So there's nothing to worry about."

"I haven't met their parents. What do you think, Carol?" Both of our mothers joined us in the living room.

"I know the girls want to be independent, but we should at least know where they live. Sarah, is your phone charged?"

Sarah's eyes fluttered, and she frowned.

"Let me see." Mrs. Neal smiled at Momma. "This is her new excuse why she doesn't call."

Sarah huffed and handed her mother the phone. "See. It's charged. When we get there, I'll call. Will that work?"

Momma paced. "How about I walk down with you? I'll at least know where you are. Once I know it's okay for you to be there, I'll leave. And you shouldn't be there all day. You don't want to overstay your welcome. Then we could go to the museum this afternoon."

Sarah and I moaned.

Dad piped up. "Let your mom walk with you. She'll make sure everything's okay. If you want me to pick you up, just call. It may be raining later."

I exhaled. "All right. Sarah, let's get ready?"

"Yes. Let's." As she headed toward her room, she said "I'm going to put on my black shorts and the blue tank top. What'd you decide to wear?"

"My white shorts and the green tee shirt from the fund raiser for the kennel. It has dog paws on the front, and it's really cute."

"That sounds perfect. And, it will match your eyes, too. Good idea."

I scrunched my nose. "Well, that wasn't what I was trying to do. I just wanted them to ask questions about the kennel."

By the time we walked out the back door, patches of sun peeked through the clouds, but the wind gusted. I called Sydney. He halted at the door, staring at his working cape. "You get to wear it today and show off."

Darby rushed to the door, but Sarah's mom called her back. Darby glanced over her shoulder, up to Sarah, and then to me.

Sarah saw my expression, whined, and put her hands on her waist. "Trina, she'll get in the way." Darby pawed Sarah's leg, and Sarah ignored her. "Mom promised to keep her."

"Oh. Don't leave her. I'll watch her."

Sarah's eyebrows lifted, and she blinked. "Are you sure?"

"Yep. Come on, Darby. Let's go."

The screen door slammed. We bounced down the steps and waited for Momma.

Sydney and I ran on the packed, wet sand. I had told him, "No water." Darby stayed close to Sarah and Momma as they chatted.

At Chase's deck, Sarah halted. Sprinkles of pink popped out on her cheeks, and then her whole face blushed. "Oh, My, Gawd. We're here!" She didn't budge.

I wrapped Sydney's cape around him and turned to Momma. "Okay, Momma. We're here. Now you know where we'll be."

Grabbing Sarah's hand, I said, "Come on, chicken. Here's your chance to be with Peyton. You've been waiting all morning. It'll be fun."

Momma crossed her arms. "I'm standing right here until I see some sign they were expecting you. You girls have fun. Use your manners. And call if you need us."

I trotted up the wide wooden deck, pulling Sarah. The closer we got, the larger the lemon yellow house seemed. It stood two stories tall on much taller pilings than our old rental house. It had a dark, leafy-green metal roof and white hurricane shutters held open, shading the windows. The large nautical-themed wooden porch had a thick rope looped between each railing.

We stood at the entrance of their long wooden walkway, drooling over the house, until the glass French door opened.

Chapter 21

A tall, slender woman in white shorts, a sleeveless turquoise blouse, and white tennis shoes approached, smiling. "Welcome. Please come in."

I waved to Momma, but she didn't leave. Sarah and I stepped onto the walkway.

"I'm Mrs. Manning, Chase and Peyton's mother. We've been looking forward to your visit."

She waved over our heads, and I assumed it was for Momma. When I glanced back, Momma had disappeared.

As we walked closer, Mrs. Manning halted, drew in a lungful of humid air, twisted her shoulder-length, brown hair behind her neck, and backed toward the glass door. "Oh!" It sounded almost like a scream. "I didn't realize you were bringing your dogs."

Sarah and I peered at each other. My stomach lurched to my throat. That wasn't the response I had expected. Sydney heeled, knowing it was time to work. I gave him a hand signal for Sit.

Even though I had planned to care for Darby, Sarah called her. Darby sprinted on the deck ready to play, and Sarah hooked her leash. Sydney stayed.

"Wow." Mrs. Manning blew out like a shout. "They are very energetic. Will they stay outside?"

My body jerked upward and froze as if playing the game Freeze. *What? What am I supposed to do with the dogs?* In a second, my mouth loosened enough for me to speak. "Do you have a gate on your deck? I can't just leave them on the beach."

Then, Mr. Manning marched outside. "Well, hello there! Logan's been so excited about Sydney. I couldn't wait to meet him. And this must be Darby. I've heard about her, too."

Mrs. Manning's glare seemed to be launching daggers at her husband. I backed up and stared at the two of them.

Afraid to interrupt, I murmured, "Sydney calms quickly, once he's greeted everyone. I'll keep him close. Will that be okay?" Out of the corner of my mouth I whispered, "Sarah, hold Darby."

Sarah nodded and murmured to Darby. She gazed at her surroundings, but didn't move.

When the door opened again, out jumped Logan, screaming. "Syd-ney. Syd-ney." His hands fluttered, and he bounced up and down. "You. Here!" Logan sprang to Syd's side. His furry body remained still, except his nose nudged Logan.

Mrs. Manning screamed at her husband, "Frank, help Logan. He's going to get bit!"

Logan flashed a gigantic smile from ear to ear.

Sydney barked once, caught my hand signal, and slid to his down position. "That's better. No barking. Quiet."

Logan's father put his arm around Logan's shoulders. "Look how happy he is, Kathy." He glanced at his wife. "He's not afraid. He's been playing with them on the beach."

"What? You didn't tell me he was playing with DOGS. Who was supervising?"

"Chase and Peyton have been telling you. Have you ever seen Logan so excited?"

I sucked in my breath. *What have I gotten into?*

On the deck, Logan sat with his legs straight, leaning next to Sydney, scratching his back. Syd's little stub wiggled and Logan giggled, trying to catch it.

As things quieted, Chase and Peyton appeared. Then the commotion repeated, but not as frantic as when we first arrived. Darby barked and jumped on Peyton and Chase. Syd stayed in his down position. When I gave him permission to sit, his whole body squirmed and wriggled. "Okay. Say hello."

Mrs. Manning straightened once more. She moved to the side of the deck, gripping the railing. I think she spoke, but none of us heard her words. She could have been crying.

"Okay." I caught myself gaping at Mrs. Manning and sighed. "I think the excitement's over now. The dogs will relax and use their manners."

Logan hugged Sydney around his neck. His mother shouted, "Frank, do something!" He didn't acknowledge what she yelled. Mrs. Manning tried again. "Logan, honey, you're choking that dog. He might bite you."

"No bite. Friend." Logan never released his hold.

His mother guzzled air and choked. She put her right hand in the middle of her chest and covered it with her left hand.

Is she having a heart attack?

Then she clearly said, "I've never heard him put so many words together."

I straightened my back and smiled. "Sydney's been trained to play with children. I don't want you to be afraid, Mrs. Manning. He's really safe." I paused to see if Mrs. Manning had relaxed. That wasn't happening, but I continued anyway. "They've already spent a lot of time together. Would it be okay for us to run on the beach?"

Mrs. Manning's skin creased around her eyes as if she was losing control of her emotions. Her husband walked over and put his arm around her shoulders. "Kathy, look at them. They're so happy to see each other."

I lifted Logan's arms gently from Sydney's neck and held his hand. "Sydney's happy to see you, too. If your mother says, 'Okay,' do you want to take Sydney to the beach?"

Logan stared at the porch floor and nodded. I squatted to Logan's face level. "Look up, Logan. Look at me. That a boy. Do you want to walk Sydney?"

He lifted his face for a full second and said, "Yes."

I glanced at Mrs. Manning and waited for her reply. She squeezed her husband's hand, nodding.

"Your mother said, 'Okay.' Let's go for a walk. Sarah, I'm taking Darby, too."

Chase stepped forward saying, "I'm going with you. When we come back you can tell my parents about service dogs."

Peyton grabbed Sarah by the hand and said, "I've got a game going on the computer. Come and watch. Then you can play, too."

Sarah glanced at me, her face glowing. She put her hand on her heart and patted the spot with her pointy finger. Her signal told me her heart beat wildly. She took a deep breath and, as she was yanked away, asked, "Trina, are you sure about taking Darby?"

"Yep! I told you I would. We'll have fun on the beach. At least till it starts raining. See you later."

Chase ran down the deck. Both dogs were off-leash with Logan following. I stopped on the sand, put my hands on my waist, and exhaled. "That was a surprise. So your mother doesn't like dogs?"

He walked over to me, his shoulders slumped, and his eyes veered off to the side of my face. "I should have warned you."

My cheeks warmed. "That would have been nice."

"I tried to call you—"

I patted my cheek and my mouth fell open. "—Oh. Sorry. I just found out this morning, my phone isn't working here. I'll give you Sarah's number. Hers works."

The clouds darkened. The wind picked up, and the smell of rain was near.

"Let's hurry." Chase started to run. "We don't have long." He yelled over his shoulder. "Mom's never been around dogs. I'm not worried. She usually listens to Dad. Once she sees how great Sydney is with Logan, she'll change her mind."

I hurried my pace. "If it's raining, will we be able to go in the house? I can't just leave the dogs outside."

"Don't sweat it. Dad will make sure they're in, and you'll have time to tell my parents about this program."

Sydney romped in the sand, knowing he wasn't allowed in the water. Darby chased at the bubbles in the foamy water. Logan followed Sydney, giggling a belly laugh. "Syd-ney! Syd-ney!"

We walked together, and then Chase turned, walking backwards. "You're incredible."

I choked, stopped walking to catch my breath, and stared at him. "Why?"

"The way you handle Logan is amazing. He's so happy, and he's talking."

I shook my head and started moving. "I'm not doing anything that different or difficult."

"But you're so into it. Determined. That's what's mind-blowing. Most girls are into other things."

"Like?"

"Oh, you know." He lifted his shoulders up and held them by his ears.

"No. What things?" I smiled. I wasn't going to let him off the hook. He had to tell me.

He let his shoulders fall. "Like clothes, flirting, being fussy. You're different." He paused and looked at his bare feet. "I really feel like you're a friend, someone I can trust, a buddy I can hang with."

This time I really did blush. And I couldn't hide my embarrassment. *A buddy? That's not what I wanted to hear.*

Chase stopped and lifted my chin. "Did I say something wrong? You looked at me so, I don't know, like I hurt your feelings."

"Nope." I looked at the wet sand, thinking about what he'd just said. He was trying to tell me he liked being with me. "I think I got what you meant." And smiled at him.

After a couple of silent minutes, I worried out loud. "I'll need some towels to dry the dogs. Maybe we can go into a room that your mother won't worry about." Chase started to speak while I had another thought. "If your parents drove us home, I could explain in our house. Oh, that won't work either because the dogs would mess up your car."

"Trina. Give it a break. It'll work out. You'll see."

CHAPTER 22

Kicking up the sand, Sydney raced straight to me on command. I unfastened his cape and waved my hand. "Go play." Sydney pranced through the water. Logan followed with a rowdy and infectious laughter. Chase and I got caught up in his happiness. We chuckled and splashed each other. My heart felt light, and I lost track of time. I hummed, "No worries."

The sky grew blacker. Lightning flashed miles out across the water. "It's coming. Trina, we should head back. I've got a plan for the dogs. You can dry the dogs in our bathroom, downstairs. When we go up, if you'll stay with them for a few minutes, I'll ask Dad where he wants us to go."

"Okay. But, if it's a problem I can call my dad, and he'll come pick us up."

"I've been so excited about my parents seeing how Sydney helps Logan. He's the happiest I've ever seen him."

"Why is your mother so afraid of dogs?"

"She told us that when she was in high school a big dog jumped on her and bit her nose. After that, she's never wanted to be around dogs."

I called Sydney. Darby stopped running and walked by my side. "Well, no wonder."

"Actually, she's the one who has stopped us from ever having a dog, even a small one. This is why I'm so excited to see Logan improving because of Sydney. Maybe we'll get a dog after all."

Just then a large flash spiked through the clouds, and Chase ran to catch Logan before it thundered. Chase made a game of lifting Logan, turning him upside down, and making him giggle as the thunder roared.

"We're going to have a race." He set Logan on his feet. "Are you ready? Let's see if you can run faster than Sydney. On your mark. Let's go."

We didn't run far before the sky opened up. The rain poured, soaking our hair in seconds. Logan didn't like being wet and screamed and ran in circles. Chase pulled his towel from his neck, caught Logan and wrapped him, tightly like a mummy, and then Chase placed his cap on Logan's head. It fell down, covering his face, so Chase flipped it around.

Logan trembled. His teeth chattered. Chase bent over, and in one sweep hauled Logan into his arms. Chase stood taller, and gave me a huge grin. "He's so light." Then he whispered into his brother's ears, "Is this better?" Logan nodded and snuggled up closer.

We raced down the beach with Sydney and Darby at Chase's heels. Logan squealed so loud, he didn't notice the next flash.

But the dogs did. They cowered down. Only their eyes lifted to the sky. Now it was my turn to calm them, to get them back. I reached into my pouch of treats, and bribed them toward the house.

Once we stood in the carport, Chase and I inhaled deeply, and puffed out a lungful of relief.

Looking into Logan's face, Chase said, "Good job, Bro. I'm putting you down."

The dogs shook. Water flew everywhere. Logan sniffed, wiped his nose with the back of his hand, and then turned in circles, waving his hands and babbling, "House. House. House."

Chase opened a door. "Here's the bathroom I told you about. On the other side, we have an elevator and we won't have to go back in the rain." Logan quieted and followed Chase.

I walked in, poking my head in each area. Every room had a border of purple and orange paw prints under the ceiling. The shower curtain, the rugs on the floor, and the towels were either orange or purple with alternating colored paws. Even the ceramic soap dish held cute orange paw pieces of soap. "Wow. A shower, a dressing room, and a bathroom." I covered my mouth and giggled. "You guys must be Clemson fans. We are, too. Well, my family is, but Sarah's are Gamecock fans. I love the orange tiger toilet seat cover. Did your mom needlepoint it?"

Chase's eyes danced with amusement. "Yes. My parents met at Clemson. Wait till you see inside the house."

I wandered through the rest of the bathroom area. "This is fantastic." Old red bricks filled with shell mortar made up the floor. Towels, soap, and even hair dryers were available. I hosed the dogs' feet in the shower with a handheld nozzle and dried them with very plush orange and purple towels. "My mother would kill me if she saw what I was cleaning the dogs with. I hope your mom doesn't get angry. I really want her to like us."

"These are actually old towels we use after doing outside chores. No problem. Are you finished?"

"Yep!" I called the dogs.

Chase pushed the button for the elevator. "Tell me about how you got started being a puppy raiser." The screech let me know it was coming down. The door opened and we walked in.

"Three years ago, after losing my old dog, I told my parents I never wanted another dog. When Momma helped plan an assembly on service dogs, the idea seemed interesting. I thought it would be a good way to never get attached, or ever have another old dog. I didn't want to ever feel that sad again. Boy, was I wrong."

Chase's face lost all expression. "I'm sorry. I don't like thinking of you being sad."

The dogs squirmed. Logan rocked back and forth, which brought Chase back to where we stood.

He snickered. "Oops. Forgot to push the button. Going up."

When the elevator door opened, Sarah's giddy laughter and her loud voice floated down the hall. "That has to be Sarah playing video games. It's her favorite thing to do."

Chase put his hand on the side of the elevator door to hold it open. "Logan, hop out. Call Sydney."

Logan bounced out. He stood in front of Syd, clapping and hopping. Chase reminded Logan to call Sydney.

I laughed at Chase. "You told Logan to hop out. He did exactly what you told him to do."

Startled, Chase stood there thinking. "You're right. Mom and Dad told us Logan takes everything we say literally. Wow. You just showed me how he does that. And I gave him two commands at one time, which I shouldn't do. I'm learning, too." He bent down to Logan and said, "Walk Sydney to the laundry room."

Darby and Sydney followed Logan. In the laundry room, Logan clapped and bounced.

Chase patted Logan's shoulder. "Perfect! Good job, little bro."

I stood in the room with the dogs. "Okay, Chase. Now what?" I found myself lifting my face to his. Our eyes connected. Little brown flecks in his green eyes came into view. I took a small breath. "What's your plan?"

He didn't respond and seemed to be in a trance.

Our eyes, stuck together, sent a slow fizz up my back. I had to break the spell. "Chase." I cleared my throat. "We can't just barge in with the dogs. I'll stay here until you talk with your parents."

"Uh. Yeah. All right. Good idea." Chase walked with his shoulders squared and his chin jutting forward. "Logan, come with me."

I sat, crossing my legs, and invited Sydney to climb on my lap. Darby sat next to me. I stroked them, speaking quietly. Suddenly their heads shot up. "Oh, you scared me."

The dogs pounced at the opening of the door as Mr. Manning had stepped in. "Hi, Trina. Sydney's gorgeous. And Darby, you are, too." He patted her head. "You sure have done a great job of training."

I smiled and found a loose curl to twirl.

"Please don't be uncomfortable here. I want my wife to get to know you and the dogs. We'll just take it slow. Follow me."

"I can leave both dogs here and close the door. Or if you have a baby gate that would even be better. They'll be okay with being left for a while. Or, I can bring Sydney and leave Darby, if you want." I couldn't stop talking, not sure if I'd made any sense. My face heated up.

"You know, leaving Darby might be a good idea. Let's not overpower my wife with two dogs. Are you sure Darby won't mind?"

"No. She'll be happy to sleep. Sydney knows to how to behave, so we'll be able to talk without him bothering anything. He's nice and clean. A little wet from the rain."

"Thank you, Trina. He'll be fine. This is a beach house. Let me find the baby gate." He started to walk away, speaking to himself. "I've got it stored somewhere. Maybe in the attic."

CHAPTER 23

Once Mr. Manning had the gate secured, I rubbed Darby's head. "I'll be right back. You stay."

Sydney, back in his cape, followed us into the main room, overlooking the entire horizon, the glittery ocean, and the beach.

"Wow. What a view." When I turned toward Mrs. Manning, my eyes went directly above her head to a painting of a tiger that stretched the length of the dark, eggplant-purple couch. I stared for a moment, caught myself, and gave Mrs. Manning a giant grin. "That's beautiful."

She sat with her hands in her lap, leaning on orange pillows decorated with either embroidered tigers or a large C and staring blankly out the window from the couch. She looked like a cardboard mannequin. Chase came in with an orange-striped, purple tray carrying cookies and drinks and carefully set it on the coffee table. His mother still didn't move.

I mouthed the words to Chase, "Is she okay?"

As I sat in the chair next to the couch, Chase lifted his open hands to the ceiling, and lifted his shoulder to his tilted head.

Out loud I said, "Sydney, down."

His nose sniffed the aroma of peanut butter cookies.

I said in a firm voice, "Leave it."

Sydney didn't think twice, and rested next to my chair.

Mr. Manning sat on the couch, facing me. "While Logan's playing in his room, you must tell us about this dog organization and how you got involved."

"Sorry, Chase. You've already heard some of this."

He shrugged and sat next to Syd.

I turned to his parents. "I'll give you the most important details. Otherwise I'll be talking all day." I smiled at Mrs. Manning to see if I'd get any response. *Nope.* I took a deep breath.

"Okay. Here I go. Three years ago, my thirteen-year-old dog died. Her name was Gretchel. I was sooo sad. I never wanted another dog. Then the following year, Momma, she's a vet tech by the way, helped plan an assembly about service dogs for fourth and fifth graders. The speaker told us how we were the right age to help train puppies. I didn't know about service dogs or puppy raisers, and I don't know why, but after the assembly something made me research those subjects.

"After reading about being a puppy raiser, I thought it might be a perfect way to always have a puppy and never have another old dog. And…" I peeked at Sydney and sighed. "I believed I could train a puppy without getting attached. But now I know that's impossible. I've worked really hard on teaching him how to help others, which has been a lot of fun. We've worked together for one year almost to the date. Last year I picked him up from the kennel on our way home from the beach. That was really exciting." My voice softened and I had a harder time getting the words to come out. "This time when we go home, I'll return him." A hammer pounded in my chest. The hurt from saying those words took my breath away. I looked out at the crashing waves, inhaled a couple of times, and tried to speak. The next words came out all choppy.

"He'll go back this Sunday for his final training. If he passes all his tests, then he'll be matched to a companion that needs him." I looked down and then forced myself to look straight at Mr. Manning. "In six months, he and the other puppies he's trained with will have a big graduation ceremony. I'll get to see him one last time." I rubbed Sydney's back. His amber eyes looked up and blinked. "I sometimes think he understands everything I say."

This time Mrs. Manning looked at Sydney.

Chase's dad patted his wife's knee. "How's that for a story? How old was he when he came to you?"

"Six months old. He was still small and so cute. He had been with a family that had to move. I had just finished my training and qualified to be his handler." I leaned back in the chair and looked for flaws in the ceiling.

Mr. Manning waited to see if his wife was going to speak. Nothing. So he continued, "Well, I'm astonished, Trina. Have you enjoyed the training? Will you do it again?"

A tear slipped out. Quickly, my fingertip wiped it away. "He's so smart and has learned so fast. I know I've fallen in love with him, but he'll be perfect for someone and change their life. That's what makes training him so special." I moved next to Sydney on the floor and scratched behind his ears.

I had asked myself the same question over and over in these last few days. I wanted to be a dog trainer, proud of each puppy, knowing they'd go to a great new home. But now I doubted my plan. I worried about losing Sarah's friendship. And having to give up another dog. After a long pause, I held my head up and looked straight at Mr. Manning.

"I loved every minute of the training. A girl at the kennel who's training her second dog says it gets easier after you've given up your first dog. But training takes a lot of my time, and it hurts getting attached. So I have to say I don't know."

Mr. Manning fixed a plate with a couple of cookies, and handed it to me. "I can understand your hesitation."

Chase's mother made a movement and our eyes jumped to her. After a few more seconds, which seemed like a lifetime, she spoke. "Trina, how do you know these dogs won't harm anyone?"

"Oh, Mrs. Manning. Their training starts soon after they're born. The puppies are carefully watched. We have to record every behavior and what skills they've learned. If there's ever a question about their temperament, they'd go back to the kennel." I tried not to glare at her. Explaining Sydney's skills had brought back wonderful memories. She wasn't helping me feel better.

Laughter shot through the hallway, breaking up the serious atmosphere. Chase smiled and said to me, "Sounds like Peyton and Sarah are having fun." Then he turned toward his parents. "Mom, Dad, do you have any other questions?"

Mr. Manning looked at his wife. "Is there anything else you'd like to know?"

Suddenly, she lifted her chin with a deliberate look. Color came back into her face. "Can you show me some of the things he's trained to do?"

I straightened in the chair. "Yes. Absolutely." I walked over to grab my backpack, and saw Logan peeking around the corner. "Hi, Logan. Do you want to see Sydney?"

He nodded, climbed on the couch, and snuggled with his mom.

"Besides following my commands, Syd's been taught to use his mouth to open the refrigerator and fetch things for people who can't move, and use his paws to open doors, and turn on lights. For kids who have temper tantrums, he's taught to lean on their thigh muscle. The pressure helps them relax. Here. I'll show you." I reached in my bag, pulled out the rubber strap for opening doors, and a carton of juice. "Chase, can you clip this to the refrigerator handle? And put this juice on a shelf." He nodded and took it. "Now, I'll show you how a service dog would calm Logan."

I scooted forward in the chair, and gave the command, "Lean." Sydney crawled under my left thigh, pushing his body against a muscle, and leaned his head on my right thigh. I rubbed his head. "Good boy. Okay." I looked at Mrs. Manning. "Here's another command that works wonders and feels really good. Hug." Sydney leaped, placing his front paws on my lap. I grinned. "He does this to me all the time. The dogs are trained to never leave their companion. One boy, before he had a service dog, would run away when he got angry. Now his service dog alerts his parents by barking, and then runs to stay with the boy."

"That's amazing." Mr. Manning glanced at his wife. "I had no idea dogs could do so many helpful things. What do you think, Kathy?"

"I agree."

Her answer stunned me. I spun my head around and stared.

She leaned forward. "Well, I can see he's very well-trained, but he still frightens me. I know it's not logical. Do you think it's possible for me to get over my fear?"

Mr. Manning beamed and patted her knee, again. "Anything's possible if you want it to happen. Let's see what else Trina wants to show us."

"Well, some of our dogs work with people in wheelchairs. They give a command with their voice or a hand signal, or type into their computer and the computer speaks for them."

Mrs. Manning shook her head and said, "I can't believe the skills these dogs learn. It's truly astonishing. Beyond belief."

"I'm going to ask Sydney to get me the orange juice. Is that okay with you? That I let him get up?"

Mr. Manning didn't hesitate. "Absolutely!"

I moved to the center of the room. "Sydney, Come." He stood and faced me. "Fetch juice." Sydney looked around the room. Then he wandered into the kitchen. He looked back at me. I nodded and said once again, "That's right. Fetch juice."

He went to the refrigerator, pulled on the strap and opened the door. Without piercing the container, he lifted the carton and carried it into the room. I said, "Take to Mrs. Manning." I pointed to her, since Sydney didn't know her by name.

She jumped backwards, tucking her legs under herself on the couch. Sydney sat, waiting for her to take the juice carton.

I broke the silence. "Good boy. Mrs. Manning, he's waiting for you to take the juice."

"Okay! I'm a believer now. But I can't touch him."

"May I ask him to give it to Logan?"

Mrs. Manning smiled. "Yes. That'd be great."

"Syd. Give juice to Logan." Sydney looked at Mrs. Manning and then to Logan. "That's right. Give to Logan."

Sydney stepped in front of Logan. He grabbed the carton, ripped off the straw, pressed it through the plastic wrapper, and popped it into the hole. Slurping loudly, he giggled.

Logan's mother sighed and smiled. "Why don't you kids go play? I need to let all this sink in. Thanks, Trina."

CHAPTER 24

Leaving Logan with his parents, Chase started to reach for my hand. A salmon color spread from his cheeks to his ears and neck, and I guess he changed his mind. I let my breath slip out and followed him down the hall.

Sydney's ears perked to attention, hearing voices down the hall. He rushed ahead to where Peyton and Sarah sat in game chairs, screaming and cheering at their soccer game. They never noticed we entered the room or that we stood behind them.

Chase's look hinted he was scheming something. He held up one finger, then two, and on three, he shouted, "Boo!"

Peyton and Sarah flinched, lost control of the game, and jerked around. Sarah gave me the squinty-look, but Peyton just blew it off. "Good try, guys."

Chase moved to Peyton's side. "Want some company?"

"Hey, Bro. Let us finish this game. Sarah's winning. And since I just lost that last play, I have to win at two more matches."

I patted Chase's arm. "Can we get Darby? She's been alone for long enough."

"Sure."

We marched to the laundry room. Darby was curled in a ball, sleeping, but the moment she heard footsteps, she shot up and stood at the gate.

Chase grinned at me. "What would you like to do while they're—" He nodded his head toward Peyton's room. "—playing computer games. Do you like music?"

"Yes. I love all kinds of music."

"Let's go to the den over the garage. My computer's there, and we can make a new play list. I'll call it Trina's Beach Music."

I smiled, crunched my shoulders, and curled my toes in my flip flops. "That sounds like fun."

Sprinting upstairs, the dogs ran ahead and halted midway. "Come on, Sydney, Darby." Their heads ducked as the rain pelted the aluminum roof like hooves galloping overhead. "Wow. I really should call my parents. They'll be worried."

On the stairs, Chase handed me his phone. "Here, use mine. Tell them we'll bring you home later."

Punching in Dad's number, I followed Chase up the rest of the stairs. It rang and rang. And then Momma answered, "Hello?"

"Oooh! I'm glad you answered since it was a number you didn't recognize. It's me, Momma."

"Yes, honey. I figured that out. Are you having fun?"

"Uh-huh. We're great. And in the house. We'll stay a little longer, and Chase's parents will bring us home if it's still raining."

"Ask them if they'd like to come over for dinner and then call me back."

I passed the question to Chase. He jogged downstairs, asked his parents about taking us home and staying for dinner. I stood at the top of the stairs, watching. Mrs. Manning looked at the floor. "That's very nice, but I'm not sure I can be in the same house with two dogs, let alone riding in a car with them. Your dad can go."

Mr. Manning's expression wilted, and he smiled at me. "Sorry, Trina. Please tell your mother, I'll take you back and come in for a quick visit. Dinner will have to be another time. Thank you, anyway."

———

Chase and I sat at his computer table. Sydney crawled to his favorite spot by my feet. Darby went under the coffee table. As Chase scrolled through his favorite bands already downloaded, he clicked on songs I didn't recognize. If I crinkled my nose, he'd move to the next song. The ones I liked, he added to the list.

Once in a while, lightning cracked and the thunder rumbled louder. Chase's forehead creased and his lips pinched. "Let's do two more songs, and then I'm going to unplug the computer."

Even though he had a surge protector, at that moment, the computer sputtered for a second, and then shut off. The room turned totally dark. He slapped the top of his wooden desk and grumbled. "Nooo! Now, we'll have to start all over."

I sat very still. *Will he try to hold my hand? Nope.*

His parent's generator chugged on, and when the lights blinked and stayed lit, Sydney had already climbed out and stood on his hind legs with his front legs and chest plopped across Chase's lap.

Choking on my laughter, I said, "Oh my. He's trying to calm you. You're getting a hug."

Chase smiled, blew out his frustration, and wrapped his arms around Sydney's neck. "You are really something, Sydney. Thanks." Restarting the computer, he found *Trina's Beach Music* intact. "Okay, I have a couple other albums you need to hear. If you don't like any of these, we're done."

He clicked on a song and the guitar twanged loudly. I shook my head, and he clicked on another. While we sat forward staring at the screen and listening intently, something gross caught our attention. One at a time, we sat back, and lifted our heads.

An awful rotten egg aroma crept up from under the desk. Chase tucked his chin, sniffed, and scrunched his face. I knew exactly what we were smelling. My skin crawled with shame. I bent down. Sydney slept curled into his front paws, every muscle relaxed. Maybe, too relaxed.

"I'm sorry." I covered my face with both hands. "This is so embarrassing."

"It's funny, Trina. Don't be."

I lifted my head and smiled. "My grandmother used to say, 'I didn't hear the train, but I sure do smell the smoke.' It's definitely time to take Sydney outside. His stomach's upset from the salt water."

I called Sydney, and he jolted awake. "Come on Darby." We hurried downstairs and out to the beach. "Wow." In the black sky, slivers of blue peeked. "It's stopped raining. No water, Syd."

Both dogs did their business, and after clean-up, we jogged back upstairs.

Chase said, "Let's listen to our list." He selected a fast rock and roll tune and grabbed my hand. Before I even had time to think about it, we were shaking and shuffling back and forth across the carpet. I covered my mouth, snorting. My stomach filled with bubbles. I was dancing. With a *guy*. But instead of it being romantic, it was hilarious. Sydney herded us, pouncing at our feet and yapping.

Chase said in rhythm with the music, "I guess he doesn't like us dancing."

"He's a herding dog and wants to control our movements."

We sat back down. Sydney crawled under our legs, and Darby went under the coffee table.

"Enough of that." Chase pulled out drawing paper. "You told me you liked to draw, right?"

"Yeah. Um." I shuffled my bottom in the chair, and turned my head just enough to see his face. "What do you want to draw?"

"I'm going to sketch your face."

I pulled on my tee shirt sleeves, flicked some curls off my forehead, and knew my face glowed. "Oh no. Please don't." My fingers found a strand of hair at my neck and began twisting it in circles.

His eyes gleamed. "Yes. I want to remember you and this day."

I made funny faces hoping he'd not be serious. I drew him as a stick figure. We laughed over my silly drawings. But Chase's picture shocked me. Even though it was a caricature of me, it was wonderful. He had added freckles over my nose and cheeks, and fluffy hair went down to my shoulders, and I didn't look comical. "Wow. Is that me?"

"That's how I see you." He sat up straight and blinked his green eyes at me.

"I don't know what to say. This has been so much fun. Especially because Sydney's with me." I wanted to smack myself. *I shouldn't be talking about Syd and how he's with me. And it reminds me of his leaving. Chase might think I'm not having fun with him. I need to talk about something else.* So I said, "I wonder what's happening with Peyton and Sarah." *That probably wasn't right either.*

"I don't know. But I'm happy they're busy." He cleared his throat, and his face blushed under his tan, and then he looked at the floor. After a second or two, he regained his composure and asked, "So how much longer will you be here, at the beach?"

"We leave Sunday morning. Kind of early. The time's going way too fast."

Chase's eyes peered into mine. He nodded slowly. My neck grew warm and then my ears were on fire. They probably matched my hair. I wondered if every part of me above my neck was one blob of rusty red. I needed air. His attention made me feel special, and yet, I needed to get farther away.

"You know, it's not raining. Maybe we should go now? We can walk back. It'd be good exercise for the dogs. Unless your dad really wants to meet our parents?"

"I'll go ask him." Chase ran downstairs, asked his father, and raced back up. "He told me he'd love to meet your parents, but if you wanted to walk home, he'd meet them tomorrow."

"Well, it'd be a lot easier not to put two dogs in your car. Sydney, Darby come." They followed me downstairs. "I'll call Sarah, and we'll head home. I guess we should say goodbye to Logan. I don't want him to get upset."

Footsteps thumped on the hardwood floors, and a rosy-cheeked Sarah burst into the living room. "Is it time to go?"

"Yep! Our dogs will want dinner."

Logan had obviously heard our conversation from wherever he was and bounced in front of us. "Syd-ney, dih-er?"

"Yes. Time for us to go home."

Logan squatted, and hugged Sydney around his neck. "Bye, Syd-ney." He stood and waved both hands. "Bye-bye," and ran to his room.

Chase and Peyton walked us down their path to the sand. Chase's chin dropped. "I sure hope tomorrow's sunny. Then we can spend the day on the beach again. We'll walk down to your place."

Peyton added, "And we'll hang out all day."

Sarah and I said in unison, "Sounds great," and snickered. Then she slanted her head and out of the corner of her eye peeked at Peyton.

Peyton winked at her, smiled, and tilted his head. "See you later." They flirted like in a secret code.

Once we were out of sight, we hooked elbows and glided down the beach. The dogs followed unrestrained. The sun played hide-and-seek behind big, thick, gray clouds. The breeze whistled. The smell of honeysuckle and salty air filled our noses. Everything that afternoon was magnified.

Sarah sighed until she ran out of air. "Wasn't it a fun day?" Then she inhaled once more, standing straight. As she blew it out, her whole body seemed to relax. "What was your favorite part?"

"There were so many. Oh, Sarah. Let's sleep downstairs tonight, so we can talk. Okay?"

"Oooh. That's a good idea. I can't wait for another day on the beach. And with Peyton."

Chapter 25

Sarah's parents had planned spaghetti for dinner, which was perfect with the dreary weather. We ate in the kitchen, and as soon as everything was washed and put away, Sarah and I packed our nighttime supplies. Darby stayed with Sarah's mom, but Sydney never left my side. He expected to be included.

On the bottom bunk we lay on our sides, talking over our parent's loud laughter and music. I shared, "Chase said I was 'amazing.'"

Sarah nodded, eyes glued on me. "Yes. Continue."

"He said I wasn't 'like other girls.'"

Off and on, I'd stop for a breath and answer Sarah's other questions. Like, "How did the other girls act?"

I told her what he had said. She laughed, but I didn't want her to think about how she was like those girls, so I kept talking. "And he liked the way I handled Sydney and helped Logan. He made me think about getting another dog. It's going to be a hard choice."

"You know, if you don't take another dog right away, you could go with me to Disney World?"

I lifted my head and stared at her. "No way! Really?"

"Wouldn't we have fun? We'd fly on an airplane."

"Wow. Disney World." I took a deep breath. "I'll ask my parents." I banged my big toes together and pictured the two of us walking down Main Street. "That's an awesome invitation." Then I clammed up. Not sure why I couldn't blurt out, "Yes!" right then and there. But after a moment, I lifted my eyes, and shifted my position. "Thanks. Now, tell me about your day."

Sarah rolled on her back and looked at the bottom of my bunk. "Peyton looked at me like I was important. It was so weird how he listened to my ideas on running for class president, and then wanting to be on the USC soccer team. He wants to go there, too. We talked about soccer camp. And then he asked me—um." Sarah took a deep breath and looked away. "Never mind."

"What aren't you telling me? What is it?"

"Naw. It's nothing. Another time. We even invented phone codes, and planned to meet up somewhere during camp, maybe at meals. And he held my hand as we walked outside."

"Oooh. Sounds kind of lovey-dovey! I guess you really like him. So, what should we do about tomorrow? We'll need to check the turtle's nest. And we don't know when they're coming down."

"I guess we should've asked." Sarah rolled back to her side and frowned. "We never got their phone number and they never asked for ours. That's kind of strange, don't you think? That they didn't ask."

"Well, Chase knows my phone doesn't work. And I guess we were busy doing other things and just forgot. You know, tomorrow, I say we get up whenever, go check the nest, and walk the dogs. It's supposed to be a sunny day. If we don't see them, let's take the bikes that are in the storage room for a ride down Jungle Lane."

Sarah sat up, careful to not bump her head. "That sounds fun. I know my parents will say, 'Okay' and that will make your parents say, 'Okay.' There's hardly any traffic. Dad said it only took them an hour to ride all the way around. They had lunch at the Hamburger Shack. Why don't we do the same? And we don't want to hurry to the beach. Seem too eager, right?"

"Now you're thinking. Sounds like a plan. Do you want to read? It'll help make me stop thinking about today. I bet we'll never forget this day."

The overhead light barely lit the pages under the bunk. We squinted and took turns reading a page. When Sarah got frightened with a part of *Nightfall*, I put my arm through hers and we huddled together.

She said, "Sure hope I don't have nightmares."

"You'll have to sleep with Sydney tonight, if you don't mind him snuggling. He can't be on the top bunk."

"That's okay with me. I'll feel safer. Aren't you just a little scared down here, all by ourselves?"

"Naw. This is fun. It was *your* idea."

"I know. I know. Sometimes I think of things, and later, I think it's not such a good idea."

"The door's locked, Sydney's here, and our parents could hear us if we screamed. Come on. Let's read."

I'd fallen asleep with the book on my stomach, and my right leg hanging over the edge of the bottom bunk. When I rolled over, I caught myself before hitting the floor, and noticed Sydney wedged between Sarah and the wall. Realizing where I lay, I stifled a laugh and climbed the ladder.

The minute my legs went under the sheet, I fell into a deep, coma-like sleep. That lasted until Sydney barked.

I leaned over the bunk to check on Sarah, but she wasn't there. My heart acted as if it had been electrified. I gasped for air. *Where did she go?* I lifted the blinds. The backyard was dark, but the porch light made shadows across the grass. Then Sydney made a low growl.

I didn't have a phone. And I didn't want to open the door. "What is it, Sydney?" He leaned his head sideways, listening. And then he wiggled and did an excited whine. A deep voice and quiet laughter echoed under the house. *What the heck?*

I crawled down the ladder and peeked out the small window in the door. Off to the side stood Sarah and Peyton, clutching hands, staring into each other's eyes, bodies two inches apart.

No way. She knows better.

The minute Sarah giggled one more time, Sydney used his alarm bark. He'd wake our parents.

I yanked the door open and said in a firm, hushed voice, "Sarah, get in here. Hurry. Someone's going to be down here any second."

Peyton kissed her forehead, shoved her in the door, and took off running.

I stepped back, out of the way, and glared. "How could you be with him, alone? What's gotten into you? You know better. We've been warned about being with strange guys and late at night. What were you thinking?"

Sarah waved her hand in my face. "Oh stop, Trina. Enough. Peyton's a good guy. He met me at our sand dune. We sat and talked for an hour."

I didn't move. "What if something had happened?"

"I had my phone."

"You just met him. You didn't know what he'd do!"

"Yeah. Yeah. Yeah." Sarah charged into the bathroom and continued talking. "I've seen all the movies, read all the pamphlets. I spent the whole day with him. He's nice." She stuck her head out the door. "Please don't tell. It would ruin the trip. We'd never get to see them again."

I leaned against the wall. "You're asking me to lie to my parents or yours?"

"Neither. But you don't have to tell them. We'll know in the morning if they heard anything. Will you promise me?" She laid on her bunk like she was dismissing me.

"I don't know. I'm worried about you being safe." I crawled up the ladder. *Let her think about what she is asking of me.* A couple of minutes later, I broke the silence. "What if something bad happened to you? It'd be my fault for not stopping you."

She kicked the bottom of my bed. "Come on, Trina. We were only talking. Please."

I leaned over the edge, and caught Sarah's eyes. "Only if you promise not to do it again by yourself."

She snapped back, "All right. I promise."

I wiggled my head on my soft pillow, getting it ready for a comfy sleep. "Are you crossing your fingers?"

After a long, loud sigh, Sarah whined, "No, silly. Now let's go to sleep."

CHAPTER 26

THURSDAY

When my eyes opened, Sydney's early morning alert seemed just minutes ago. Remembering my fright, I shuddered and became wide awake.

I separated the plastic slats in the blinds. *Oh, yes! What a pretty sunrise. Another new day.*

The wooden ladder squeaked and groaned as I stepped down. Sydney, never off duty, woke and sprang over Sarah.

In no time, I had dressed and unlocked the storage room. Sydney crept in, inching up to each item, putting his nose to the test, seeing if it was safe. After nothing leaped out and bit him, he wandered courageously.

I rummaged through old chairs with missing parts, moldy coolers, ripped umbrellas, and found six bikes piled together. Two men's bikes lay on top. I pulled out a red girl's bike with no hand brakes, a small tear in the seat, and a cute basket on the handlebars. I searched through the other bikes, and found a blue boy's speed bike with hand gears. Both bikes had rusty spokes, but their wide tires seemed okay, just a little low on air.

"Okay. Syd. Progress. Now I just need to find the air pump." I searched until I spotted a hand pump hanging on a hook. "Gotcha!"

I squatted, and spun each tire around and around, looking for the tire valve. Steadying the pump with my feet, I pulled and pushed the handle, whooshing air into the tires until they seemed firm.

"All right, Syd. The bikes are ready. Now. Let's see if we can wake sneaky Sarah."

Standing over sleeping beauty, I said, "I'm going to run with Sydney. Do you want to come?"

Sarah moaned and rolled over.

I clinched my mouth tight, shrugged my shoulders, and almost tripped over Sydney. His front legs and nose were under Sarah's bunk. He lifted his head, looked at me, and then stared under the bed. "Oh, I know what you want, Mr. Syd."

I slid my backpack out, grabbed his Frisbee, and buried it under my sweatshirt. While walking on the beach, Sydney kept his eyes on my hidden hand. He pounced at me. I ignored him, giggling inside. I ran in the sand, letting him circle me.

A ways down the beach, I turned my back to him and pulled out his favorite toy. When I turned around, his eyes flew to my hand. He panted, bouncing left and right.

I held it in the air. "Are you ready?"

His mouth stretched over his teeth, grinning. I launched his orange Frisbee, and he glided after the disc. Sydney leaped like a dancer doing a pirouette, crossing his back feet and pointing his toes, catching it in the air. He brought it directly back, dropped it at my feet, and bowed, wiggling his little stub in the air. Staying in that position, he looked down at the Frisbee, and then up, telling me, "Here it is. What are you waiting for?" This game continued until he panted so fast, his tongue dangled sideways. The Frisbee fell to the sand and he flopped on top of it, smiling.

"Good job, Syd. Time for breakfast."

We hurried up the stairs to the outside deck. He lapped water as I dashed inside for his food bowl. No one had oiled the screen door, so there was no way to sneak in. Jerking the door open, I tried making the squeaking noise quick, closing it softly, not letting it bang.

Inside all was quiet. I tiptoed to the kitchen, filled Sydney's dish, and stuffed my pockets with two juice boxes and a package of powdered donuts. I let Syd into the screened porch to eat and headed downstairs.

I repeated the quiet opening and closing of the door and then bounced down the steps, hoping Sarah was awake, but I knew before opening the door probably *NOT.*

"Yep! I'm right. Come on, Sarah. The beach is waiting."

"Oh, Trina. Why are you always in such a hurry? Don't you ever sleep in?"

"You're the one who chose to stay up all night, and yesterday it was cloudy. I got rested then, even though you woke *me* last night. We're only here for a few more days. Let's not waste any more time sleeping."

Sarah covered her head with her pillow. "Go away. I want to sleep. Just a little longer. I'm sure you can find something to do. Without me."

"Nope. You have to get up. I found bikes. And the turtles need to be checked. Remember the storm yesterday." Just then the dogs started barking. "It sounds like Darby's up. I'll go take her to the beach, and then if you're not dressed, I'm letting both dogs in. They'll get you up and make you remember not to wander around at midnight, again."

After another romp on the beach, I rushed upstairs with the dogs and told Momma, "Sydney has been fed, and Sarah and I are going to check the turtles." I closed the gate and ran down to our room. As soon as I opened the door, I yelled. "Are you awake? Do I send in the dogs?"

"Oh, all right. Okay! Okay!" Sarah rubbed the sleep from her eyes. "You're really obnoxious this morning. I get more sleep upstairs."

"Yeah. And I know why."

Sarah's face crumpled.

"Come on, sleepyhead." I waved the donut package in front of her face. "Look. I've got breakfast. All you have to do is get dressed."

Sarah shuffled to the bathroom. In a couple of minutes, she came out with her hair pulled through the back of her cap, and wearing yesterday's clothes.

I snorted. "Oh, my. You're in the same outfit."

Sarah narrowed her eyes. "I'll change later. After I wake up. Did I hear you say you found bikes to ride?"

"Yep. I even filled the tires and wiped off all the cobwebs. It'll be fun." I ripped open the plastic wrapping. "Here, have a donut. I have juice in my pocket, also."

She shook her head. "I'll eat while we walk to see the turtles." Sarah glanced outside. Under the deck, it was dark, but the sun shined cheerfully over the backyard. "Oooh, it does look like a pretty day. I wonder what Peyton's doing?"

"Sounds like you're waking up." I tried not to gloat, bit my lip to keep from grinning, and headed out the door. "I'm excited about seeing the guys, too, but we need to do what we want since we don't know their schedule. Right?"

"Uh-huh." Sarah nodded and followed. After a few steps down the walkway, she spoke. "Maybe we'll see them on our way."

"Yep. Maybe."

Sarah cheered up as we splashed our feet in the water, talking about the day ahead. The debris covering the top of the turtle's nest had blown away. We laid extra reeds on top, straightened the splints that protected the nest, and then sat next to it, talking to the unborn turtles.

"Well." Sarah lifted her head and stared toward the guys' direction. "No sign of the boys. Let me change clothes, and then we'll go explore the island."

Our parents rocked on the porch as we stormed into the house. Before we disappeared inside, Sarah's mom asked, "So what have you girls been up to?"

Sarah froze. No questions were asked about last night. She stood in front of the door, and told about the nest and its needed repairs.

I shared about the bikes and our plan to go to lunch, and opened the door.

"Now wait just a minute." Momma stopped rocking, and her voice grew louder. "You girls can't go gallivanting around the island by yourselves. When did you both start getting so independent?"

I straightened my back and shoulders, and turned around. "It's happening, Momma. I'm almost fourteen." And gave her a smug smile.

Momma was now sideways in her chair. "Well, I'm not sure I like this happening so fast. I don't want to pop your bubble, but it could be dangerous for you girls riding around by yourselves."

"What are your plans, girls?" Sarah's mom leaned forward.

Sarah told her, folded her arms and waited, tapping her foot on the floor.

Mrs. Neal said, "How about your dads go with you?"

I copied Sarah, and folded my arms. We said in unison, "No."

Then I got quiet, and Sarah went on, "We want to go by ourselves. There are only two roads and Jungle Lane."

We stood our ground, glaring at them. Momma looked at Dad for help. He offered another suggestion. "I know this island seems remote, but I'd rather be safe than sorry. How about we ride behind you, part of the way. You'll never know we're there. We'll let you go up Jungle Road, and we'll meet you at the Shack."

Sarah moaned. "We wanted to have lunch by ourselves."

Her dad chimed in, "You can sit at your own table, and pretend you don't know us."

"Come on, Sarah. Let's get fixed up. I think it's our only way." I pulled her arm until we entered her room.

I was catching on to the idea of not being the ugly duckling. I borrowed another cute tee shirt with lots of swirls of colors. In my room, I tried to shake out the wrinkles in my white shorts since they had been on the floor all night. My mother's words bopped through my brain. *If you'd fold your clothes instead of dumping ..."*

Once I was dressed, I spoke to Sarah's door. "Okay. I'm ready. Meet you downstairs." I grabbed the boy's bike, rode in circles on the scruffy front yard, and watched our dads fill their tires.

Finally, Sarah appeared in her crisp white shorts and a pink tank top over the white one with lace. She wore a white cap with pink lettering, a cute beaded bracelet with lots of pink and purple, and clean white tennis shoes with pink-striped anklets.

I dipped my head and pretended not to care. *Why does she always have to look so perfect?*

Sarah pranced toward the girl's bike, wrinkled her face, and stared at me. "These look kind of old. Are you sure we'll be safe?"

"I tried them both out. They're fine. Which one do you want to ride?"

"I'll ride this one. I can put my purse in the basket. Are you taking a purse?"

"Nope. I have money" And patted my back pocket. "Let's go."

Our dads crossed the street with us after we waited for two cars to putt down the road. Then they let us pedal ahead. Sarah and I rode together on the bike lane of Palmetto Blvd. In between houses, the ocean sparkled, and the waves swelled before breaking and crashing on shore.

Sarah said, "The waves are really big today."

"Yeah. It'll be perfect for riding my raft."

Sarah gave me The Look.

I returned it. "I didn't say you had to do it."

After riding a few more blocks. Sarah pointed. "There's Jungle Lane." She waved to our dads.

We crossed over small dirt roads, followed the path, and viewed high tide creeping through the green marshlands. Full creeks invited birds for lunch, and a breeze sent a salty, fishy odor into the air.

At the other end of the island, the road dead-ended into another lane that followed the golf course. Our legs pumped up and down as we whooshed past a foursome of two guys and two girls playing golf.

Without saying a word, Sarah braked her bike, planted her feet on the ground, and pouted. I kept riding, but slowed and twisted my head around to ask why.

Then she ordered me. "Go. Trina! Just GO!"

I glanced over at the golf course. One guy had black hair and the taller one had long brown hair. They looked just like...

Oh, no! I squinted. Two blond-headed girls seemed about their age and were goofing around with them. I gulped. *Peyton and Chase are playing golf, not on the beach looking for us.*

Sarah stood on her pedals, leaning over her handlebars. Her legs couldn't pump fast enough. "I can't believe it," Sarah huffed. "No wonder we haven't heard from them." Her ears, sticking out from her cap, grew hot pink, and then rosy blotches appeared on her neck.

Having trouble keeping up, I yelled ahead. "Sarah. Stop. Please. I need to catch my breath."

She pulled her bike over to the edge of the sidewalk and halted. When I caught up, her face reminded me of the momma turtle. Salty tears had stained a path down her red cheeks.

"Sarah, there has to be an explanation. Neither of them sounded like they had any other plans. It just doesn't make any sense."

Her face paled, and then she was puffing mad. Her nostrils flared and her whole face looked like a wrinkled prune. "Do you think it was because I met him last night? I bet he thinks I'm too young."

"If he thought that, he wouldn't have visited you last night."

Sarah bent her head. "Maybe he was testing me?"

"If that's true, he found out who you really are. Whatever happened last night, I'm not letting them ruin our trip. Nope. Let's go have lunch. And then we'll go to the beach."

We stood, straddling our bikes on the sidewalk. A car passed with its radio banging out an obnoxious drum beat.

Sarah's sad eyes followed the car, and then returned to me. "I'm not very hungry."

"Me, either."

A couple pushing a stroller walked around us.

Sarah watched them disappear. "I guess, since we have nothing better to do, let's get a Coke."

"That's the right attitude. And I'll have an ice cream cone."

Fifteen minutes later, we parked our bikes next to a table under an umbrella. Sarah put her purse over her shoulder and walked up to the window to order. She pulled a napkin from the silver holder and wiped her streaked face. "I'll have a Coke, please. And one vanilla cone." She turned to face me. "Do you want a coke, too?"

"No thanks, but I'd love a bottle of water."

Sarah paid, handed me my bottle of water, and then my cone.

"Thanks, Sarah. Here, I have money."

"My treat. Let's sit and rest. I don't think I've ever been so mad in all my life."

"I know. I can't believe they lied to us."

Sarah leaned over her drink, sipping her Coke from a long straw in between saying, "How dare they…" Sip. "They left us…" Sip. Her face lost all color, and she stopped talking. Her straw had stuck to her bottom lip. In slow motion, her tongue lifted the straw so she could slide her mouth away from her drink, while never moving her head. "You won't believe who just got out of their car and is walking over here."

"Well, it can't be our dads."

CHAPTER 27

Girls' and boys' chatter grew closer. I kept my head down just like Sarah, and we stared at each other. She wasn't giving me any clues, but I could tell this wasn't the time to ask questions.

A car door slammed, and two girls ran ahead to the counter. Then Chase and Peyton walked ahead of their dad and another man.

Sarah whispered, "Let's go."

I shook my head. "They'll see us."

"I don't care if they see us. I want to get away."

My front teeth scraped my bottom lip. "What about our dads?"

"I'm sure we'll bump into them."

Sarah squeezed her paper cup of Coke, splashing Coke all over her hand, and threw it in the trash can. My half-eaten cone followed. I kept my water but had to place it in Sarah's basket. We mounted our bikes, pumped our pedals, and sped down the road. Breathing heavy, we didn't say one word, until we passed our dads.

Sarah waved without stopping, "We're heading back. We decided we weren't hungry."

Mr. Neal and Dad shared a startled look, but it was Sarah's dad who spoke. "All right. We're going for a burger. Call as soon as you get back."

"Okay, Dad. Later." She turned to me. "We can sit on the porch and do those dorky puzzles or the craft stuff that you brought." Her legs slowed, pumping just fast enough to propel the bike forward and not tip over.

I passed her. "Well, I love doing those things, but we need to go to the beach. You know how much I like to swim."

"Maybe there'll be other guys on the beach. Then if Chase and Peyton come down, they'll see us with new friends." Sarah stopped pedaling, put her feet on the ground, and groaned. "That'd make me feel a whole lot better."

I turned my bike around, and straddled it in front of Sarah. "You know, I don't think we should be so angry. We just met them. And yes, you shouldn't have met him last night, but I don't think that had anything to do with today."

Sarah closed her eyes and nodded. "We talked and laughed. He didn't even hold my hand until we came back to the house."

"So, no biggie. Maybe we'll never see them again. I bet this is how you learn about boys. You meet one, and then you meet someone else. Come on. Let's go."

Sarah, ready to move, started pedaling and talking. "I guess after you've met a hundred boys, one day you meet one that likes you the same as you like them. You know, Trina, I think boys are going to be a lot of work."

"Duh. It's like in the movies. They make the girl all happy and then sad. And to think this is what you wanted to do for vacation."

"Maybe the rest of our beach trip we should just do girl stuff."

I almost crashed my bike. I squished my hand brakes, and Sarah rolled past me. "Did those words come out of YOUR mouth?"

Sarah turned around, grinning. "Yep! That's what I said." Then she continued riding.

We rode under the house, parked our bikes, and ran upstairs. The house was silent. I looked out to the beach. "Our moms are on the beach. So, do you want to go down?"

"Yeah. That would be more fun that sitting up here."

"Okay, beach—here we come," I shouted and hurried toward the bedroom. "Meet you in one minute, maybe two. I'm wearing my new bathing suit again. How long do you need?"

"I'll wear the same suit I had on yesterday. You must be wearing off on me. I'll be quick, too."

"Well, you always look nice. And I like that bathing suit."

We rushed into our rooms and came out at the same time, looked at each other, and laughed.

"See, Trina. We'll be friends forever. Let's see what's happening on the beach."

While walking down, Sarah's phone played her parents' tune, *You Are on My Mind*. "I guess Dad's making sure we're safe." She ran up behind her mom and said, "Hi."

Sydney nosed Momma, wiggling his nub and whining.

Mrs. Neal jerked around with her phone to her ear. "Oh, Trina. Thank goodness you're back."

Sarah smiled and said, "Well, hi to you, too, Mom. I thought Dad was calling."

Her mom's eyes scrunched, making her forehead wrinkle. Her eyes wandered to me, to Sarah, and back to me.

My stomach clenched. "What's wrong, Mrs. Neal?"

Momma stood and grabbed my hand. "Honey, Mrs. Manning called about five minutes ago. She found your Dad's number on a scrap of paper by the phone. Logan's missing and she's hysterical. Her husband's supposed to be golfing, but they've already left. He hasn't returned her call."

"What happened?"

"I guess Logan got upset when all the others left and snuck out. She's begging you and Sydney to find him. I told her we'd be down as soon as I found you."

"Wait a minute. Mr. Manning is at the Hamburger Shack. Our dads are there, also."

Sarah paced and called her dad.

"I'll take Syd upstairs and get his cape. I take it you have Dad's phone?" Momma nodded and showed me her hand. "Call Mrs. Manning. Tell her I'm hurrying. Come, Syd." We raced up the stairs. I filled my waist pouch with his favorite treats, located his water bottle, and snapped it onto my belt. "Okay. We're ready."

In the carport, Momma had the engine running and handed me the address. "I think it's only four or five blocks down the road. Your dads are talking with Mr. Manning. Carol's going to walk up the beach toward their house. We'll go the other direction. Sarah's staying here in case he should come this way."

"I wonder what happened."

"I didn't waste any time asking questions. You'll get all of the information you need once we're there."

Mrs. Manning stood out front, waving her arms. We bolted from the car, and Mrs. Manning blubbered information in between blowing her nose and hiccupping. "Logan had a meltdown when his brothers left to play golf. There's no way Logan can handle sitting in a golf cart all morning. He has a very short attention span."

Momma held Mrs. Manning's hand, stroking her wrist. "Kathy, Trina's only practiced playing hide-and-seek with other children. Sydney's not a search and rescue dog, but maybe he'll be able to find Logan. I'll go with her, but you need to stay here." Mrs. Manning's wild eyes widened and her face whitened. "Kathy, you have to be here in case he comes home or someone finds him. Call us if you need to, and we'll call you as soon as we find him."

She sobbed. "Okay. Thank you."

A load of gravel hit the pit of my stomach one stone at a time. I had to ask. "Mrs. Manning, I haven't seen Logan swim. Will he get in the water?" I sucked in my breath and held it.

"Not without his life jacket. He doesn't like to get his face wet. He may walk a long way and forget how to get home. He doesn't know his phone number and can only say his first name."

"Oh." A relieved breath blew through my lips. "That's good. He won't get in the water. Can you give me an item he wears a lot? I need his scent."

While Mrs. Manning rushed in the house, I wrapped Syd's cape around his back. He knew at once he was on duty. His eyes grew bright amber, and his mouth spread across his teeth.

Huffing and puffing, Mrs. Manning rushed back, carrying Logan's ball cap. She caught her breath in between words. "I'm surprised he ran off without this. He loves wearing it to keep the sun out of his eyes."

"That's perfect. We're ready."

CHAPTER 28

The three of us jogged toward the sand dunes. I held Logan's ball cap up to Sydney's nose and said, "Find Logan."

As Sydney inhaled the scent, his golden eyes looked into mine. He backed up, jiggled his stub, and shoved his nose once more into the empty space inside the cap. That was his signal, "I know what you want me to do."

"Good boy, Syd. Find Logan."

Momma and I stepped back. We let him run freely, getting his bearings. He lunged into the bushes behind Logan's house. He circled the sea grass in the dunes. He dashed toward the water, his nostrils opened and closed at the the wet sand, and then he spontaneously made a U-turn. He raced on to dry sand and sniffed his way up the coast. After each inspection, Sydney woofed. I knew Logan would recognize Syd's bark and would come running.

If he heard. Or if he could? That thought sent shivers up my neck. I clasped my hands in front of my chest, squeezing them, hiking my shoulders to my ears. I took a deep breath and blew it out with my eyes closed, and prayed, "Please, keep Logan safe."

Momma and I peeked around the dunes, calling Logan's name, hoping Sydney might have missed him. High tide was moving down, but there were no footprints, no trail of food, and no way to know which way he might have gone.

I headed up a wooden path and called, "Syd, Come." Again, I put the cap under his nose and said, "Find Logan."

We walked under the house and up to the front yard. Sydney lost interest, so I let him lead me back to the sand. We repeated this search, checking the dunes, and then under each house block after block after block. After searching for an hour, I gave Syd the command, "Down," in someone's empty carport. He panted heavily and rested. Once his breathing slowed, we shared the bottle of water.

"Any other ideas, Momma?"

She shook her head. "Let me go ahead and wander down the beach while Sydney takes his time doing what he's been doing. He takes a lot longer sniffing every inch."

"What if Logan's gone up to someone's house, Momma? What if he knocked at their door, and they took him in? I'm getting scared. What if we can't find him?" I wiped my damp face.

"Hold on, Trina. Mrs. Manning's calling." She listened with her eyes glued to a spot on the cement floor. "Okay. That's great." Putting Dad's phone in her pocket she said, "The boys and their friends are going door to door. And the island police have one car patrolling the streets. So we'll stay on the beach."

I shook my head. "Did you say, 'friends?'"

"Yes. I never got to tell you. Mr. Manning called just after you left this morning. He wanted you and Sarah to know they had company show up and had a change of plans for the day. Since they missed you, he asked if we'd all meet for dinner. We thought you'd enjoy that, so we agreed to meet at 6:00 for pizza. Now, of course, I'm not sure what we'll be doing."

"Oh, that's makes me feel so much better! I told Sarah there had to be a good reason." I blew out another long breath. "Okay. Syd, Find Logan."

He turned in circles, excited to be back on the job. We walked and walked. I gasped when I saw The Pavilion, the pier in the back, and the souvenir shop. Hope bounced through the gravel in my stomach, shoving some of the pebbles to the side. I wanted to scream, but my voice had grown hoarse. A little giggle tried to come out. *Maybe he's up there watching the seagulls or looking for dolphins. Wouldn't that be wonderful?*

But we were at the end of the beach. On the other side of this pier, strangers camped in tents or in trailers at the state park.

We climbed the wooden stairs, checked out the restaurant and the bathroom and asked the manager if he'd seen a little, black-haired boy. We walked behind the building, and down the wooden planks. My stomach quivered. I swallowed the nausea. No sign of Logan squealing at the seagulls or staring out to sea.

I collapsed on the pier. Sitting cross-legged, my hands covering my face, and I cried. Sydney put his nose under my arms, lifting my hands and began licking my tears. Momma sat next to us, weary.

She lifted my chin. "It's time to go back, honey. We've done all we can do."

CHAPTER 29

Walking toward Logan's house, we continued searching. The tide had lowered, so we checked for small footprints. The sun blazed, making the dry sand too hot for bare feet. The breeze had stopped blowing. I worried about Sydney's feet and about him overheating, and what about Logan? Where would he take cover if he got hot?

My eyes scanned the dunes. The sea grass stood tall and fluffy, blowing in the breeze. Tucked in next to the stems, six-inch wide boards and wire fences restrained the sliding sand.

I squinted, thinking. *Hmm. If I was small, I might find some shade next to them.* Looking toward the backyards, I noticed Palmetto trees and wide bushes sparsely covering the walkways. Under the decks would be cooler, also. "Momma, let's look in all the shaded places we can find. Logan's got to be hot and tired by now."

"Good idea, honey."

I called Sydney to me. "Sydney, Speak." As he woofed, I counted for him. Holding up my thumb for one, then he woofed again and I added my pointy finger. On the third bark, I held three fingers in the air, nodded to him and said, "Good boy. Maybe Logan will hear you and find us."

Every second house I repeated that command. Sydney woofed, and then we searched. Sydney went under every deck built above ground. I checked behind each sand dune. Momma looked under trees growing in the yards.

We stopped at Mrs. Manning's house. I had to show Momma the restroom downstairs. "Isn't this amazing? You should have seen the towels we used to dry Syd." Then we walked up to the deck.

Mrs. Manning stood in front of her glass French doors. The moment she saw us, the door flew open. Her eyes were red and swollen. "Nothing?"

We shook our heads no.

She clasped the railing. "This is the longest he's ever been gone."

My eyes widened, and my voice squeaked out. "So he's done this before?"

"Twice. He's never gone very far, but each time it's happened, he's walked a little farther away. It's been two years since the last time."

"Did he have a special hiding spot?"

She shook her head, side to side, too weak to speak. She inhaled and then forced words out in one breath. "But we've always found him close by."

"Oh." My chest relaxed like someone had untied me. "That's good to know. We'll find him. He's getting older and has more energy. I bet he's just found a better hiding place."

Momma put her arm around my shoulders, pulling me close. "Kathy, have you heard from anyone?"

She bent her head and mumbled, "No," never letting us see her eyes.

"Well, I'm sure everyone is looking hard. I'm taking Trina and Sydney home for a rest. Please call if you hear anything."

This time, Mrs. Manning lifted her face to us. "I can't thank you enough. I'm so sorry you had to spend your day this way."

Momma moved forward and wrapped her arms around Mrs. Manning's shaking body and let her weary head lean on her. "Kathy, I can't even imagine how difficult this must be. But, I'm so glad we could, well, try to help. He's going to show up. Let's go inside. Once I know you're okay, I'll drive back home."

I had forgotten we drove. An idea sent a shockwave shot through my body. "Momma, I'm walking back. You stay here with Mrs. Manning. We'll head home from the beach."

Mrs. Manning pushed away. "Trina, you and Sydney need to come in and rest. I'll be okay with Sydney in the house. He's a marvelous dog. How can I be afraid of him after all he's done?"

I lifted my chin and smiled. "I'm glad, but I want to check some other places before I give up."

Mrs. Manning wouldn't hear of us leaving before we had a break. She filled a beautiful glass bowl decorated with large, orange paw prints around the entire bowl with cool water for Sydney. He lapped until it was empty.

Momma and I sipped a glass of water and ate slices of apple. I broke three slices into small pieces and fed Sydney his favorite treat of all time. He deserved it.

Refreshed, Sydney and I zipped down the walkway. I undid his cape and slung it over my arm. The hot sun was heading west. That took my breath away. I swallowed a couple of times, inhaled and blew it out. We had to find Logan before it grew dark. The tide was lower, the waves smaller, and the beach had more wet sand, making it firmer and easier to walk. Sydney dashed at the small waves, popping the white bubbles in the foam. I didn't care if he got wet. He was free to relax, and have some fun before going back to work.

After we passed the turtle's nest, I called, "Sydney."

He rushed to meet me.

I strapped on his cape and put Logan's cap up to his nose. "Okay, Mr. Syd. This is it. We've got to do this. Find Logan."

He turned in circles, wiggled his rear end, and ran. He darted up to the dunes. He sniffed and looked at me. He sniffed again. Then he put his nose close to the sand. He looked like a hound dog. Chills went up my body. He was onto something. It better not be a fish.

Sydney ran to the next dune and up to a tree close to someone's backyard. He turned around and circled me like he was saying, "Hurry up."

"What do you smell, Syd?"

He barked, raced to the wet sand, and showed me foot prints. They were small, bare feet.

"Okay. Syd, show me."

He explored the soft, sandy dunes. It looked like part of the sand had been pressed into a body shape. A small body. My heart pumped even faster. I started huffing, filling my lungs. I scanned the area. *If Logan's been here, it's been since the tide's gone down. Maybe he's on the way to our beach house.* "I bet he wants to see you, Syd. Thank goodness, Sarah's there. Someone will find him. Okay. Let's keep going. Find Logan, Sydney."

Sydney put his nose to the ground. His rear end pointed to the sky. I followed. He circled the dune once more, double-checking the footprints from the ocean to the trees. He wouldn't move forward.

"What is it, Syd?"

He turned around and repeated his steps. I glanced between the dune and the trees. Sky blue wooden steps led to someone's two-level house. Hidden underneath was a three-sided outdoor shower matching the wooden steps. An ocean-blue plastic shower curtain decorated with colored fish hung across the opening. I stood back and let Syd repeat his steps. This time he crept toward the shower stall.

I wanted to scream, "Yes. Yes." But I stayed quiet. *Could Logan be inside? Was he hurt?*

Sydney knew to stand at attention when he came upon what he was looking for.

"Good boy."

He sat.

I whispered, "Quiet."

Syd's little body squirmed, making an indentation in the sand with his bottom.

I slid the curtain back, an inch at a time. Not wanting to startle who or what was in there, I peeked inside. There was a small bench on the back wall and shaded by the tree. Sleeping, curled in a ball, one arm under his head and one arm hanging off the ledge, Logan breathed in and out. Slowly and peacefully. He had no idea of the ordeal he had caused. He'd been angry and fled.

I stepped back and inhaled. My eyes overflowed. I bent face to face with Sydney and whispered, "Good boy." I wrapped my arms around him and whispered in his ear. "You get to wake him. He'll be so excited to see you."

Sydney sat, waiting for his command. His eyes sparkled and his tongue drooped sideways. "Okay. Syd. Find Logan."

He slinked in, put his nose under Logan's limp arm, and lifted it. Logan stirred. Then Syd moved close to his face and licked his cheek.

Logan's eyes opened. He squealed, "Syd-ney. Syd-ney. Want see." Logan sat up and hung his legs over the side of the bench. He lifted his face to me, grinning, showing two missing teeth on the top and on the bottom.

I lifted Logan off the bench, lightly cuddling him before setting his feet on the ground. He had no idea he had been missing. He had only wanted to find Sydney. He must have gone the wrong direction and turned around, grew tired, and took a nap.

I snatched Logan's hand and said, "Sydney home."

He ran toward our beach house.

Logan shook my hand off and chased after Syd. I'd call Momma from there. Sarah had a phone.

Rushing toward the house, I saw a blond head on a beach towel sound asleep. Getting closer, it was hard not to notice that Sarah's back, shoulders, and legs were fire red. "Sarah, wake up. You're really burned."

Sarah lifted her head. "What?" She looked at her arms. "I must've fallen asleep. Oooh. Ouch!"

"I can't believe you fell asleep while we've been worried about Logan all day."

Sarah's expression showed confusion. "What? Oh. After searching around here for hours, I thought I'd watch for him on the beach. I guess I fell asleep."

Sarah recognized Logan, and tried to bend her knees. Moaning, she stood and bent from her waist to be face to face with Logan.

"Oh my." Sarah clapped her hands together and pointed her face to the skies. And then she looked at me with wet eyes. "You found him!"

"Sydney did. Just a few minutes ago. I need to use your phone. Like now!" I paced, waiting for her phone. "Sarah, you've definitely had enough sun."

"Here, it's in my beach bag." Sarah handed me her bag. "I really did help look. Oh, Logan, I'm so happy you're okay."

Logan stared at his feet, but we heard, "Logan, okay."

"He has no idea everyone's been looking for him. He's the lucky one."

I phoned Mrs. Manning.

Her frightened voice answered, "Yes."

"Hi, Mrs. Manning, I have Logan." She cried into the receiver. I'm not sure if she understood a word I said, but I told her where and how we found him.

Momma must have taken hold of Mrs. Manning's phone. "Hi, honey. Mrs. Manning is speechless. We're on our way. I'll call Carol, and she'll call the others. See you at the house."

Sarah, Logan, Sydney, and I stepped into the screened porch about the same time Mrs. Manning and Momma walked through the front door. Mrs. Manning rushed in, picked Logan up in a death grip, and squeezed.

He squirmed and said, "Off."

I smiled at Mrs. Manning. "He was looking for Sydney the whole time."

Mrs. Neal came up the back stairs, opened the screen door, and stifled a scream. "Oh, Sarah. You did it again. I trusted you to use lotion. You look like a lobster. Let me see if I brought the aloe." She hugged Mrs. Manning on her way inside. "What a happy day!"

Momma said, "Wait, Carol. I know I have some. I'll get it. Trina, please get Sarah a big glass of water. She needs to be hydrated."

As I handed Sarah the glass of water, I whispered, "Mr. Manning called us this morning. They had surprise company."

Her eyes squinted, and she mouthed, "company" while tilting her head. I nodded.

Mrs. Manning stopped crying. "Please accept my apology for all the worry and the time you spent on your vacation day. I'm horrified that you had to be a part of all this." She held Logan's hand. "Oh, here comes your daddy."

The door flew open. Mr. Manning stood inside, staring at Logan. "Hey, little buddy!" As soon as he was at an arm's distance, he reached and lifted Logan's small body to his chest. After gaining control of himself, he looked at each one of us. "I hope you'll still plan to have dinner with us tonight. We need to celebrate."

CHAPTER 30

S arah lay on her stomach, letting her mom grease her sunburned parts. Waiting for the lotion to soak in, I sat on the bed next to her.

Mrs. Neal explained the phone call. "Mr. Manning said their friends had arrived unexpectedly. We agreed to dinner, thinking you girls would be excited, but Sarah, if you're not up to it, we can forget it."

Without moving her head, Sarah mumbled, "I feel okay right now."

"Trina, please keep her still for five more minutes. I'm going to get a drink of water. This has been a long day! Thank goodness it had a good ending."

Sarah lifted her chin as her mother disappeared. "Friends? Hmm. Maybe they're girlfriends from home? And they're double-timing us. We could go and not mention that we saw them."

"Well, you could also use your sunburn as an excuse, and stand them up."

Sarah's smile grew to a huge grin. "Not a bad idea. Would you go without me?"

"No. Of course not. We'd just cancel. Never see them again."

"Well, let's think about it for a minute. They really didn't stand us up, even though that's how it felt." Sarah laid her head back down and stared at the wall. "If we never talk to them, we'll never know what happened."

"Yeah!"

"Besides being hot and my legs don't bend well, I guess I'm okay." We remained silent, thinking. Then she said, "I sure did like the pizza, and I'm kind of getting hungry. How about you?"

"Uh-huh. Oh, Sarah." I turned my body and folded a leg under me. "We both want to go. Let's just do it. I can't wait to hear their story."

"I can't wear jeans tonight. Want to wear a sundress? I brought two. Just in case you didn't bring one. I knew we'd share."

"I'm glad you did. I thought you were crazy bringing so many clothes. Will you help me with my hair? Maybe, I can be beautiful, too."

"Yeah," Sarah grinned, lifting her head an inch above the bed. "And then we can act like we're not interested in them."

The door opened again. Mrs. Neal came in to examine Sarah. "Oooh, honey. You already have little white blisters. Are you sure you're feeling okay?" She paused and shook her head. "Let me get you another glass of water. Be still. You're still drying." At the door, she added, "And if you start to feel bad tonight, we won't stay long. I know you and Trina are anxious to see your friends, but there's always tomorrow."

"I'll go shower, Sarah. Be right back."

After I had blown my hair dry, I knocked at the door.

"Come in, Trina. I laid the dresses out. And I already know which one you'll want."

The sun dresses would have been identical a year ago. But this time, one was swirled in purple, green, and blue, and fitted and pleated around the bust area. The skirt started from there and flared to above the knee. It had wide straps over the shoulder, crossing in the back. The other dress was pink, blue and purple, fitting at the waist, with the entire bodice of alternating colors of elastic, and ribbon ties for the shoulders.

"I also know which one you want. I'll wear the one with purple and green. It's really pretty. Thanks." I held it up to me and looked down. "It's going to feel funny wearing a dress. My shiny legs will stick out. Good thing the Band-Aids are gone." I jiggled one bare leg, and we giggled.

"Do you want me to French braid your hair?"

"Yeah. If you're up to it. Will you wear yours the same way?"

"Not exactly. I'll have a small French braid on top and wear the rest down."

Just a little before six, Dad's voice boomed through the house. "Load 'em up. I've turned on the air conditioning in the carriage, and it's waiting for our two Cinderella's."

We walked out of the bathroom. Our parents did a double-take. "Wow. Are these girls our daughters?" Momma's smiling eyes connected with me.

I bent my head and hunched my shoulders. "Don't make me blush. It'll make my freckles stand out."

Sarah stiffly modeled her dress before heading downstairs to the car. Everyone, except Sarah, hustled into our van. She moved slowly and needed a hand getting in.

Momma turned halfway around. "It's been quite an exhausting day. When Frank called this morning, he told me their company would be here for one night. They were on their way home from a trip, and so close to the island, they decided to visit."

Sarah asked. "Who's their company?"

"I didn't think it was any of my business to ask. I'm sure you'll get all your questions answered tonight."

Sarah and I stared out the window, watching the parking lot appear. It was almost time to confront the boys. We had made a plan and were ready to implement it. We hung back, letting our parents enter the restaurant. The hostess remembered us and made no fuss about Sydney.

Momma nodded and smiled toward Peyton and Chase, who were sitting with the two girls. "We'll sit with their parents. Order anything you like."

Sarah and I glanced at each other, wearing blank faces. We were ready to begin Plan A: Cold Shoulder. We walked up without saying a word, making no eye contact. I told Sydney, "Go under. Sit." I sat in the empty chair at the closest end of the table and Sarah went to the opposite end.

Then Logan crawled under the table.

Not making plans about Logan baffled me. I looked straight ahead at Sarah. She shrugged and didn't look at Peyton. I made a quick decision to crawl under the table.

Logan was petting Sydney, saying, "Good Sydney," over and over.

In my fussy dress, I sat with my legs crossed. "Logan, we can't eat under the table. How about you sit close to me and help me with Sydney?"

Logan peeked at me, and then hid his face.

I grabbed his hand saying, "Come on Logan. Out you go." Before I knew it, Chase was under the table, and our eyes accidentally locked.

He surprised me with his expression, and then he whispered, "Please don't be mad. I wanted to see you today. I'll explain later." Louder, he said, "Logan, out. We don't eat under the table."

Logan obeyed. Chase pulled Logan's chair next to mine at the end of the table. Then put his chair to the right of Logan, and before long everyone had played musical chairs. Sarah wanted to be close to me so she went to my left side. Peyton moved his chair next to Sarah, and the taller girl faced me from the other end, but was still close to Peyton. The other girl was on Chase's right toward the end of the table, and next to her sister.

"Okay. Now that we're all seated," said Peyton with a smirk, "Let me introduce our friends, Shelby and Henley. They live down the street from us. Our parents have been friends since college, and we've grown up together."

"Oh," said Sarah. She eyed the girls, trying to figure out if they were just friends, but used her grownup manners and said, "It's nice to meet you. Did you have fun playing golf today? Uh-oh!" Sarah grabbed a napkin, trying to cover her glowing face that now matched her dress. Then she turned to me.

I glared at Sarah, which meant, "Shame on you." Then I spoke straight ahead, looking at a spot on the wall. "We rode bikes today all over the island. And then we went to the beach."

Chase smacked the table with his hand, forcibly saying, "I knew that was the two of you at the Hamburger Shack." Sydney popped up and lay across Chase's lap. "Oops. I'm getting a hug."

I told Sydney, "Good boy. Down." He lay next to Chase, staring at him.

Chase turned back to me. "You took off like a flash, and I told Peyton you'd be upset. I'm right, aren't I?"

"Well," I stammered and looked down. "What can I say? We had planned on seeing you at the beach, and then we saw you playing golf. So how do you think we felt?"

"Angry? I'm sorry. We never got anyone's phone number. By the time Dad remembered you had called on my phone and found your Dad's number, you had already left for your bike ride. He wanted to invite both of you to play golf with us."

Henley, who looked about the same age as Peyton, giggled. "Trina, Sarah, I'm sorry you couldn't join us today. We've been friends with Chase and Peyton forever." Henley looked at each one of us as she spoke. "All day Peyton talked about going to soccer camp with you, Sarah. And Chase went on and on about your service dog, Trina."

I watched her expressions. *Was SHE jealous? Was she pretending to be polite?*

"And I want to hear more about Sydney," added Shelby. I sensed she was about our age, maybe younger and okay with me being friends with Chase. "He's really cool."

The grownups sat at the table next to us. Mrs. Manning continued glancing over, smiling. Mr. Manning kept the conversation going, asking my parents about the kennel and about raising a puppy for service.

Momma was the first to answer. "Since I've always worked with animals, it's been fun and a lot of work. But mainly for Trina. Yet, she's done such a wonderful job of training."

Dad added, "I'm really proud of her. She's always dreamed of riding horses competitively, but we could never afford owning one. This has given her a new reachable goal of being a dog trainer. Sydney's going to be perfect for someone. We'll sure miss him, though."

"I suspect she'll do it again." Momma's voice fell almost to a whisper. "So, we'll fall in love with another new little personality, just like Trina, and have to let it go. Again."

Realizing my parents felt the same heartache I did and didn't know about my doubts, made my heart sag.

I bent my head and sighed. *They're hurting, too.*

While Mrs. Manning listened, she never took her eyes off of Sydney. The moment she spoke, everyone at their table hushed. Even our table quieted. "I've made up my mind. I'm going to visit this kennel when we get back home. After today, how could I ever be fearful of such a special dog? I want Logan to have a service dog. He's like a new little boy around Sydney." She looked at her husband. "If everyone else in the family can care for the dog, I'll learn to deal with my anxiety."

A smile grew on Mr. Manning's handsome face as he gawked at his wife. "When she makes up her mind to do something, she's a force to be reckoned with."

The guys hooted and hollered, making so much noise, the restaurant vibrated.

Dad stood, trying to calm the group. "Since we're finished with dinner, maybe we should change venues. How about everyone come to our house? We certainly need to celebrate this day. We can sit on the porch and listen to music."

Mrs. Manning shook her head. "No, please come to our place. We have lots of room." She looked at the faces around the table. "The kids can use the computer, watch TV, or go for a walk."

All of us shouted, "Yeah," and "Great idea." And then we discussed the evening plans.

Sarah and I sent signals with our eyes. We knew what the other was thinking. Time for Plan B: Make The Girls Jealous.

CHAPTER 31

Inside the Manning's house, Sarah asked Peyton, "Can we play the same computer game we played yesterday?"

"Sure." He grinned from ear to ear. "But I'll beat you this time."

Henley stood back, watching their interaction. "I'll watch you two play, and then play the winner."

Peyton clapped his hands. "You're on, Hen."

I patted Chase's arm. "Sydney needs a walk, and then he'll be nice and quiet."

He grabbed my hand this time, and pulled me toward the deck door. "Good. I need a walk, too. Come on, Shelby. You can keep us company. And Logan. Want to go for a walk?"

Logan ran ahead, flapping his arms and calling, "Syd-ney, Syd-ney."

Chase walked between Shelby and myself. I kept the conversation on Logan and Sydney, and how his mother was coming around. As long as Chase and I chatted, he didn't pay any attention to Shelby. When she tried to change the discussion, I called Logan, and told him what a good job he was doing. With a new confidence, I wanted to show Shelby who Chase really wanted to be with. I had learned how to talk to a guy. "All right. I think Sydney's tired and ready to go back."

Chase did an about turn. "Good. I'm ready for dessert. How about you two?"

Shelby and I smiled at each other, but didn't say a word.

Chase walked backwards, taking turns focusing on us. I knew then, Chase was enjoying being the center of attention.

—————

After a couple of hours of hanging out, Dad rounded us up. "It's late. Time to go."

Everyone thanked Mr. and Mrs. Manning, and I politely nodded at Henley and Shelby. "Have a good trip home."

Off to my side, I noticed Sarah's crossed fingers behind her back while she smiled sweetly. "It was nice meeting you."

On the way home, Sarah leaned over and in a hushed voice said, "Can you believe those girls? We've got to sleep downstairs again. Want to?"

I nodded. "Yeah. And I promise I won't wake you." In between yawning, I added, "You can sleep as late as you want."

We collected our supplies for the night, headed downstairs, climbed into the bottom bunk, and couldn't stop talking. Sarah started first. "When I won a game, Henley grabbed the controls and screamed, 'My turn.'"

I blinked. "What'd you do?"

"I looked at Peyton, and he snickered, and shrugged his shoulders. Then he said, 'You girls go for it.'" Sarah turned to me, puffing her pillow. "I shot him a nasty look. He knew there was a war going on."

I rolled on my side and tucked my hand under my head. "I think those girls were a lot jealous. And that they do like Chase and Peyton, even if they've been friends since they were babies. They just couldn't believe they had some competition."

"Well. I'm going to see Peyton at camp for one week, and maybe you'll see Chase at the kennel if you decide later to get another puppy."

I returned to my back, dipped my chin on my chest, and closed my eyes. My stomach played leap frog, and I struggled to catch my breath. "Let's not go there tonight. I don't know." Looking up at the bottom of the top bunk, I stopped hyperventilating, and changed the subject. "We sure learned a lot about guys this summer. I doubt I'll ever see Chase after this week. But you'll have fun seeing Peyton again." I looked at her, reining in my emotions. "I've learned nothing lasts forever. Even in all the movies, the girls are dumped because of other girls or the girls meet other boys and dump them. But it's been fun."

"See." Sarah sat up as far as she could, and smiled from cheek to cheek. "And you fought me on wanting to meet guys. It's been cool, hasn't it?"

"Uh-huh. Exhausting. And a little scary, too. But we're learning together. Just like best friends should. Right?"

"Of course, silly." And she wiggled back down on the bed.

"You promise not to go wandering tonight?" I stared at her. Was she hiding anything from me?

"Only if you come with me." And linked her arm through mine, giggling.

I moaned. "Oh. Not tonight! I'm way too tired.

Sarah grinned. "That's good. I've already told Peyton no."

I faced her. "Wow. I'm proud of you. Okay, we have two more days. What should we do tomorrow?"

"Sleep in, first." Sarah pleaded with her eyes. "Trina, you promise to let me sleep as late as I want?"

"Yep." I crossed my heart and pretended to throw away the key. "I'll sneak out, if I wake before you."

"That's funny. You know you'll be the first one up." She looked over at me. "Do you want to read? It might help us stop thinking about the guys."

"Yeah. Then we'll dream about werewolves."

"No, we can't do that." Sarah inhaled a long, deep breath. "I want to dream good thoughts. Maybe we'll find another lovey-huggy part in the story."

I held the book up, and we took turns reading a page. Finally my arms grew weak and I whined, "I can't do this anymore. I'm going to sleep. See you in the morning."

Sydney snuggled in next to Sarah.

When I glanced back, my heart skipped a beat. "I miss Sydney sleeping with me. Tomorrow we need to sleep upstairs."

"I agree. I'm all squished in this bed. And it's so hard. But hasn't it been fun being all by ourselves? Doesn't it make you feel more grown up?"

Exhausted and weak-legged, I struggled to climb the rungs. "I don't think it's being by ourselves that makes me feel more grown up. I think it's because I am growing up."

"Oooh, Trina. That's awesome." During another huge yawn, I only heard, "—morning. Late! Okay?"

And, I drifted off into dreamland, until Sarah was shaking me.

"What in the world? Wake up, Trina. Are you okay? You've been screaming, 'Sydney, Sydney!'"

"Oh, Sarah. I had such an awful dream," I blubbered and quivered inside. "I dreamt about Chase and Peyton changing into werewolves and chasing Sydney on white sandy beaches. I could see through the clear blue water. Pelicans flew at the werewolves trying to save Sydney. I guess that's when I started screaming." I smeared the wetness into my cheeks with my fists.

"You know, Trina. I think your feelings about giving up Sydney are coming out in your dreams. It's got to be hard."

"Yeah! You're probably right. But maybe it's worse because we're fussing over guys, and I have to choose between the trip and another dog. All these worries are making me crazy."

Sarah stood on the ladder, stroking the side of my face as I stared at the salmon-colored wall. She laughed and told me, "I dreamt of making the final goal at a soccer match, and Peyton was on the sidelines, cheering."

I whispered, "Well, that's nice." And rolled onto my back and stared at the ceiling.

"If you're okay, Trina. I'm going back to sleep. The sun's not up, and I'm still tired."

"Me, too." I listened to her climb down the ladder, and let the tears trickle down my cheeks.

CHAPTER 32

FRIDAY

For the second time that week, I overslept. Momma lightly tapped my shoulder and murmured, "Trina. It's 10:00 in the morning."

My head popped up. "Oh, My Gawd! I've never slept this late." I looked around, blinked a few times, and lifted the blinds. The bright sun shined hot rays on the grass. "I've even missed my run on the beach, and the day feels like it's half over. I'll be up in a sec."

Inside the house, Momma hugged me. "You obviously needed the rest. The only reason I woke you, honey, was because of a phone call." She gave me a silly grin.

I leaned forward, propping my elbows on the kitchen table, holding my head up. "Okay. Who called?"

Momma filled her cup with coffee. "It was Chase. I told him you'd call back as soon as you woke."

I didn't budge, and my words came out in a monotone. "What'd he want?"

"He invited us to go for a ride on their boat, including Sydney. He said the boat was quite large."

I straightened in my chair, suddenly wide awake. "On their boat? Cool! Today?"

At that moment, Sarah hauled her limp body into the kitchen. "Did you hear, Sarah?"

She nodded and sat.

"Well," Momma sipped her coffee. "I told them we were trying to find some activities that would keep Sarah out of the sun. Maybe, we'd go to Charleston and take a buggy tour of the city. Go shopping?"

Sarah jerked awake, and we said in unison. "What?"

I looked at Momma like she'd lost her mind. "Why would we want to go to Charleston instead of going on their boat?"

"Well, I didn't say no. I just said you'd call them back. Chase said there's a large covered area on the boat so Sarah could stay out of the sun, except if she went swimming."

Sarah sagged. "I really want to go on their boat, but I'm NOT swimming."

Mrs. Neal walked in to the kitchen. "If you girls want to go boating, your fathers can take you." She looked at Momma and said, "Let's make it a ladies' day into Charleston. We'll stay 'til we're shopped out."

"That's a wonderful idea, Carol. Let's go."

Dad plopped into Momma's empty chair with his cup of coffee. "Your mother said Chase's company was still sleeping, so they're not in a hurry."

"Chase still has company? I guess I should call him."

When Chase answered, I said, "Hi. Sorry it's so late, calling you back." I listened to him explain about the day. He only mentioned the boat ride. I said, "We'd love to go. Our mothers are going shopping, so they'll pass on the boat, but our dads will join us. And it's okay to bring Sydney?"

"Yes! Mom wants Logan to have him aboard. The boat is already docked. Have your dad meet us at the marina around 12:30. We'll plan on having lunch on the boat."

He never mentioned their company, and being too embarrassed, I didn't ask if they'd left.

After I told Sarah what Chase had said, Sarah's eyes begged me. "I've got to stay out of the sun. My skin is all crinkly, and it stings. I sure hope they don't expect me to go swimming. Come on. Let's figure out what we'll wear."

In her room, she said, "Wow." She snatched my hands and we bounced around in a circle. "What a great way to end our trip."

"Yes, yes. I can't think of anything more perfect. And Sydney will have another boating experience."

Sarah's look changed from smiley grins to deep frowns. "Will you help keep me from swimming? I don't want them to know."

"I'll keep your secret." I gave her my serious face. "Aren't you're glad you told me?"

Sarah bent her head. "Yeah!"

"I know your sunburn hurts. You stay here. I'll run and check the turtle's nest really fast. Then we'll get ready."

After melting in the hot sun, I showered and dressed in my other new swimsuit, a striped purple and orange tankini. Then I put my hair in a ponytail and grabbed my Clemson cap. Some curls did their own thing, sticking out around my neck and ears. I pulled a purple cover-up overhead, and slipped on my flip flops. *Oooh! This is going to be sooo much fun!*

Sarah was still in her room, so I knocked at the door. "Hello in there."

"Come on in, Trina. Let me see your bathing suit." I lifted my cover-up. "Oh, I love that suit." She dashed from corner to corner looking for items. "Are you taking a change of clothes?"

"Naw! I'll dry out. But *you* can, if it makes you more comfortable."

"Okay. I've packed a few things. I'm ready. Do you think the other family went home?"

"I guess we'll find out soon enough."

Mrs. Neal had packed a cooler of goodies for us to share. "See you all later. Darby can stay on the porch. She's worn out. She'll be happy to sleep the afternoon away."

Momma added at the door, "Just keep Sydney safe and have fun. Bye."

Sydney heard his name, and jumped to attention. "That's right, Syd. Come. Since you're such a special dog, you get to have another adventure."

He watched me wrap my treat pouch around my waist, turned in circles, and then stood for me to attach his cape.

At the marina, I gasped. The beautiful white boat tied to the dock was not a boat. "Sarah, *that* is a yacht. Look at it!" It had a wide navy blue stripe all the way around and a big navy blue bow on the right side, the starboard side. The back of the yacht, the stern, had FOR US, written in large navy blue block letters. And tied to the stern were two wave runners.

Sarah concentrated only on the wave runners. All color from her face vanished.

"Relax, Sarah." I put my hand on her shoulder. "You won't have to ride them, if you don't want to." I wanted to shake Sarah's shoulders. "Come on, Sarah. We get to ride on a yacht!"

Then we heard, "Hi." It was a girl's voice from above. "We've been waiting for you."

CHAPTER 33

Right on cue, Sarah and I tossed our heads upward. Sydney squeezed between my legs and had the same response.

Without moving, Sarah whispered, "Well, Trina. There's the answer to our question."

"Yep!" I poked her in the ribs. "Let's grab our stuff."

From the top level deck, Mr. Manning called, "Please, come aboard."

Our dads cheered, offered compliments about the yacht, and brought their supplies to the main level. Sarah carried her backpack in front of her with both hands, between her stiff legs. She walked to the boat like the Tin Man needing oil. I could almost hear her squeaking.

Sydney and I stepped aboard, buzzing with excitement, our eyes gleaming. I had a great excuse to nose around. Sydney wanted to explore.

Chase and Peyton sprang up the stairs from the bottom deck, which turned out to be the kitchen, bathroom and sleeping area.

Peyton handed us an orange soda. "Welcome aboard. Our friends were having so much fun, their parents decided to stay longer."

Sarah couldn't help herself. She peeked up at Henley and Shelby on the top deck, and then her eyes went to the water. She staggered to the pole by the stairway, and gripped it with both hands.

"All aboard!" Mr. Manning called from the steering compartment. "Let's get moving." And hollered to our dads, "Can you fellas help launch us?"

They grinned and nodded, and returned to the dock. Dad went to the bow and Mr. Neal went to the stern to untie the ropes, and then leaped back on deck.

Mr. Manning idled out of the harbor and into the main channel. The warm breeze carried the scent of salt and fish.

I closed my eyes and inhaled. Sydney stood on the bow, lifted his nose to the breeze, and made his doggy grin. I squatted, and we looked into each other's eyes.

"Isn't this fun? I think you were meant to be a water dog."

He got closer and licked my lips.

Logan hopped up with both feet, one step at a time from below. He screamed, "Syd-ney!" Syd's little stub waggled so hard he turned sideways. Logan scratched behind Syd's ears, and then Logan pointed. "Boat. Wah-der."

"That's right, Logan. You're teaching Sydney new words."

Mrs. Manning stood at the top of the stairs, watching. "It's amazing to watch them together. Thank you for coming."

"Gosh." My insides bubbled, and I could hardly keep myself still. "Thank you for having us. This is really a special treat. I'm sorry our moms didn't make it. They decided they'd had enough sun and water. I can't ever get enough. Neither can Sydney."

"Well, I'm glad you came. I've laid out sandwiches and fruit up here under the awning. Please help yourselves while we cruise around the island. We'll stop after a while, and then you can go swimming and ride the wave runners."

Sarah's hands clamped tighter to the post, turning her knuckles white. I moved to her side. She spoke without ever taking her eyes off the water, "Oh, Trina. I've probably made another terrible decision. I'm sorry. I'm going to ruin this trip."

"No you're not. There's no rule that says you have to go swimming. Or ride the wave runner. Look at me."

Sarah rolled her eyes off the foaming waves, stared at me, gulped, and swallowed.

"What is the scariest thing about the ocean? You used to swim in Mrs. Brown's pool."

"Her pool water was crystal clear. And I scooted around wearing a ring and could touch the bottom. This water is dark. I can't see the bottom. It's really deep and I have no control of the waves coming over my head. And, there are sharks out there. I don't want to be a sissy or show my fear, but I just can't get in that water. What am I going to do?" Tears blurred the blue of her eyes.

"We'll figure it out."

Henley and Shelby raced down the stairs, holding a cookie in each hand, nodding to us, and went below.

"Come on. Let's go up top." I scooted around the table and let Sarah slide in.

Sydney went to my feet. Logan sat on the other side of me, rocking back on the cushion and bouncing forward.

Sarah stared into the wide open space.

My face brightened. "Sarah, did you know that if you see dolphins that usually means there are no sharks in the area? We'll watch for dolphins. Maybe that'll make you feel safer."

"I don't think anything will make me feel safer. I heard being on a big boat can make me sea sick. What if they tease me?

"Just stay up here, take deep breaths, and relax. Think about having fun. All you have to do is tell everyone your sunburn hurts, and you don't feel like getting wet and salty. No one will know anything different."

"Okay. You really think that'll work?"

"I do. Come on. Let's munch, and then if you feel better, we'll explore the boat. Isn't this beautiful?"

From the top deck, the view was breathtaking. Water sparkled under the sun as far as we could see. Pelicans soared in circles, diving for their midday meal. Off in a distance, Mr. Manning pointed out a shrimp boat to Mr. Neal and Dad. "They bring in fresh shrimp to the island every night. So if you like shrimp, this is the place to indulge. Maybe we should all go out for shrimp tonight. What do you say?"

Mr. Neal laughed. "Sounds great to me."

Seagulls circled the shrimp boats.

Mr. Manning steered and turned to us. "Ok, girls. The boats stir up the fish, and the birds will stay close to catch a meal. Keep your eyes out for dolphins. They like the fish and shrimp, also."

A few minutes later Peyton walked up. "Look to your left. Just in front of our boat. There's a school of dolphins. The biggest one just leaped into the air. Did you see it?"

Login stood and pointed. "Doll-pin."

Henley, Shelby, and their parents hung over the railing down below, and started counting bodies just like Sarah and I had done on our first encounter. "See, Sarah." I whispered. "That means we'll be safe out here."

"I don't care. There's way too much water out there for me."

Then Peyton started calling. "Come on, everyone. Let's go swimming. If there are dolphins, we can swim, and ride our wave runners. Who's game?"

Chase called up, "Come on, Trina. Do you like to ride?"

I looked down at him from the balcony. "I don't know. I've never done it before."

"Well you can ride with me. They're made for two anyway. Do you want to try?"

"Yeah! I think so." I patted Sarah's arm. "Will you take Sydney, or do you want me to ask my dad?"

Sarah hesitated, took Syd's leash, and followed me downstairs to the cushions at the front. "Will you be okay, while I ride?" She nodded and looked away. I faced Chase. "Will you go fast?"

He shook his head and grinned. "Here, put on a jacket. It'll keep you afloat. I'll start off slow, and let you get your sea legs. I won't scare you. I promise." He turned to Shelby. "I'll give you a turn next."

She smiled, and moved toward the back steps.

At the same time, Peyton had moved over to Sarah, trying to persuade her into riding. She shook her head, "No. My sunburn hurts and I don't want to get it wet and salty. Maybe Henley will go."

Henley leaped up. "I'll go. I love riding with Peyton."

Peyton pleaded with Sarah one more time. But she hung her head, "No, thank you."

I kept my eyes on Sarah as I buckled my cape. Henley glanced over her shoulder before following Peyton, and purposely waited for Sarah to look back. Then Henley gave Sarah a look that said, "Ha, ha! He's mine, now."

I clenched my fists, tucked my chin, and sent bad words with my eyes at Henley.

Peyton, oblivious to what was going on, grabbed Henley's hand, "Let's go, girl. We'll give them a race."

That gave me an idea. *I'll be brave. We'll show her a race!*

My last view of Sarah was of her talking to Sydney. Then I was in the water. Logan's and Sarah's faces peered over the railing. Shelby had stayed by the back ladder, awaiting her turn. Logan had been told to wait until his brothers were finished. He had to ride with his father.

Mrs. Manning yelled from the front of the boat, sitting with Logan and Sarah. "We'll be the cheering squad."

Sarah had to be dying a thousand deaths. I knew she wanted more than anything to be out there with Peyton but just couldn't do it. The laughter and kidding around probably made her even more desperate, especially watching Henley riding with Peyton. But after a few minutes in the water, I wasn't thinking about Sarah any longer. I was hanging on.

Chase didn't push the throttle all the way. At first he drove straight over little waves.

"Okay, Chase. I'm ready. Let's get 'em!" The wind blew in my face, stretching my smile from ear to ear.

Salty water slipped into my mouth, but I grinned and laughed. The motor roared as we spun in circles, rushing through waves. I screamed, "Go, Chase! Go!" Chase and I beat Henley and Peyton to the buoy. Then we raced back to the boat.

I giggled so hard I got the hiccups. "Wow." Hiccup. "That was so much fun."

Chase turned around, laughing, too. "You did great. Next time I'll let you drive."

"Whoa! I don't know about that." Hiccup. "Oooh. That one hurt."

The four of us climbed aboard just as Sarah staggered up from the bathroom. "Are you okay?"

She nodded a whitish face and glanced at Peyton. "Did you have fun?"

Peyton flashed his charming smile, and Sarah inhaled a deep breath. He asked, "Are you sure you don't want to try? The sun's not as strong, and the jacket will cover your back."

Sarah looked once more out to the horizon. There was nothing, but water and blue sky for her to see. Then she stared at Peyton. "Well, no one went under. Your hair isn't even wet." She stiffened her shoulders and locked eyes with me. "Was it fun?"

"Yeah. I laughed so hard, I got the hiccups." Hiccup. "See. The wave runner is bigger than being on a bicycle. We didn't go very fast at first. Chase didn't bounce over any waves, until I screamed, 'Hit it!'"

Sarah gave Peyton a look that said "I'd like to do it, but I'm afraid."

"Watch." He put on his jacket, clicked the buckles, and jumped into the water. He floated without using his arms or legs. Then he kicked, rolled over and over, and went back to lying perfectly still. "See. It keeps my whole body up. Logan can do it, too. Why don't we all just float for a while, and then if you want a ride, later, I'll take you for a spin."

Sarah spotted a hot, pink jacket on top of the pile. "All right. I'll try that one."

CHAPTER 34

For Logan—and all the adults agreed—swimming was a super idea. I waited for Dad to get in the water, and then handed him Sydney. Dad held Sydney's wiggly body for a moment and then let go. Sydney dog-paddled in every direction, looking for Logan. After finding him, Syd swam in circles, determined to keep Logan safe.

Mrs. Manning never took her eyes from Logan, even while asking me, "He won't hurt him, will he?"

"No. He's very gentle. But, I'll stay right here and make sure his nails don't scratch him."

Sarah climbed down the ladder, one leg at a time. She let go of the ladder with one hand, hung on for a few seconds, taking quick short breaths. Her sunburned face turned a softer shade of pink.

Peyton swam over, pried her other hand loose, speaking to her the whole time. He talked about soccer camp, and all the things they'd do in a couple of weeks.

She kept her eyes glued to his, took one long breath, and squeezed his hand.

He held her jacket, and continued talking for a little longer.

She started giggling. "Okay, Peyton. You can let go. I'm okay. I have no idea what you've been telling me, but I'm okay. Look, Trina. I'm really doing it."

For Sarah's first time in the deep ocean, she played tag with Henley and Shelby, got her hair wet, and seemed to forget where she was.

Finally, Mrs. Manning called, "Let's get Logan and Sydney back in the boat. They've had enough."

Putting my hands under Syd's stomach, I held him a few inches out of the water. Dad wrapped his arm around his chest and carried him up the ladder, and I followed. Peyton handed a shivering Logan to his mother, and dove back in the water.

Logan started screaming. "Want swim! Want swim!"

Mrs. Manning mummy-wrapped Logan tightly in a towel like Chase had done, plopped him in her lap, and hugged his slim body.

Logan's words quieted, but he continued to mumble and gently rock. "Want swim. Want swim."

Mrs. Manning spoke to me while looking at Sydney. "Please, Trina, help me."

I called, "Sydney, Come." We followed her upstairs, as she carried Logan snuggly in her arms. Up front she unwrapped Logan, and sat him on the cushion along the side of the boat. She remembered the command I had given Sydney. While never getting close to Syd, her kind eyes made eye contact with him, and she said, "Sydney, Hug."

Sydney blinked at her, and then looked to me. "Yes, Sydney. Hug." He moved next to Logan, putting both paws across Logan's lap. Logan stared at Sydney and petted his head. "You best friend." He sobbed and gulped air, repeating, "You best friend."

Mrs. Manning continued glancing at the two best friends and checking the refreshments. She yelled down to the rest of the group. "Time to get out. I put dry towels by the stairs. Peyton, Chase, please show them the hose on the third step, and how to rinse off the salt water."

As they climbed aboard, Peyton's conversation floated up. "Sarah, do you want a quick ride?" I glanced over the railing.

Sarah looked at the wave runner and shook her wet hair. "I've had enough swimming. I'm really cold right now. Maybe later. Okay?"

"That's fine. I'm just happy you had fun. Here, let me show you where to rinse off."

I turned to Mrs. Manning, "Are you okay with watching Sydney while I rinse off? Oh. Dad's on his way up."

Mrs. Manning gave me an expression I'd never forget. Her smile widened and her eyes sparkled. "Trina, seeing the two of them together, and Logan so calm. Well, it's making me a believer in service dogs. He's absolutely an amazing dog." She paused, and got closer to me. "I must tell you, Trina. I called

P.A.A.L.S. this morning and told them what's been happening during our beach trip."

I caught my breath. *Oh no. What has she done?*

Mrs. Manning continued. "Your trainer is thrilled. She's faxing me an application to put Logan's name on her list. I'm hoping you'll have some influence on their decision." She patted my arm. "Go on down, Trina, and rinse off. Here's your dad. I'll be fine. Wow. That feels good to say. I am fine."

I could hardly stand, let alone walk downstairs. I went over to the cushion where Sydney and Logan sat. They didn't even notice my presence. I stroked Sydney's back and his amber eyes glowed at me. My heart ached from happiness to sadness. It was already happening. Only a few days left before he moved on, but he'd be a happy dog.

I inhaled and looked out to the sea. I thought back to a day when a rock had hit Dad's front windshield and made a hole the size of a teeny dot. As we drove, the window slowly cracked, inching down in a crooked line. By the time we arrived home, tiny pieces of glass had shattered onto the floor. That was how my heart felt. The invisible hole had just been made.

Watching the waves form and roll relaxed me. I had to really concentrate. Then I walked to the bottom deck. Sarah was grabbing a plush yellow towel, and starting to dry. I whispered to her, "After I rinse off, I'm going up. Sydney's with Mrs. Manning. You'll never believe what she just told me."

Sarah stared at me, but I didn't have the energy to tell her, yet. It wasn't the right time.

On my way up the stairs, I froze in my steps, gazing at Logan and Sydney. What a perfect sight. They were staring at each other, and Logan had his hand on Sydney's head. A small crack moved down my heart. Then Mrs. Manning spotted me. Her face lit up the whole deck. I used my fingers to pretend I had my camera.

Mrs. Manning beamed as she held hers in the air.

With the radio turned on to our popular songs, everyone hummed or sang with the music until an announcement interrupted. "A storm is brewing out at sea..."

Mr. Manning shouted, "Okay. You all eat up. It's time to head back. If there's a storm out there, we don't want to be stuck in it." He glanced out to sea, and his face turned serious. "We may be fine when we get closer to shore, but it's not a lot of fun being in deep water during a storm."

Sarah and Peyton had climbed upstairs and slid across the cushion, surrounding the table. Sarah giggled and said, "We know all about being in a boat during a storm, don't we Trina? This time we'll have a covered area."

Peyton reassured Sarah. "These storms happen all the time during the summer, but they don't last long."

The clouds swirled, and the ocean swelled, growing choppy. Waves broke, leaving behind white surf before rolling into a wave again.

Henley and Shelby had moved to a side cushion on the middle deck with their parents. I guess they figured out whose attention the boys wanted.

The storm did stay farther out. The clouds teased each other, and the lightning flashed, but we never heard thunder. Our fathers discussed dinner and decided they'd probably buy a few pounds of fresh shrimp, cook at home, and enjoy a quiet evening.

Chase and Peyton asked if they could come and hang out. Our eyes pleaded with our dads.

They smiled and said, "Of course."

Mr. Neal said, "We don't have a television or computers, but we have music."

When we arrived home, Darby sulked. We had interrupted her nap. Ready to play, Sydney poked her with his nose.

Dad looked out the window, smiling. "Your mothers must be buying out Charleston. Come on, Neal. Let's surprise them with dinner. Do you girls want to come?"

"Nope!" We said together.

Heading to the screen door, Mr. Neal said, "We'll have a feast tonight. Anything special you girls want?"

"Oooh. Ice cream. Chocolate. Is that okay with you, Sarah?"

She shoved her fist into the air. "Perfect."

Darby didn't want to move, but after Sarah teased her with a treat, Darby found enough energy to jog down to the backyard. It was time for her to do her business. Sydney joined us, but he was the first one back up the stairs, wanting dinner.

The closer the thunder got, the heavier the air smelled of salt. Sarah stared out the screen. "It may rain here, but at least we're inside." She turned to me. "I sure had fun today. Peyton knew without asking that I was afraid. But he never once mentioned it. We lucked out. Our first time with guys. And they're nice!"

"Yep. I wonder if this is just a fluke. We may not be so lucky next time."

Sydney pawed me.

"I know. I know, Syd. You must really be hungry. I'm fixing your dinner, right now."

"Oh. I hear a car." Doors slammed. I ran to the window. "Our moms are back. With lots of bags."

Sarah opened the back porch door. "Wow. Looks like you enjoyed yourselves. Did you buy me anything?"

Her mom walked around her. "Nope. It was our day, and we did just what we wanted to do."

Momma followed with her arms full. "Tell us everything while we put our stuff away. Where are your fathers?"

"They went to buy fresh shrimp and whatever else they think we need for tonight. Chase and Peyton are coming over."

Momma stopped moving and blinked. "Um, okay." She shook herself and forced a smile. "So, did Sydney behave?"

"Yep. He and Logan played all day. You'll never believe what Mrs. Manning did." Momma lifted her head with a puzzled look. "She called the kennel and told Ms. Jennifer all about what Sydney's done with Logan. She's applying for Logan to have a dog."

"Wow, honey!" she said, smiling. "That's wonderful. Logan will really do well with a service dog. Wouldn't that be wonderful if it turned out to be Sydney?"

"Yeah. If that can happen?"

"I guess we'll find out in six months."

Mrs. Neal walked up to Sarah. "Were you okay, sweetie? Did you get in the ocean?"

Sarah straightened her shoulders and her chin popped out. "I wore a jacket and swam all by myself. Peyton knew I was afraid, but pretended that he didn't. You wouldn't believe how he treated me."

"I'm so glad." Mrs. Neal squeezed Sarah. "Oh. I hear your fathers."

Sarah and I ran down the stairs and the dogs followed. "Want some help?"

"Yes. Grab some bags."

By the time we were in the house, Mr. Neal had described our appetizers, and how they were going to make a low country boil.

"Trina," Dad called from the kitchen, "Take the iPod to the porch and choose some music. Let the party begin."

Chapter 35

M r. Neal brought out peeled shrimp and a cocktail sauce to the wooden picnic table. I dipped my first shrimp, took a big bite, gasped, and started coughing. "No way! What's this sauce? It looks like catsup."

Dad chuckled. "Maybe we got a little carried away with the horseradish. Go get some catsup and another bowl. We'll fix some milder sauce for you girls."

Momma brought out the onion dip, chips, and other leftovers. "Oh! I like this music." She danced on the porch as she set the food on the picnic table. "Okay, everyone. Eat up. I'm not taking any of this home."

Sydney crawled under the table, and Darby lay next to Sarah's feet. Their eyes squinted at us as we rocked back and forth, singing the words out loud, out of tune, and being silly. All of a sudden we heard laughing from below. I grabbed Sarah's arm, and we both clammed up, growing pink in the face.

Peyton's voice cracked high and low. "What's going on up there? Are we crashing the party?"

Both dogs rushed to the door, wiggling, and adding a couple of woofs.

Sarah chuckled and called down. "No, your timing is perfect. My dad may poison you with spices, but we have lots of food. He's got a large pot on the grill, boiling shrimp, corn on the cob, red potatoes, and sausage in special seasonings."

Mr. Neal brought us strawberry slushies with an umbrella stuck in the middle. "Hold on, guys. I'll make a couple more."

I laughed, and directed my comment to Chase. "I hope you like beach music or oldies. It's all Dad has."

"Sounds great. Our parents play this kind but only quietly because it bothers Logan."

"Watch out for the cocktail sauce. It's really spicy." I strangled my neck with both hands. "It scorched my throat."

"I like spicy. Let me see." Chase grabbed a shrimp, dipped it, and put the entire shrimp in his mouth. "Wow! This is great." His eyes watered, but he never flinched.

"Liar!" I smirked and covered my mouth.

"No. It's really okay. After each bite, it gets easier to swallow." He sniffled and cleared his throat. "It's making my nose run, though. I need a napkin."

"Move over, bro. I need to try this special recipe. Oh, man. It's hot." Peyton took a quick swig of his drink. "I'm not as brave as Chase. I'll dip in your milder bowl, too. The shrimp are great, though. Isn't it cool that we watched them being pulled in today? They're really fresh. Can't get this at home." He coughed and wiped his nose. "More catsup here. I'll stir."

Mr. Neal called. "Dinner's ready."

We ate tons of low country boil along with warmed cornbread from the bakery. I poured honey on mine.

Too full for dessert, I retrieved my brand new scrapbook. "Who wants to draw?"

Sarah gave me The Look.

But I continued, "We can try out all these new, squiggly pens and glitter sticks, and draw things we've done on the beach."

Sarah moaned. "You go ahead. I can't draw a stick person, but I'll give ideas." She pulled out her game player. "Peyton, do you want to play?"

Chase's eyes lit up. "We can make a picture album to keep as a memory of your week with Sydney."

I stared at him. How could he know how hard it's been doing all these things and wanting to remember every moment? A tiny flood filled my eyes.

Peyton patted Chase on his back, and headed over to Sarah.

"Momma and Dad, wait till you see Chase draw. It's amazing." Air bubbles tickled the inside my stomach. I couldn't wait to see what he'd draw. I set the huge tablet in the middle of the table.

Chase flipped pages. "Wow. This is all empty. Where do you want me to start?"

"On the first page!" I giggled and Chase blushed.

I tore out a piece of paper for me before Chase started sketching. "Draw you and Peyton, making your sand castle, and Logan petting Syd." I laid my sheet on top of a stack of newspapers, picked up a pencil, and glanced at Chase's sketches. "Wow! That's wonderful. I'm going to do our little boat trip to Pelican Island." I drew the little skiff, docked on the sand. Down a ways from the boat sat one blond and one red-headed girl in the sand, hugging their legs, and looking at the brown point filled with pelicans.

Sarah leaned over me for a moment, while Peyton played on her game player. "Put some pelicans in the air with fish hanging from their mouths."

I looked up. "Can anyone draw Darby and Sydney making figure eights in the sand?"

Chase glared at Peyton. "Stop playing that game. You're good at drawing dogs. Give it a try. I'm almost finished. There's plenty more room at the table." Peyton continued clicking on the game. "Naw. You go ahead."

"Sarah. Here's the box of crayons. You have to add something to the picture. Put in some seagulls. If you make a swirly M, pulling out the legs, it'll look like a seagull."

"Not interested."

Chase finished his first drawing of Peyton and himself, building a sand castle, and then took another sheet and started with Logan and Sydney staring at each other, right in the middle of the page. "This is when Logan met Sydney."

Chills climbed my arms, and I stopped drawing. His picture started coming to life. "Momma, come here. You have to see what Chase is drawing. Dad, you won't believe it."

They stood over Chase, oohing and awing.

"Thanks." Blushing, he still continued to concentrate. "Does anyone have any other special memories?"

"I have one, but you may not want to draw it." I laughed. Everyone looked at me. "When your mother answered the door and saw the dogs coming toward her. I thought she was going to faint."

"Yeah! That was funny, but probably not to her. Hmm." He stared up at the ceiling with his finger on his mouth. "How about when Sydney and Logan were under the table at the restaurant?"

"That was hilarious," said Sarah, lifting her head from the game. "We were so mad at you. And then we played musical chairs." She stopped talking for a second, looked at the game, and closed the lid. "Maybe you can draw your beautiful yacht, Chase? That was special for me because I went swimming in the ocean."

I paced on the deck. "This is turning out to be a masterpiece. Maybe we'll have more ideas tomorrow. We could always come up here to get out of the sun.

The wind had really picked up, and lightning spiked through the clouds in the distance.

Sarah counted. "It's only a couple of miles away. But it's getting louder."

Peyton turned to Chase. "Are you at a stopping point, bro? We should head home."

"Let me finish this last part."

Dad piped up. "Oh, no. You're not walking. I'll drive you."

When Chase finally put his pencil down, Logan and Sydney looked like a photograph on the page. "I'm finished. Are you ready, Peyton?"

Dad grabbed his keys after a quick look at the sketch. "Fantastic, Chase. Let me take you home."

Sarah and I followed Chase and Peyton to the car.

Peyton put the side window down. "See you tomorrow. We'll be in front of your house all day. We'll have to bring Henley and Shelby."

"Whatever! We'll be nice." Sarah leaned her head, put both hands palms up, and shrugged. "It's our last full day.

Chapter 36

After saying goodbye to the guys, we climbed the stairs as the rain splashed on the deck, and the sea air whooshed through the screen. Away from our parents, Sarah and I rocked. Sarah leaned over, whispering, "Who could have imagined this trip would be so fab. I'm so glad you wanted to train Sydney. I wonder if we'd have met Chase and Peyton without him."

"Maybe." I leaned in and kept my voice low. "But I must admit. Without Sydney, I'd never have had the courage to talk to them."

The air cooled so much that we took turns going inside to grab our hoodies. We weren't ready to end our dreamy day and stayed on the porch.

"If the storm gets too close, Sydney will be in my lap again. I may have to go inside and hold him. As a service dog, he's not supposed to be afraid of noises. I haven't told Ms. Jennifer yet, but it'll disqualify him from some jobs, so I'll have to add it to my last report."

"Uh-oh!" The skin around Sarah's eyes crinkled. "That's not good. Maybe this'll be good practice."

Darby snored under the table. Her legs squirmed, and occasionally she squealed or snorted. "The beach has worn her out." Sarah chuckled and climbed under the table to watch Darby's legs jerk. I joined her. Darby made so much noise we barely heard our mothers' conversation.

But we did.

We stared at each other and stayed very quiet. Momma was saying, "If it's raining when we get up, maybe we should pack up and go home. That'd give us a day at home before we have to return to the kennel."

My heart stopped. I wanted to scream, "Stop talking about returning Syd!"

"I've done everything I wanted to do," Sarah's mom added in a defeated voice. "And I'm ready to be in my own bed."

Our dads agreed. Mr. Neal had another suggestion. "We could get up leisurely, pack and clean, and then go out for breakfast, and head home."

Sarah and I puckered our faces. We wobbled our heads, calling out, "No. No. No."

We scuttled out from under the table as fast as our legs could untangle, and stood in front of our parents.

I cried, "We have to see our turtle's nest, and Sydney needs one more run on the beach."

Sarah rubbed her head where she had bumped it on the table leg. "And we need to feed the seagulls. And of course say goodbye to Peyton and Chase. We have a lot to do before we just up and leave."

"Okay, okay, girls," Dad moaned, looking directly at each one of us. "Don't get all worked up. Let's wait and see what the day looks like tomorrow."

Mr. Neal caught Sarah's eyes. "If it's sunny and a great beach day, we'll stay. But if it's raining, I'm ready to go home."

Sarah and I stared at each other with long faces. We couldn't change our parents' minds.

"I hope the sun pops out in the morning." I wiped a tear from my face. "Sarah, let's stay upstairs tonight. We can read on my bed for a while. Maybe Sydney will get comfortable and can work through the noise. I want him close to me."

We settled back on my bed, at the same time a huge bolt of lightning shot through the sky. I started to count, and couldn't get one word out before another big boom sounded from outside. Sydney jumped onto the bed, and sat on my stomach, quivering, looking every which way. I wanted to name the noise. Find a way for him to understand he was safe.

"Sydney, rain." I hugged him around his entire body, and said, "Okay. Good."

He slinked between Sarah and me, circled close to our shoulders, and laid with his front legs stretched forward, watching and listening.

"He understands so many words," said Sarah, stroking Sydney's back. "I hope this story doesn't scare him."

"I know. He might not like the part where the werewolf bites the dog. But I think—" Boom. "—the thunder is more scary—" Boom. "—than werewolves."

"The storm is right on top of us." Sarah sighed and squished the pillow over her head. "That's the loudest thunder I've ever heard."

"I don't think I've ever seen lightning like this except on the Fourth of July." I glanced at Sydney, who was lying still, but panting. "Good boy, Syd." I stroked his trembling back. "Rain."

"The Fourth of July was more fun. Sarah snuggled closer to Sydney. "Try reading again. Maybe it'll take my mind off the noise."

As I opened my mouth to read, the thunder and lightning hit at the same time. The windows rattled, and we stared out the blinds. Every few seconds it boomed even louder. Sydney rushed to sit on top of my hands, preventing me from being able to read. Sarah couldn't have heard me, even if I'd tried.

I squeezed him, using the "Hug" method. He panted so fast, his heart thumped like a snare drum roll. "It's rain, Syd." Holding him tight with one arm, I rubbed his head and stroked his soft ears, calming him. "Sydney okay."

Then new footsteps tap, tap, tapped on the floor. Darby's nails clattered keeping beat to Sydney's drumming heartbeat as she danced around the corner, missing the rugs on the floor.

"Someone else is scared. Oh, Sarah. I've never seen her so frightened. And she's not very good at sneaking in."

Sarah patted the bed. "Come on up, Darby. Syd's already here."

She launched herself straight into the air and landed on the bed, panting. After another big boom, she circled around twice at the end of the bed, collapsed by our feet, and faced us. Her head lay on her paws. Then her ears fell forward, hiding her paws, but her red, droopy eyes never left us.

We sat quietly, waiting for a few more minutes. Nothing happened. Sarah, Darby, and Sydney relaxed.

"It sounds like the storm's going away." After the next flash, I counted to one thousand one, before the thunder roared.

Sarah saw the next flash and counted to one thousand two. Then the noise banged again, but not as loud. "Hooray! It's moving away."

As the storm quieted, Sydney moved to my side. Sarah and I took turns reading a page, and slowly stretching out. After we read two chapters, our eyes grew heavy.

Sarah sat up. "Come on, Darby, I'm going to bed." But Darby didn't move.

"She's okay, Sarah. Just leave her here. If she wants to get up later, she'll go." I wiggled down under the sheet, putting my feet to the side of Darby.

Sydney squirmed back and forth until his body molded next to mine. His head lay on my pillow, breathing a fishy breath into my face. "Are you comfortable?" I rubbed his head, and then slid my fingers through his beautiful freckled fur.

His stub waggled.

I stared up at the ceiling, not able to move. I made myself listen and not think. The gush of rain crashed like a waterfall hitting the roof, and the wind propelled the drops into the window. It even had a rhythm. Ping... Ping-ping. Ping... *Will it ever end? I'm not ready to leave.*

Sometime in the middle of the night, I found our door cracked open. The light from the kitchen lit up our room enough that I noticed Sydney and Darby had made a puddle of bodies and legs at the foot of the bed. They snuggled together, looking calm. I rolled over, curled into a ball, and fell back to sleep.

It seemed liked minutes since I had closed my eyes, but when they opened, white stripes gleamed across the floor.

The sun was shining.

CHAPTER 37

Hoping for a great sunny day, I had left the blinds open last night. I shot up in bed, my heart racing. "We can stay. We can stay." The words flew out. I covered my mouth, but too late.

Momma lifted her head and whispered, "Trina, take the dogs and go out quietly. Don't wake anyone else."

Sydney lifted his head and pulled his legs from the pile. He crept to my nose, stretched like he was bowing, stuck his bottom in the air, and wiggled his little stub.

"Oh, Syd. We get to go to the beach one more time."

After a couple of licks on my face, he pawed Darby. They stood on the bed, and shook the sleep from their heads. The mattress wiggled and squeaked. One at a time, they jumped to the floor.

I giggled and tip-toed to the living room. "Who's ready for our last day at the beach?"

Our last day. And only the dogs and I were awake.

I couldn't wait any longer to walk on the beach. Sarah had to get up. I grabbed my hoodie, tee shirt, and shorts that lay at the end of the bed, still warm from dog bodies. Tip-toeing to the deck, I shook the sandy clothes over the railing and dressed in the living room. The dogs huddled together, panting and waiting.

In Sarah's room, I shook her. "Wha? What?" Sarah mumbled as she opened her eyes.

"It's sunny. We get to stay. Let's go!" I whispered as softly as I could.

Sarah rubbed her eyes and sat up. The sun barely leaked through her closed blinds. I went to the window and lifted a corner of the blind. Sun blasted through the window and made her blink.

"Okay, I'm up. I'm up." Sarah's clothes lay on the floor. She grabbed the same outfit from last night and put it on. "We're in a hurry, right? See, you're rubbing off on me."

The dogs turned in circles on the wooden floors and Sydney grumbled and whined. "Sydney, shhh. You're supposed to be a quiet service dog. Quiet." He sat, gazing at me.

Sarah shook her head, "He's amazing. He understands everything." Then she caught herself and stopped talking.

I closed my eyes to get control. Today, everything I did would make the crack in my heart grow. I had to make this last day the best of my memories.

The screen door squeaked as Sarah opened it. Single file, we scooted out.

I closed it quietly. "Let's see what's on the beach." We carried their leashes while the dogs ran free on their final morning run.

At the top of the dunes, we looked out. "Oh my." I put a hand on each cheek. "That was quite a storm last night." We spied seaweed, driftwood, lots of shells and, for the first time, starfish.

Sarah looked in all directions. "I've never seen starfish on the beach. Look, they're everywhere."

"We should definitely take a few of these. But maybe we should pick them up on our way back. I'm afraid their legs will break." The dogs ran sniffing the ground. "There must be lots of new smells this morning. I sure hope Sydney doesn't find anymore dead fish." I scanned the area.

We walked toward the turtle's nest. "Look at these shells," Sarah said. "They're fantastic."

I handed Sarah a paper bag. "I have too many already, but they're so pretty. It's hard leaving them."

Sarah smiled. "My parents told me there wouldn't be room in the car for all the stuff I've collected and me. They may have to choose."

"On our way back, we'll be pickier."

The wet sand grabbed our footprints and the dog's.

"Today, I want us to leave our prints on this beach, too." I walked backwards and sideways. Sarah walked on her toes and then on her heels. Being silly, we made figure eights with our footprints until we arrived at the turtle's nest.

The storm had blown the top of the nest apart. One orange ribbon was torn and hung from a leaning stake. After straightening it, I tied the ribbon together and back on the stake. Sarah used her flip-flop to hammer it deeper into the sand. The dogs came up to the dunes and sniffed, but weren't interested in the mound.

Sarah patted the sand down.

I collected more stems from the marsh grass and covered the nest and said, "I guess it's camouflaged as well as it can be. The babies have a long time before they hatch."

We walked backwards, staring at the nest. Sarah sighed. "Bye, baby turtles. Hope you make it to the water."

I yelled, "Walk fast and swim away."

Before we turned to race back to the house for breakfast, voices called. "Sarah. Trina, wait." Sydney and Darby recognized the voices, and barked.

Sarah gasped when she saw who it was. "Oh, no. I knew I should have fixed up. Look at us."

"Relax, Sarah. Do you really think they care? They've seen us swimming and playing in the hot sun."

The dogs rushed toward them, wiggling and bouncing as Peyton and Chase ran to meet us.

Sarah asked, "What're you doing out here so early?"

Peyton smiled and leaned in close to Sarah's face. "We thought you'd be up early since this was your last day, and we hoped to see you. Have you already been to the turtle nest?"

"Oooh, you should have seen it." Sarah described everything we repaired. Darby pranced between Peyton's legs.

Chase listened intently. Grabbing my hand, he said, "You've got to show us."

"Okay! It's over here." I pulled him a ways up the beach and then stopped.

Sydney halted next to me, listening to our conversation.

"Maybe while you're still here," I dropped my chin and lifted my eyes with a hopeful expression. "You could check it. We know the Turtle Patrol checks all the nests every day, but this morning they didn't fix our nest. Thank goodness, we did. Now it's safe. But while we're not here…"

Chase put a hand on each of my shoulders, and gave me a stern look. "I promise, Pretty Green Eyes! We'll check it every day. Maybe Mom'll bring us back before the turtles hatch and we'll count the babies heading to the water."

Flushing, I stared back. Shivers flowed up my neck and then down my arms and legs. My heartbeat raced. I swallowed, and shifted my left shoulder to the right, kind of shoving Chase's hands away. "I wish I could see them. But I already know I can't come back. This was my one vacation for the summer." I looked down at Sydney. His warm amber eyes were like shards of glass stabbing at my heart. I had to catch my breath. I couldn't go there in my mind. I returned my eyes to Chase and let him distract my pain. "This was a special trip. And way too short."

My stomach rumbled. Everyone heard it and laughed with me.

"Do you want to follow us back? It's time for me to fill my tank. When I get hungry, I have to eat. Have you seen all the starfish?"

Both boys looked at each other and shook their heads sideways.

"You've got to see the beach down our way. It's covered in them."

"Let's do, bro." Peyton grabbed Sarah's hand, and tugged her toward our side of the beach, laughing.

CHAPTER 38

Sarah released Peyton's hand and joined me, stacking piles of stranded starfish in our hands. The guys helped sort, looking for the best ones. Chase tried to revive a few in the water. He walked back to us with a puckered face and moaned. "They're all dead."

Sarah turned her newest starfish over in her hand, checking for signs of life. She shook her head and added it to the top of her stack. "These'll be perfect for a science project."

I looked at my tall pile balancing next to my chest. "Yep. And we'll have enough to share with everyone." Then I frowned at Chase. "Are you sure you don't want even one?"

He chuckled, shaking his head. "We've been coming here for so many years. Our parents made us promise to stop collecting. It's hard though. Every once in a while we'll sneak something home."

Under our house, mosquitoes swarmed as we cleaned our feet and the dogs. "This is awful," I fussed. "Dad said, 'A hatch occurs after every storm.'" We swatted our cheeks, shoulders, and legs. "You guys are so lucky to have a bathroom under your house. See what you're missing."

"Enough!" Sarah shouted. "I'm out of here." We ran to the sunshine, leaving the mosquitoes in the darkness, hungry and lonely. Outside in the sunlight, laughter caught my attention.

"Sarah, our parents must be awake. Maybe they fixed us a special breakfast, since it's our last day."

Peyton halted by the stairway. "We need to get back. You have a good breakfast, and now that I have Sarah's phone number, we'll call when we're heading down."

"Don't you want to come in?" Sarah pleaded, using all her charm. "There's enough food for all of us."

"Naw!" Peyton looked down the beach. "We promised we'd be back to visit with our company. We'll be down, after lunch. Are you still okay with Shelby and Henley hanging?"

Sarah and I shrugged and smiled at each other, and then turned to Peyton, and said together, "Absolutely."

Chase waved. "Okay. Later."

We watched them walk away. When their bodies turned into tiny specks in the sand, we climbed the stairs, and went inside.

The smell of bacon drifted to my nose. "Hooray! I'm sooo hungry."

"Me, too. But I wish they could have stayed."

"It's okay. You know they'll be back."

Inside the kitchen, I shoved an entire piece of bacon into my mouth. "We've already checked on the turtles, Momma," I said, mumbling with a full mouth, and then swallowed. "The boys met us there. They survived the storm."

Momma laughed and said, "The boys or the turtles?"

"You know who I'm talking about." I made a silly face at her. "The turtles, of course."

We all laughed. "I can't believe the Turtle Patrol didn't fix our nest after that terrible storm." I leaned my head, narrowing my eyes. "I wonder how they could have missed it." I paused and shook my head. "It's a good thing we hurried down. Sarah redid their nest, and I fixed the stakes and ribbon."

Sarah scrunched her eyebrows, and made her voice whiny, exaggerating her sadness. "Just think, we'll never know how many make it to the water."

After a deep sigh, I changed the subject. "The boys are coming back here sometime later. Sarah and I want to feed the seagulls after breakfast."

Momma set bacon, eggs, and grits on the table. Sarah's mom brought coffee cake and orange juice. They both fought back a smirk.

Sarah winked at me. I shrugged my shoulders. Our mothers were hiding something.

I stuffed myself until I couldn't eat another bite. "Are you ready Sarah?"

"I'm so full it's going to be hard to move," she moaned.

We stood, and slowly rummaged through the cabinets. Our parents continued their morning routine, drinking coffee and talking, but Momma interrupted their conversation to call to us. "Girls, look on the counter for a brown bag. I saved some snacks for the sea gulls. If you see anything else, take it."

I found an almost empty bag of potato chips, and Sarah dumped leftover pretzels into the bag. "Now, when you girls come back, plan on cleaning up," Momma said. "We'll go looking for souvenirs and books."

"Thanks, Momma. That'll be fun." I walked out the door.

Sarah followed. "I can't hurry this morning. I feel like I've got a bowling ball in my stomach. I sure hope our flying friends are still waiting for us."

"Me too. We have lots of goodies. It'll be our last time feeding them."

With no dogs running at our feet, we splashed in the water, chatting.

I sighed. "I'm going to miss being at the beach. And the guys. I never thought I'd be interested in guys. Did you hear Chase call me Pretty Green Eyes! See what you've gotten me into."

Sarah eyed the ocean. "Yeah! That was cool."

"And you'll see Peyton at camp. Whoo-hoo! Won't that be fun? I can't believe the week went by so quickly." A sharp jab in my chest startled me. I took one more breath and said, "I'm glad I got to see Sydney on his first beach trip." That didn't cheer me, but it was the truth.

"Darby, too. Maybe we can come back next year. By then you'll have another puppy, right?" Sarah immediately grabbed my arm and hugged me. "I'm so sorry, Trina. I know you don't want me to mention—I'm saying all the wrong things."

"It's okay. So am I." I put the bag on the sand, and used both hands to clear my eyes. "I may lose it a few times today, but I'm trying to enjoy every detail. I keep telling myself how wonderful he's going to be for his special—"

I didn't get to finish my sentence. A swarm of seagulls flew over our heads, shrieking. It was like they were telling us to hurry up. Sarah picked up the bag, and ran with the bird's flight. She reached in the bag, and tossed crumbs into the air. The biggest seagulls were bullies, grabbing the crumbs first. Then I reached in the bag, and threw crumbs another direction for the littler birds. As the bag emptied, the birds surrounding our legs took off. I called up to the sky. "Goodbye, seagulls. Hope you have a good summer. See you next year." I pitched the last of our food.

Sarah had named some of the birds. "They won't let us get close enough to pet them, but they sure liked our snacks."

The sun burned directly overhead. "I'm ready for air conditioning. Let's go and see what our moms have planned. They're acting like they have a surprise for us, but we're not supposed to know."

"They have a hard time keeping secrets, don't they?" Sarah blinked her soft blue eyes and giggled. "Let's play along. Like we have no idea. Then when we get back, we'll meet the boys. And, maybe I'll go for a swim."

"Wow, Sarah. Really?"

"Yep." Sarah held her head high. "Now that I know I can wear that jacket, I feel safer."

"Do you think Darby will swim, too?"

"I don't think she'll go any farther than her legs, but I want to be able to say I rode the raft."

I did a little jig. "Yes, yes, yes. You have to do it. Maybe the boys will bring their wave runners. You should try that, too."

We went from a walk to a run, heading into the house and startling our moms as we dashed to our rooms. I found a clean tee shirt bunched up in my suitcase. I laid it on the bed and tried to press the wrinkles out with my hands. "Oh well, maybe the heat will make them go away," I said, giving up. I found a pair of green shorts under the bed, and pulled on the same white socks I'd worn bike riding, and then my tennis shoes. I brushed my hair, and pulled it into a barrette at my neck. Some curls still got away.

Sarah came from her room looking fresh. Her pink tank top matched the pink design in her shorts. Her hair was neatly combed.

"Don't you look nice! You win the fashion prize for the week." I laughed own at my clothes. "I'm out of clothes that even begin to match, even after sharing with you."

Sarah smiled, "I thought I might as well wear everything I brought. I still have some other tops. Do you want to wear one?"

"Naw. It's not like I have to be perfect."

Sydney lay on the rug, fighting to keep his eyes open. I knelt near him. "Sydney, you look like the beach has finally worn you out." His eyes opened, and he stared at me without moving his head from his paws, and exhaled a deep, loud sigh. "Come on Syd. You can do it! This our last adventure. Here's your magic cape."

CHAPTER 39

Momma drove into the state park office parking lot, and Mrs. Neal squirmed in her seat. I opened my door and said louder than expected, "Oh. Wow! I bet they have information inside about sea turtles."

"Yeah!" Sarah plunged out her door. "And maybe, they'll have pictures and postcards we can take home."

As we entered the red brick building, a medium height, black-haired ranger hurried to greet us. Her long, pony tail swished side to side, and a giant smile grew on her freckled face. She wore brown slacks, a matching short-sleeved brown shirt, and a beige tie with a loggerhead turtle embroidered in the middle. "Hi, girls. Let's see. You must be Sarah. And you must be Trina. And this has to be Sydney. It is so nice to meet all of you. I'm Ranger Jeanette."

Sarah and I froze. Our mouths hung wide open. I didn't know what to say. Sarah was speechless, too.

"Your moms kept us informed on how you've been checking on a certain turtle's nest all week. Once we felt confident you'd be inspecting the nest, we actually left some of the caretaking to you. Want to follow me?"

We followed like baby ducklings in a row, but with our mothers behind. Sydney walked, glued to my side.

In the office, the ranger laid a brown, three-ring binder on her desk. "I wanted to share these pictures with you. You girls already seem to know how important it is to protect the sea turtles. They'd be extinct, if it weren't for people like you."

She opened the picture album. "Here. Take a look." She moved away.

Sarah and I turned page after page, staring at every detail.

There was a turtle pulling its big body onshore. There were photos of a turtle laying her eggs, just like we had watched. It could've been our turtle.

We saw pictures of two rangers making the square protector barriers. And then pictures of baby sea turtles hatching. "OMG! Sarah, look. That's what our turtles are going to look like!"

Sarah tried to count the babies. "How many will hatch?" She looked up at the ranger.

"It's different every time, but there can be a hundred or more. Not all of them will make it to the water. Some will be eaten by birds or fish while swimming."

Sarah and I couldn't take our eyes from the photographs.

Then the ranger said, "I plan to send you pictures of your hatchlings, crawling out to sea. You've been a great help, and I want you to go back to school, and share this experience."

I wrapped my arm through Sarah's. "Is that cool or what?" I turned to Ranger Jeanette. "Well. I'm not sure what to say. This is fabulous. Thank you for letting us help."

Sarah grinned. "I've been so sad not knowing what's going to happen to the baby turtles. This'll definitely make me feel better. Thank you."

While heading back to the car, Sarah and I jabbered on and on, telling our mothers what a wonderful surprise they'd sprung on us.

After giant bear hugs, we climbed back into the car. Before starting the ignition, Momma turned. "Now what else is on your To Do list for your last day at the beach?"

I tapped my pointy finger on the car's armrest. "Hmm, for *my* last day, I guess, besides swimming with Sydney and the guys, I want to eat shrimp and hush puppies one more time. Can we go out to dinner tonight?"

Momma bobbed a happy face.

Sarah's mother stared at Sarah. "What about you?"

She lifted her shoulders and a toothy grin exploded. "Well. I have a surprise for you. I told Trina I'm going to swim and ride on the raft."

"All right!" Mrs. Neal almost bumped her head on the car roof. "We're going to have a marvelous last day." Somewhere in the middle of Mrs. Neal's sentence, Sarah's phone sang a new tune. It sounded like Surfer Boy.

"Oooh! It's Peyton." Then she answered it. "Hey."

Her face lit up. She kept her eyes locked with mine, smiling, and nodding.

I fidgeted in the seat and whispered, "What? What's happening?" I couldn't stand listening to a one-sided conversation.

Sarah pushed the speaker button. The rest of the conversation was loud and clear.

Peyton croaked out, "Our company left. No more Henley and Shelby."

Sarah punched the air with her fist like you do when there's a touchdown at a football game, and mouthed, "Hooray!"

Both guys spoke at the same time so some of the conversation got jumbled, but we sort of understood. They were going to spend the rest of the day with us and ride their wave runners up to our beach.

Then Peyton added at the end, "Sarah, I'm bringing the pink jacket."

Her eyes sparkled, and she answered in a huffy breath. "All right! I'm going to ride your wave runner. I'm really going to do it. We're on our way back to the house. See you in an hour."

I put my face close to the phone, "Bye-ee."

"This will be our best day ever." Sarah inhaled and blew it out.

"Yes. We'll do everything we planned. And more. Momma, please hurry. Get us home."

We leaned back in our seat. Silent. For a couple of minutes, Sarah and I didn't move. I knew how the day was going to end. I scrunched my face, struggling not to show any emotion. "I'm certainly learning how to say goodbye."

Sarah smiled. "But, it may not really be goodbye. Invite Chase to come up to Greenville when Peyton goes to camp. And if Logan gets Sydney, he'll have to stay in touch."

"Maybe?" I tried to smile. My words came out softly, "There's no guarantee that Logan will get Sydney. His family has to qualify, and then train. And Sydney's going back tomorrow. The timing may not be right." I put my head in my hands, and sobbed.

Momma looked in her rear view mirror. Her voice quivered. "Oh, honey, I know this is going to be a hard day."

Sarah scooted over, as far as the seat belt allowed, and rubbed my back. Her warm tears dripped on my knee.

Momma tried again. "Think about how happy he'll be doing what you've trained him to do. And you talked about getting another puppy before we came to the beach." Momma stopped.

Sarah whispered in my ear. "I'll do everything I can to keep you busy and thinking about other stuff. Okay?" She winked at me, and mouthed the word, "TRIP."

I couldn't respond. I hadn't said anything to my parents about the trip. Did I want a trip or a new puppy? My time was running out. But today, I'd make every second count.

CHAPTER 40

After several attempts, I finally calmed my emotions. I really did want to be excited about our last adventures, our last full day. Every minute rushed into the next. The day became a blur, like a movie on fast forward.

Still talking about Ranger Jeanette and all the pictures and souvenirs, Sarah and I dashed into the house to change into our bathing suits. We sprayed sun lotion where we could, and then on each other's backs. Gently, I applied an abundance of lotion to Sarah's sunburned back. I couldn't talk her into wearing a tee shirt over her bathing suit.

We raced out the screen door and let it bang, our final statement that we were here.

Sarah and I tossed one end of our beach towels into the air, and giggled as they floated down in unison to the sand. We plopped on our bottoms, wrapped our arms around our bent knees, and waited for the boys to drive their wave runners ashore.

The roar of their engines grew louder as they raced into view. We shot up and met them at the water. My stomach did a somersault. This day had officially begun.

With quick instructions from Chase and Peyton, we slipped on our safety jackets and clicked the buckles.

The thrill of the day was watching Sarah bouncing over waves in her pink jacket, laughing and hollering. I bet her voice echoed across the island.

Sydney was told to stay. He raced back and forth on the wet sand, yipping. Darby chased the birds, oblivious to what we were doing.

As teams, Chase and I won all of the races against Sarah and Peyton, except for one. We let them win.

Peyton blamed Sarah for making him go slow. She laughed and finally agreed.

As the sun floated westward, we hauled our tired bodies once again under the house. It would be our last time to fight with the mosquitoes. Sarah and I hooted about saying goodbye to the pesky insects. It was nice knowing we were leaving them behind.

Everything that happened on Saturday was final. The end.

Peyton and Chase happily agreed to join us for our last dinner. Sydney, the celebrity of the island, intrigued the diners at the Pavilion. Most customers wanted to meet him and asked many questions. I gave Sydney the command, "Touch." He eagerly sat and nosed their hands.

All of this attention kept me occupied, explaining the wonderful things about Syd's job. It pushed my sad thoughts away, and made me aware of why I had chosen to be a puppy raiser. It made the unavoidable decision loom like a dark cloud overhead. I was so confused. And by the end of dinner, every part of my body screamed, "No more."

Chase and Peyton wouldn't let the evening end. They begged Sarah and me to wander up and down the beach.

Last night I had told myself, "Remember each moment." And I did try to capture all the things happening around me, but my insides were numb. And the words in my brain froze. Chase only saw a happy mask. He held my cold hand, and coaxed me to walk. We drifted off at our own pace, and left Peyton and Sarah to themselves.

Out of the entire week, our last night was the most beautiful of all. With a clear sky, thousands of stars shined brightly. A burst of energy pushed my thoughts from my brain into words. "Look at all those stars, Chase. Maybe those stars are spirits, blinking us well-wishes. I'd like to believe they're telling me to be happy and not afraid. That good things will happen."

Chase squeezed my hand, and we gazed off into the sky.

A slight warm breeze of salty air whispered around us, making me feel giddy and yet hollow inside.

"Trina, you are the bravest person I know. I could never do what you're doing. If Logan gets a service dog, it will be because of you."

"Thanks. I hope he does. He's made so much progress this week. I'm terribly depressed about letting Sydney go, and it hasn't helped that I don't know if I'll do it again."

"What? You're the perfect dog trainer. I know it hurts to let go of Sydney, but think if Logan had never met him. You've found your special skill. Your purpose. Don't you *ever* forget why you're doing this!" Chase's bright green eyes shined with energy.

"Thanks, Chase." I sobbed through my words. "I needed that pep talk, and I will think about what you've said, but I'm so tired I can't take another step."

"I'll walk you to your stairs. And then I'll head home. What time are you planning to leave?"

I swallowed and caught my breath. *I can't talk about leaving.* "We need to be in Columbia by one o'clock for the celebration. It will only take a couple of hours to get there."

Chase interrupted me. "What kind of celebration?"

I stopped walking. "It's to celebrate the dogs' success. The four other puppies that have trained together are returning, also. They'll spend the next six months doing special training. The last three weeks will be with their chosen companion. And if they make a good match, they'll go home together."

"Do you think it's too late for Logan to get his name on the list?"

"I have no idea. I'm not sure how the selection is made, or how many others are on the list ahead of him. Some dogs are more suited for different jobs. I'd say Sydney is well suited for Logan."

Chase looped his arm through mine, and we started walking again. "That'll be good. So you'll have a party. I hope that makes it easier."

"I hope so, too. I'll get to see my friends that I've trained with and—" I sighed a long breath. "—I guess we'll share our sadness and happy memories."

"So what time are you leaving?"

"Dad wants to go out for breakfast tomorrow morning before we leave the island, after cleaning the house. I'm guessing we'll be done by 10:00. I know I'll be up early, if I even sleep. I'll probably go for one more walk in the morning."

"Can I meet you in the morning?"

We were almost to the stairs. I took another deep breath. I wanted to say no, but I really wanted to see him one more time. "I guess we can do that."

He dropped his arm from mine and halted. "What time do you want to meet?"

"Let's say 7:30. Just in case I fall asleep and don't wake up early."

"Great." He grabbed my hand and got us walking again. "I'll have something to look forward to. It won't be the same after you leave."

At the steps, I hung my head. I didn't know what else to say.

Chase waited for my response, and finally said, "I'll see you in the morning." He put his finger under my chin, and lifted my face to his. "I really hope you get some sleep." My eyes stayed down. He moved away, and twisted around one more time. "Be thinking about you."

I saw only his feet. He turned and ran.

I heard Sarah huffing up the stairs behind me. "See, Trina. I'm not staying behind. Are you okay?"

"Yep. Just tired." I took each step painfully slow. "I'm heading to bed. I want to sleep with Sydney. Is that okay with you?"

"Yeah. I kind of thought you'd want to do that. I'll see you in the morning."

"Okay. Did you have a good evening with Peyton?"

"Fabulous. I'll tell you all about it tomorrow." At the top of the stairs, Sarah leaned over and hugged me. "Try and get some sleep."

"Thanks. I will." Sydney, always by my side, lifted his head, waiting to hear what came next. "Let's go to bed."

He followed me to the bathroom. I washed my tear-stained face, brushed my teeth, and searched for my dirty white socks. I had made sure Momma wouldn't find and wash them before we went to the kennel.

Uh-huh. They're just where I left them. Bunched in the corner of my suitcase. After shaking them a couple of times, I put them on for the last time, and climbed in bed.

CHAPTER 41

SATURDAY NIGHT INTO SUNDAY

M y parents stayed on the porch for a long time that night. I lay with Sydney, cuddling and listening to their voices. I could only guess what they were talking about.

Earlier in the day, my parents had whispered how they needed to be brave in front of me. They had given up a lot for me to do this job, and yet they encouraged me.

Tomorrow had crept up like a silent ghost. I didn't know how I was going to say goodbye. Sydney had been left with Ms. Jennifer for a week here and there for extra training, and an occasional weekend with foster families to help with separation anxiety. Those times I'd say, "I'll be back." But this time I couldn't say those words.

Momma and Dad climbed into bed.

Lying perfectly still, I pretended to sleep, and stared at the full moon through the open blinds.

Memories popped into my head. I whispered in Sydney's ear, "Do you remember, Syd?" I stroked his fur. His eyes glistened, staring into mine. "When I brought you home, you still had a lot to learn. Sarah and I taught you to play hide and seek in the house during the summer. You hated the hot sun. We'd take turns counting out loud to a thousand ten, and then one of us would scream, 'Ready or not here we come.' You learned to count that summer. Whenever you heard the word, ten, you'd run through the house, scouting behind doors, under beds, and in the dining room. You always got a treat when you found Sarah, or me, and couldn't wait to do it again."

My pillow soaked up the river of sadness. "Oh, Sydney. I know you'll have a wonderful new home, and love your new person. I'll always remember you.

I just dread the drive to Columbia." I sat and dried my face with the sheet. "Let's get up, and let Momma and Dad sleep."

As we walked out, Momma asked, "What are you doing, honey?"

"I can't sleep. I'm going to sit out there, and talk with Syd."

"Do you want some company?"

"No. I'm enjoying these minutes with him alone. I'll be okay."

I made a cup of hot chocolate, and gave Sydney a large biscuit. He climbed onto my lap and pawed me. "Do you want to hear one more story?"

He licked my face. "I was so proud of you when we did our first Rally competition. That was such a good experience. I hope I get the courage to do it again." Syd's eyes grew large. "Oh, don't look so surprised. One day I'll have another puppy. And I'll do all of this over again. It just may take a while for me to put the broken pieces of my heart back together like doing my jigsaw puzzle.

"I can hear the announcer now. 'Next is junior competitor, Miss Trina Ryan with her dog, Sydney, a one-year-old Australian shepherd.'"

Sydney tilted his head when they said his name.

"The judge asked if I was ready. I nodded. But my insides really trembled. She said, 'Begin.' And the timer clicked. The judge gripped her clipboard and took notes. I said, 'Halt' and you sat. Then we did a 'Front.' You halted in front and turned on my command. You walked, heeling like a pro, even while going slow and speeding up."

My head throbbed as I spoke. Not seeing clearly through my flooded eyes, I blinked and smiled down at Sydney. "Our last exercise was walking around three orange cones, and then we circled only two cones, and then finally one. I remember now how amazed I was that all my butterflies had vanished. No outside sounds ever entered my brain. I had concentrated on only what I needed to do, until we crossed the finish line."

I blew my nose in a wadded up napkin I was shredding. "Oh. My. Gawd. That memory told me what to do." I caught site of the stars, blinking through the window. "Tomorrow, or I guess later today, I'll concentrate on the best acting job I can do." Sydney's glowing eyes connected to mine. "You won't know I'm upset. I don't want you to be sad, too."

Suddenly, a calmness entered my mind.

I stretched out on the squishy couch. Syd snuggled between me and the back of the couch, and we both fell into a sound sleep. It seemed like seconds before the rosy sun slipped under my eyelids. The day had dawned. I sat up, and walked to the porch.

It was low tide, perfect for walking. I still wore my shorts and tee shirt. My white socks had squished down to my ankles. I pulled them off, and stuffed them into my pockets. My scent had to last on them for a long while.

In the kitchen the clock glowed, 6:30. Syd gobbled an early breakfast, giving him time to digest his meal before we drove to Columbia.

I scrounged around in the kitchen for something to eat. It was slim pickings for sure. I found two leftover cookies and an apple. *That'll do.*

Just before seven o'clock, Sydney and I walked on the beach. "No swimming. No water."

His eyes squinted, but he listened. "You're clean, and groomed for another trip." His ears perked, hearing the word "Trip."

"Okay, which way should we go? We have lots of time."

Syd glanced left and right and started running toward Logan's house. "All right. I know where you want to go."

We both jogged a short distance, and then I slowed to a walk and eventually stood still.

The sun sprinkled golden glitter on the water. Waves broke onshore, sending ocean smells into the air. I poked my nose upward and inhaled. At the same time a salty mist floated over my face, and I licked my lips.

Seconds later, the seagulls swarmed overhead, and squawked. "Sydney, all we're missing is the flock of pelicans diving for their breakfast." We both looked to the sky.

Without warning, I heard Chase and Logan calling, "Syd-ney. Trina."

I caught their shapes running toward us, and we dashed ahead. "I didn't expect to see you."

Chase panted. "I had a feeling you'd be up earlier than you said. And I didn't want to miss you. Even Logan woke early to say goodbye."

"Well, that's nice. I'm trying to store all the sights in my brain. I'm sure we'll be back next year. Edisto's the best, but that's a long time from now."

Logan darted up to Sydney, and patted his head, saying "My friend. My friend."

Sydney and Logan ran in figure eights. I would always remember the sound of Logan's wild laughter. I stood and watched.

Chase stayed next to me, gently taking hold of both of my hands, and turning me to face him. "Did you get any sleep?"

"A few hours. I remembered something in the middle of the night. When I concentrated really hard during a task with Sydney, my butterflies always floated away. I got amazingly calm. That's what I'm going to do today. Concentrate on not being sad."

"Good for you. I'm going to call you tonight, if that's okay? And I've already asked Dad if he'd drop me off at your house when he takes Peyton to camp. Would you like some company in two weeks?"

"That sounds wonderful." I straightened, and a rush of happiness started at my heart and traveled down every limb. I smiled. "I'll have something to look forward to. I'll probably take a break from training. Sarah has invited me to go on a trip with her after her soccer camp. Then sometime later, maybe, I'll get an eight-week-old puppy. That'll be a new experience."

Little by little, he inched forward. "Well, we'll stay in touch. I won't ever forget this summer." His face moved closer, his breath puffed out peppermint toothpaste. He leaned forward, lifted his chin, puckered his lips, and then his eyelids began to close. I blinked. A flutter in my stomach made me stiffen. *What am I supposed to do*? I swallowed, and turned brave. *Why not?*

I pursed my lips, and closed my eyes, just like in the movies. Quivering inside, I slanted forward. We bumped noses like bumper cars, jolting us backwards. In a fit of laughter, we turned sideways, and bent over snickering, hiding our embarrassment.

Chase's words sputtered out one by one to the sand. "I guess I need practice. I'm sorry." He stood, pink-faced, and looked me in the yes. "That was my first time."

"Me, too." I cackled some more, and then straightened. "I've never even talked to a boy." Our eyes caught, one more time. "Do you want to try it again?"

His eyes opened wide. "Yeah. Would you?"

"Yes." I wiggled my shoulders and threw my head side to side, loosening my neck and smiling. "I like learning new things."

Chase's eyes stayed glued to mine. "Okay. What do you think we did wrong?"

Giggling inside, I tried to be serious. "We came straight at each other." I used my thumbs to point. "You go to your right and I'll go to my right."

"Okay. On the count of three." He started to lean in, and squinted. "Are you going to close your eyes?"

"No. I think I'll leave mine open so we don't bump."

"One, two, three."

We met in the middle. Our lips touched for a second. We backed an inch away, staring into each other's green eyes, smiling, and did it again. Longer this time, and after a second, I closed my eyes, too.

Chase pulled away first. "Wow." He put both hands on his chest.

I tugged on each sleeve of my tee shirt, swaying from side to side. "I guess neither of us will forget." I sighed, bent my head, and swept the sand with my big toe. "I really need to head back. Will Logan be okay after we leave?"

"Yep. I promised him if he said goodbye without getting upset, we'd play some computer games. That makes him happy."

Chase called Logan, and I called Sydney. They both came running.

"Can I have a hug, Logan?"

He nodded once and stared at the dry sand.

"Bye, Logan. We have to go home."

Rubbing Sydney's head, Logan said, "Bye, Syd-ney." He lifted his head for a second, catching Sydney's eyes. He smiled before bending his head again.

Chase and I held each other's eyes like in a trance. I couldn't stop my lips from shivering, and made myself turn around.

Sydney and I jogged as fast as our legs could go, wanting to flee. At the stairs, we sprinted up. Voices echoed from inside. I wiped my face, straightened my shoulders, and walked in.

Everyone scurried around packing and cleaning. Mrs. Neal had banished Darby to the screened porch while the vacuum howled. I grabbed a broom, and put Sydney on the outside porch, too. After sweeping sand out the door, I went to my room to pack. My suitcase lay on the bedspread, closed. On top lay my *PINK & PURPLE* concert tee shirt and my jean shorts.

I went looking for Sarah.

She was rinsing the tub and wearing her *PINK & PURPLE* shirt and white shorts. She heard me gasp, leapt to her feet, and hugged me, wet rag, and all. "I thought if we looked alike today, you'd feel better."

"Thanks, Sarah." My shoulders rose up and down as I blubbered. "Won't you feel silly?

She shook her head.

"I'll go change."

Before returning to the tub, she said, "Meet you at the restaurant. Okay?"

All I could do was nod.

We finished cleaning the house, loaded the cars, and drove to the only cafe that had breakfast.

Everyone ordered giant meals. I didn't think I could eat, but my pancakes and two sausages disappeared before everyone else finished. I drank an entire glass of milk and had two bites of Momma's omelet. Sarah had jabbered all through breakfast, not letting me go off into my own thoughts.

As Dad paid for breakfast, I walked Syd to the grassy area and said, "Go potty. We're going on a trip." He sniffed for the perfect spot, and then lifted his leg. "Good boy. Let's go."

He was ready. I wished I was.

196 — Sheri S. Levy

CHAPTER 42

S arah had one more surprise in her. After breakfast, she hugged her parents, and walked toward our car. I halted and watched her walk to me, my heart racing. She smiled. "Can I go with you?"

My face must have shown confusion.

"Please, Trina! I just want to be with you. I'll miss Syd, too, and I don't want you to drive home by yourself. We can talk about the trip after leaving the kennel. It will take your mind off of Syd."

I stared at my friend I'd known for years. She really was my BFF. "Okay!" That was all that came out.

Sarah went to the left side of the car, and climbed in. We drove in silence. Chase popped into my mind, and then Sarah chatted. She was great at making conversation. We laughed about incidents that happened during our week, meeting the boys, shaving my legs, doing my hair, and meeting the other girls at the restaurant and on the boat. But I wasn't ready to share about my first kiss.

Our drive whizzed by. And then unexpectedly, I recognized our surroundings. My stomach turned upside down. My heart pumped so fast I could hear it in my ears like gushing water.

I squeezed my clammy hands together, swallowed, and told myself, *Mind over matter. No sulking until after.*

As we drove up to Ms. Jennifer's house, streamers with the word CONGRATULATIONS flew across the porch, and balloons floated from railings. Many, many people mingled outside.

I saw Scott, Jessica, Patrick and Donna. We had worked together for one year. A sting of excitement about seeing everyone spurred me forward. I opened my door and stepped out, Sydney by my side.

Ms. Jennifer announced, "Please take your dogs and all their belongings to the new playroom. Many volunteers are there to help carry items and get your dogs settled. Then it's time to say your goodbyes."

We walked toward the group, the dogs whining and pulling to greet each other. Tension filled the air, but we all wore our happy faces.

The entire crowd sucked in all the air from outside. There was a quiet hush.

I grabbed hold of Sarah. "Okay, Sarah. This will be the best performance you've ever seen. I have to be strong for Sydney. He won't understand I'm leaving and not coming back."

She held my arm. "Come on. I'm here to help."

Dad went to the car and carried Syd's bed. Mom had his Frisbee, and I had my socks tied into a knot, stuffed in my right pocket.

The new room was a long rectangle with lots of windows on the left side. Under the windows, two huge baskets held an assortment of toys. Overhead, white fans spun and hummed. On the right, a separate area looked like bedrooms for the dogs. Sections were separated by gates. Each dog had its own space with a crate but could come and go whenever the gates were open.

Dad chose Sydney's spot, set the bed down, hugged him, and stepped outside of his area. I walked Syd to his space.

Mom dropped the Frisbee and a ball on the bed, held his face up to hers, kissed his nose, and said, "You are such a good boy." Her head drooped, and she took baby steps out.

He sniffed his bed and the toys, and then looked up at me with a puzzled face. I'm sure he smelled my sadness.

"Look what I have!" I sobbed out. I pulled out my smelly socks. He sniffed, then grabbed them with his mouth and tugged. I played tug with him for a several seconds, and then opened my hand.

The socks dangled from his mouth. I squatted to his level. "I have to go." I nuzzled my face into his fur, inhaling his own special scent for the last time. "'Bye, Sydney. I love you."

Sarah led me away. Her pink cheeks held tear drops, but she held on to me until we got into the gathering room and saw Momma and Dad.

We all had a huge circle hug. I closed my eyes and remembered Mr. Walker telling me, "Thank you for all that you did. Your dog will change someone's life for the better." I inhaled, and let my breath slowly drift out.

Tables held an assortment of yummy snacks, and cold drinks sat in coolers filled with ice like treasures in a pirate's chest, but I couldn't swallow a bite.

Mom and Dad mingled with other parents trying to be brave.

I moved the other direction.

A few minutes later, Ms. Jennifer stood at the front of the room. "I want to thank—" She made eye contact. "—Scott, Jessica, Trina, Patrick and Donna, and your families for your courage and hard work. What you have done for the last eighteen months is remarkable. Every time we start another training session, I'm always amazed that I have more people waiting than we have trained dogs. I could never pull this off without your involvement."

"Your work is so beneficial, not only to me, but to the people waiting, and hoping to have a special helper. I know today is terribly difficult, but as you feel sad, please try to remember why you chose to do this. You all signed on to help someone else. You gave of yourselves, so unselfishly and your reward will be in six months. At graduation you will see your dog with its companion and doing the job they were meant to do. Please applaud yourselves, your friends, and your family for supporting you in this commitment."

It was quiet for a moment, and then one by one, each of us began a slow, quiet clap. Then the rhythm picked up, and the noise bounced from wall to wall.

Ms. Jennifer's hand signaled for quiet. "Thank you, everyone. In just a minute, I want you to mingle, eat, and congratulate each other on a job well done. The schedule for each dogs' training will be on my website along with their pictures."

Great! Now I'll have pictures of the baby turtles and my first dog heading off to their new lives.

Except for the ruckus the dogs made in the back room, the room stilled. The end was coming. Relief swelled through me. This was almost over.

Then Ms. Jennifer interrupted the hush. "Most of you have shared that you planned to train another puppy. If anyone is ready today, please go to the nursery. I have two adorable puppies ready to go to someone's home."

I stiffened. I had told myself it'd be nice to have a break, to go with Sarah to Disney World. I thought about Sarah's comment about how I was always busy with training. I wanted us to be friends, forever.

Sarah peeked at me and must have read my mind.

"I *know* you want to do it again." She grabbed my hands. "Oh, Trina! Why not get a little puppy today? You said the next time you'd like an eight-week-old."

Seeing my reaction, Mom and Dad walked over.

Speechless, my eyes filled again. I cracked a small smile. "How can my body have so much water?"

Momma sort of smiled.

Dad wrapped his arm around my shoulder and turned me to him. His serious face never balked from looking directly in my eyes. "Honey, if you want to go see the puppies, it's okay. If you want to wait, that's up to you, too. It's your choice."

I stared back at him for a moment and then broke loose. I grabbed Sarah's arm and blurted out, "I can't believe what you just said. What about our trip together? I've been afraid if I took another puppy to train—"

Sarah ended my sentence. "—We'd lose our friendship." She squeezed me and spoke softly in my ear. "I've been selfish. I shouldn't have tempted you with the trip. I've been afraid of losing you, too. I'm sorry. I have soccer, and you'll have dog training, but we'll still make time to be best friends. What you've done with Sydney is amazing."

My parents listened and gazed at Sarah. Their eyes grew large. "You invited Trina on a trip?"

"Mrs. Ryan, I'm sorry. We're going to Disney World after soccer camp, and I hoped Trina would come, but if she's brave enough to get a new puppy, that's what she ought to be doing. After watching Sydney and Logan together, I realized she's a great trainer and should be training another dog, not worrying about our friendship." Sarah's face creased. "I did invite her, but I think it was for the wrong reason."

Momma embraced Sarah and peered at me. "But Trina, it's your decision. You're the one who'll have all the responsibility. You can get another puppy later, and go on the trip, or never train again. It has to be what YOU want."

Pulling Sarah by her hand, I ran into the nursery. Behind a window, two Labrador retrievers tumbled and tackled each other. One was black, and the other yellow. I leaned close to the glass, seeing their soft baby faces, floppy ears, and black noses.

Brown eyes stared back at me, little pointy tails wagged, and then the black Lab lost interest. He scooted under the yellow Lab, rolling her onto her back. Using his head, he nudged her side. She leaped to her feet, teetered back and forth, and finally caught her balance, and trotted to the other side of the room. The black Lab shook his small body with no fur flying, held his head high with a smug expression, and chased after her.

Relief swelled through my body. A new puppy that looked different from Sydney. I'd have a new start.

Patrick and Jessica wandered in. I listened to their conversations.

We had all just finished our first, long training period. It would be easier the next time, since we knew what we were doing.

I turned to them. "Are you planning to take a puppy?"

Jessica shook her head. "I'm going out to Arizona to visit my grandparents for the whole summer. So, I'll wait. How about you, Patrick?"

"I had so much fun training my first puppy, and I'm going to be lost without him. I'm going to say YES!"

Sarah moved in closer. "That leaves one for you."

Seconds later, my parents walked in. Dad peered at the puppies, "So, what do we have here?"

I walked away from the window, my mind reeling.

Pacing for what seemed like an eternity, I returned. And then walked away again, once, twice. Everyone stared at me, waiting for me to speak. I twisted my ponytail in circles.

From a distance, I peeked at the cute faces and small bodies now snuggling together. I moved closer. Gradually, my nose touched the window. The tiny black Lab lifted his head, and his dark brown eyes stared at me. My heart flip-flopped. I took a slow, deep breath, and blew it out.

Our eyes stayed locked.

While not moving my head, the words came out. "All right. Okay."

Mom, Dad, and Sarah froze. I felt their eyes on me.

"I've made my decision." No one moved. I blew out a deep breath, fogged the glass, and smeared it away. "I'm going to do it again! This time with the black Lab." I jerked around, and caught Ms. Jennifer standing in the doorway.

Rushing over, she wrapped her arms around me and squeezed. "Oh, Trina. I'm so happy you're taking the black Lab. He's going to be a handful. But after training Sydney, you'll be the perfect one for him. Come on. Let's meet your new puppy."

Around the corner, she unlocked the door, and both pups stood, wiggling every part of their bodies.

I moved in slowly, and sat cross-legged on the floor. The yellow Lab stayed in the corner, but the black Lab pounced on my lap. I bent my face to his, and he immediately placed his miniature front paws on my shoulders and a wet nose to mine.

"Well, hello there, little boy!" My heart raced, and a tear trickled down my cheek. "Would you like to come home with me?"

A long, sticky tongue swiped my cheek. He straightened, lost his balance, and flopped across my lap. His eyes glanced up with a playful, frisky look. And then the pupils of his eyes blended into the milk chocolate brown, and his adoring, warm gaze melted the jagged edges of my heart.

"I'll take that as a 'Yes!'" I closed my eyes, breathing in and breathing out, calming myself.

I opened my eyes and lifted the small bundle of short fur close to my chest, feeling our hearts beating to the same rhythm.

I was ready, too.

- THE END -

༄

Coming Soon from Sheri S. Levy

Starting Over

༄

www.SheriSLevy.com

ACKNOWLEDGEMENTS

Thanking my family and the many friends who have supported my new writing life is as difficult a task as writing the story. My writing journey began years ago as a dog story whispered in my mind and soon became a long conversation with my close friend and walking companion. Thank you, Jennifer Warner, for listening and brain storming with me for days on end.

After retiring from teaching special needs children and learning about service dogs, the idea for my emotional plot developed. I researched online and found PAALS, a local organization. Its founder, Jennifer Rodgers, eagerly answered my questions and allowed me to observe her training process. Next came the idea for the setting: Our close friends, Frank and Kathy McGee, introduced us to Edisto Island and Clemson activities, and Neal and Carol Sopko spent many long weekends with us in an old house on Edisto Beach.

When Frank and Neal suddenly passed on, I longed to remember them, and our lost dogs. After I began this story, our Frodos critique group formed. We have made lasting friendships, allowing us to be critical of each other's work, and most importantly, to support and encourage our dreams of publishing. I'm indebted to Jo Hackl, Caroline Eschenberg, Landra Jennings and Marcia Pugh for their patience and skill in pushing my story in the right direction. You guys are the best!

One final step was a critique from Kirby Larson, the award-winning author of *Hattie Big Sky*. She saw deeper into the story and made me realize I didn't need two dogs. That night, my husband and I toasted the second dog, Jake, and *Seven Days to Goodbye* was recreated. And then came the publication offer from Barking Rain Press and my dream became a reality. Cindy Koepp, my editor, transformed the story and patiently taught me many new skills. Thank you, Cindy, for bringing my baby to life! Another big thank you goes to Stephanie Flint for creating an amazing, eye catching cover. And finding

Sue Goetcheus was a special gift! Your skill with web design and promotion ideas have been a miracle!

My love and gratitude goes out to my parents, Conner and Lillian Shepherd, who taught me to never doubt being myself. My daughter, Trina Alvarez and her children, Chase and Peyton, who loved the idea of their names used as fictional characters. My son Ryan, who created my first website and business card. And to Jeanette Smith for being my forever friend.

And to my husband, who has always boosted my confidence and encouraged me to reach for the stars. I could never have done this without your undying love and unwavering commitment.

It takes years, and many treasured friends that I have not named, who asked," How's the story coming?" Your support meant the world to me. Thank you from my heart!

SHERI S. LEVY

ABOUT SHERI S. LEVY

Sheri S. Levy's magazine article about a Diabetic Alert dog, *Scent with Love*, was published in *Clubhouse Magazine* in July, 2010. This story was nominated for a Maxwell Medallion Award with the Dog Writers Association of America's competition and received the Special Interest award at their February 2011 awards banquet in New York. As a member of the Society of Children's Book Writers and Illustrators (SCBWI) Carolinas, Sheri helps coordinate critiques and has written for their regional newsletter and for the Southern Breeze region. In addition to teaching a six-week Creative Writers Club after school hours for elementary students, Sheri also volunteers with an accredited, non-profit service dog kennel, Palmetto Animal Assisted Life Services (PAALS). Sheri and her husband have enjoyed many years of married life, and their two children have become remarkable adults; their two grandchildren are very special readers. She has loved five past dogs and now owns two Australian Shepherds. Find out more about Sheri at her website or Facebook page.

WWW.SHERISLEVY.COM

ABOUT
BARKING RAIN PRESS

Did you know that five media conglomerates publish eighty percent of the books in the United States? As the publishing industry continues to contract, opportunities for emerging and mid-career authors are drying up. Who will write the literature of the twenty-first century if just a handful of profit-focused corporations are left to decide who—and what—is worthy of publication?

Barking Rain Press is dedicated to the creation and promotion of thoughtful and imaginative contemporary literature, which we believe is essential to a vital and diverse culture. As a nonprofit organization, Barking Rain Press is an independent publisher that seeks to cultivate relationships with new and mid-career writers over time, to be thorough in the editorial process, and to make the publishing process an experience that will add to an author's development—and ultimately enhance our literary heritage.

In selecting new titles for publication, Barking Rain Press considers authors at all points in their careers. Our goal is to support the development of emerging and mid-career authors—not just single books—as we know from experience that a writer's audience is cultivated over the course of several books.

Support for these efforts comes primarily from the sale of our publications; we also hope to attract grant funding and private donations. Whether you are a reader or a writer, we invite you to take a stand for independent publishing and become more involved with Barking Rain Press. With your support, we can make sure that talented writers thrive, and that their books reach the hands of spirited, curious readers. Find out more at our website.

WWW.BARKINGRAINPRESS.ORG

Barking Rain Press

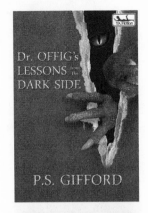

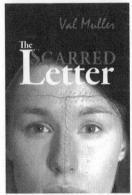

Made in the USA
Charleston, SC
28 August 2014